# Words Don't Come Easy

J.M

Michael Andrews

S.J. Gibbs

# CONTENTS

# ACKNOWLEDGMENTS

To Alan, Mike and Stephen. Thanks for putting up
with the after effects of the writers group meetings.

.

# Introduction.

Our DH Writers Group was formed in the spring of 2015. We are a small group of aspiring writers, at different stages of our careers, who meet every couple of months or so, to support each other with our development as writers.

For each meeting, among other things, we write a short piece of fiction, following a defined brief, on a title that is selected at random. We selected a book which Michael had found on Amazon, "1000 Awesome Writing Prompts" by Ryan Andrew Kinder. This is a book which we would suggest any aspiring writer (or group) purchase and try out for themselves. You can find a copy on Amazon.

We read these short pieces of work aloud at the meeting offering constructive critique in a safe environment. Initially group members used these exercises to help develop their own projects, we now challenge ourselves to write about topics and in genres that are outside of our comfort zones and have helped build our confidence to expand and extend our personal writing projects to new areas. We believe that the process of reading each other's work and receiving feedback has helped to improve the quality of our writings. This book is a compilation of the outputs of this exercise in date order accompanied by some of our thoughts and observations. The pieces are published as they were on the day they were read at the meeting and have not been edited or corrected. In this way, the book should reflect our individual journeys as writers over the past few years.

The group currently has four core members and this book contains their work only. Other members have come and gone but their work is not included in this compilation. The four core members are AJ Jones, J.M. McKenzie, Michael Andrews and S.J. Gibbs. What follows is a short biography written by each writer.

At the end of the book is a bibliography of the writers' works, and in the kindle version, hyperlinks will take you to the respective product pages.

## **AJ Jones**

AJ has always wanted to write but, like many other budding authors, her busy lifestyle allowed very little time for it. Then, one day, when she was driving home from a business meeting, she had an idea for a children's educational picture book. It took all her concentration to hold onto that idea long enough for her to splurge the bones of it into her notebook before it escaped forever into the Great Ideas Bank in the sky.

This was in 2006. Three years later, on the advice of a friend, she bought the Children's Writers' and Artists' Yearbook and submitted her manuscript to 30 different children's publishers. A few *"Dear John"* replies trickled through her letterbox and her life continued much as it had before until, one rainy Wednesday afternoon, she answered the phone to a *lovely* lady from Hachette Children's Books who asked, "Has anyone contacted you yet about your *lovely* book?".

"No", she breathlessly exclaimed, whence began a very long journey which finally led to *"I am here! Where are you?"* being published in November 2017, having been delightfully illustrated by the renowned children's illustrator, Sarah Horne.  has since been carrying out book signing events at local schools, libraries and bookstores, including Waterstones, and is in the process of writing a second book in the series.

AJ has been married for 47 years and has three grown up children and two beautiful grandsons, Oscar and Jacob. She has had a varied career path including teaching, project management and IT consultancy, but is now using her retirement to hone her writing skills. She is a proud founder member of DH Writers Group and believes that she has developed substantially as a writer since the group was formed in 2015. She has many other writing projects on the go but also enjoys proof-reading and editing other people's work.

She hopes that this collection of the group's homework assignments will give other aspiring writers an example of what can be achieved when a few committed and enthusiastic friends join together to exercise their writing muscles.

## <u>J.M. McKenzie</u>

J.M. has had a long career in healthcare but, like many people, has always had a personal ambition to write a book. As a child she aspired to be a writer but was never encouraged or supported to follow this career path. She has always written as part of her healthcare career, but this has largely been on commercial and scientific subjects. When she took a career break between 2011 and 2015 she began to write her first novel, "The Ice Factory". She also met AJ Jones during this time and discovered that she was an aspiring children's author, very close to publishing her first book. They agreed to meet from time to time to support each other. AJ already knew Michael Andrews, who had already successfully published a number of books. After a conversation in the pub, Michael was keen to get involved as well, offering to lead the meetings, and so the fledgling DH Writers Group was formed.

Feedback from the group on the first few chapters of J.M.'s budding novel, including some wise advice from Michael as an established author, persuaded J.M. to stop and change direction, and she began a new novel on a less serious subject than the first, and written in a more natural style. The first draft of that novel, Wait for Me, the story of one woman's journey to get home to her husband in the first few weeks of a zombie apocalypse in the UK, was completed in June 2017. At the time of writing J.M. is working on the second draft of "Wait for Me", and has resumed work on "The Ice Factory". She is also close to completing the Writers Bureau Comprehensive Creative Writing course.

## Michael Andrews

Michael Andrews had always dreamed about writing a novel, ever since a school assignment at the age of 14 was writing the start to a book. An avid reader of fantasy and science fiction, Michael's imagination was stretched by the likes of David Eddings, Raymond E Feist and Orson Scott Card.

However, it was only after a thirty year career in logistics and planning that Michael finally sat himself down and started his first novel in earnest. With the advent of the Kindle, Amazon opened up the doorway to independent authors and nine months later, Michael's first child, "For The Lost Soul" was published. A poetry collection inspired by the bullying theme within For The Lost Soul soon followed, receiving recognition with publishing within The Canon's Mouth, The Bully Book by Alisha Paige, reaching the final of the Mary Charman-Smith Poetry competition and finally, "The Empty Chair" was published.

Wishing to write a shorter read, but still keeping a long term plot in process, Michael started work on a series of novels, "The Alex Hayden Chronicles" with titular character Alex, a thousand year old vampire trapped forever in the body of a fourteen year old boy. Set in modern day Blackpool, he teams up with Detective Harry Shepherd to stop a serial killer in the first volume, "Under A Blood Moon". "The Howling Wind" and "The Cauldron of Fire" have since been released while at the time of writing, Michael is working on book four, "Dragonfire".

Michael was approached by AJ and J.M. to help set up the writers group and, with his experience using the Amazon platform and that he already had published books, he agreed to chair the meetings. He is delighted with how the group have transformed themselves not only as writers but as friends and happily agreed to work on collaborative books within the group.

Since the conception of putting this book together, Michael's assignment number 23, has been accepted by Severance Publishing into their "Cathartic Screams Anthology" due to be published in the Autumn of 2018. That is an edited and slightly amended version of the piece in here, and will be entitled "Reanimated Horror".

With several other backburner solo projects, as well as the group projects, Michael is sure to be kept busy at the keyboard for the foreseeable future.

## S.J. Gibbs

S.J.'s love of reading and writing started at a very young age and as a teenager would often be found with her nose in a book and used to read under the bedclothes with a torch after her father used to turn out her bedroom light.

After leaving school, in her spare time, she wrote short stories for her own pleasure. Reading was still her passion.

In 1987, her first daughter was born and diagnosed with profound cerebral palsy. This prompted her to start writing a novel about the struggles of bringing up a daughter with a severe disability.

At the beginning of 2015, S.J.'s writing began in earnest, after she joined a local writer's group. She had been struggling with the emotions of trying to write about her daughter's life and through the group found a love of writing fiction.

Along with another member of the writer's group, she formed a travel blog drawing on her extensive travel knowledge. She is also involved in a collaborative novel started by the writers group.

She also started working on her own novel "Ixagion", which is a story of a serial killer who is possessed by a demon.

Encouraged by J.M., she joined a comprehensive creative writing course, which she has almost completed, and has thoroughly enjoyed. This has taken her writing down another route and she is now working on another novel, "The Cutting Edge", which is aimed at the young adult market, and is her current main focus.

While the group were compiling this anthology, Michael encouraged S.J. to write a short story so that she could experience the joy of publishing her own work. "Fighting A Battle With Himself" has since been written, edited and published on Amazon.

## Assignment One - The main character is going to die. Begin and end with the same sentence.

### 3rd June 2015

Although J.M. and AJ were the two people who came up with the idea of starting the writers group, they asked Michael to become the chairperson and take charge, as he already had some of his books published through Amazon.

Whilst setting up the first agenda, Michael came up with the idea of setting a short piece of writing for each meeting... or "homework" as we have come to love calling them.

Initially the group was horrified that they would have to write pieces of work which they had no control over the topic but in time, all members have come to look forward to them.

This first assignment was tasked at being "more than ten sentences" with the added rule of the first and last sentence being the same meant that we had to think a little about how we were going to create the plot.

Whilst J.M. and Michael's pieces were received well, it was AJ's which had the group talking, especially as she read it out in her own indominatable style.

S.J. had yet to join the group at this point, so we have the first pieces of writing from the group by AJ, J.M. and Michael.

# The main character is going to die. Begin and end with the same sentence.

### by

### AJ Jones

Is it hot in here, or is it me?

Well, of all the cheek! They've only gone and tied me to a stake and put me on top of a bonfire. I wouldn't mind so much, but I was planning to use some of this wood for a barbie at the weekend. You know – invite some of me mates over to watch the match – should be a good one as well, Lourdes Voice over Artistes against the Barcelona Inquisitors. Nooobody expects the Barcelona Inquisitors to win!

What's that they're shouting? Burn Joan, the Cross-Dressing Witch! Nobody said that about Paul O'Grady. But then he's a dog lover, isn't he? Everybody loves a dog lover, especially the English. Well, you only have to look at Britain's Got Talent!

Oh no. What's that tickling me toes. Feels quite nice actually. I've always liked having me feet tickled, me - especially when I was wearing a full suit of armour. The Dauphin seemed to like it, too. I reckon he's got a bit of a foot fetish. Or maybe, it's a fish fetish? Dauphin - Dolphin?! (Boom-boom!)

It's a bit hotter than it normally feels though. Probably because it's a little yellow flame that's tickling my feet. Ouch!

Oh no, now it's a Big Red Angry one!

Is it hot in here or is it me?

# The main character is going to die. Begin and end with the same sentence.

### by

### J.M. McKenzie

Shame, sorrow, pain, anger and self-loathing. These were the emotions that had dominated his life and were now dominating the moment of his death. He had had moments of happiness, and fleeting glimpses of joy. There had been pleasure and some satisfaction, all be it, tinged with deep guilt. He knew he was near the end now and there was relief, but no sense of peace. He was aware of his own slow agonal breaths and of people around him but could not distinguish who they were. Sorrowful faces were fading in and out of focus. Murmuring voices and someone's hand gently stroking his own were soft and soothing. His breaths were less frequent now, his whole body shuddering with the last few reflex gasps. There was no floating sensation, no tunnel or bright light, only an enveloping blackness that started as a dark swirling mist that slowly got denser and darker until there was nothing but his own dark emotions escorting him from the world. Shame, sorrow, pain, anger and self-loathing.

# The main character is going to die. Begin and end with the same sentence.

## by

## Michael Andrews

"Why is it always me?"

George groaned as he muttered the words, thinking that once again he would have to come to the rescue of a random stranger who was taking cover behind a wooden crate as a barrage of bullets flew across the open warehouse. George's life as a Time Lord had given him plenty of opportunities to help those in need.

"Throw down your guns and surrender and we can sort out a deal," George shouted across to the six man crew of Don Juliano, the vicious crime boss who ran the underworld of Chicago.

"Eat lead, pig!" came the response, followed by a staccato of gunfire.

George ducked as the wall behind him exploded into a snowstorm of plaster dust. Spotting one of the thugs creeping unseen towards his partner, George knew that he had to act fast. Firing off a shot, he smiled as the man fell to the ground, clutching his chest where George's aim was true.

His victory was brief as, to a man, Juliano's crew concentrated their fire on the aged detective. Finding himself pinned down with no escape, George fired random shots, trying to distract the men and give himself cover to escape. However, when his gun clicked empty, he knew that it was bad. A bullet caught him in the neck and as he felt his current life begin to shimmer, he moaned to himself.

"Why is it always me?"

## Assignment Two They'll Never Find Me Here

### 12th July 2015

This was the first real test of people's writing skills, with the group having agreed to put a maximum limit of five hundred words. S.J. had joined the group but at that time hand wrote her homework. Unfortunately as we had no idea at that point that we would be publishing these works, no copy of S.J.'s work was kept. It was agreed that any missing pieces would not be re-written as the new versions wouldn't reflect the standard of writing at the time.

AJ had started work on her first novel, Max and the Riddle of the Marbles, and this showed up with the first appearance of her alter ego, the twelve year old boy. It was at this point that AJ's dark humour started to shine.

Michael's style of action thriller writing bore prominence along with the twist which he enjoys adding to his stories.

Having previously been given advice about her love of zombies, J.M. delved into her first fiction of that genre.

S.J. had been very nervous coming to her first meeting, had met J.M. and AJ for the first time and had some dutch courage beforehand. Michael had to read out S.J.'s work and the group could not stop giggling about the descriptive use of words about the male sexual organ.

## They'll Never Find Me Here

### by

### AJ. Jones

I know they'll hate me, but I just can't do it. The thought of them strapping that disgusting vest onto me and then blowing myself up isn't for me after all. I know they think I've been buying into all that Jihadi shizz but I'm not sure about it now. So I've hidden in this old fridge to have a think about it. And they'll never find me here.

The Imam says I'll go to heaven and  have 72 beautiful virgins if I martyr myself to the cause, but I'm only 12 and I don't really know what I'd do with 72 virgins or even one for that matter! Maybe I could get them to make me some lovely chapattis? I do love chapattis, especially when they're nice and hot and just off the griddle.

Anyway, I'm not sure I like the idea of "having power" over women. They say it's my right, but what about their rights? I'm British so I've been taught at my school in England to respect women. The Imam here says that men have been put on this earth to take care of women, but the other stuff he's told me is making me worried. He says that women shouldn't be independent or show any part of themselves to men who aren't their husbands, except their eyes. (Wouldn't it be funny if they couldn't show their eyes? Always bumping into stuff!)

He says that women who don't obey the rules must be flogged or even put to death. That's not what I want for my Mum or my beautiful sisters. I want them to be happy and go out to work if they want to, like the women I saw at school in England - Miss Patel, my lovely teacher, and Mrs Khan who looked after us in the playground, who put a plaster on my knee whenever I fell over. But that was before my Dad brought us to live in Syria.

Shhhh, I can hear them outside. Don't even breathe . . .

Sounds like there's one right outside now.

What's that? Sounds like gunfire! Screaming?

"Aaaaagh!"

English voices all of a sudden!

Is it safe to come out now? I'll push the door open a tiny bit.

Oh no! It won't budge! I'm trapped! Can't . . . Breathe . . . Running . . . Out . . . Of . . . Air!!

"Hey, Lads! There's a young'un in here. Looks bad. Get the medics! Quick! I'm losing him."

<u>2 weeks later - back in England</u>:

So, am I glad they found me there? 'Course I am.

But it <u>was</u> a good hiding place, wasn't it?

I actually think Allah saved me from being "radicalised", as they're calling it. I really don't think He wants all the Infidels to die. The Imam here says we <u>can</u> live in peace together, as long as we learn to tolerate each other's differences. Who knows, we might even learn to like each other!

## They'll Never Find Me Here

## by

## J.M. McKenzie

"They'll never find me here!" Jodi silently told herself as she frantically squeezed herself into the small cupboard, fitting herself in between brooms, brushes and cleaning products.  There was no handle inside but she pulled the door closed as best she could, until she could only see a tiny thread of light from outside. The broom cupboard was built for brooms and not an adult woman, even of she was only just over five foot and under eight stone dripping wet. Her neck was slightly bent, but the pressure on the top of her head from the roof was comforting, as it helped to steady her trembling body, allowing her to regain some control over her breathing.  Her feet were pressed into the angle where the wall met the floor, sharing the space with a plastic dustpan and brush. She was drenched in sweat and panting loudly, the only sound she could hear, her own pounding heartbeat that drowned out anything else.  The cupboard was dark but she could still see enough to do a rapid damage assessment.  Although her jeans and trainers were splattered with blood and gore, they seemed intact, no rips or tears.  A quick pat down of her jacket revealed similar for her upper body. She took off her bandana and wiped the worst of it from her hands and face, examining her hands back and front in the process. As the effects of the adrenaline that had been coursing through her blood stream began to subside, her heart rate and breathing gradually returned to normal and she felt no new pain. She began to feel quietly confident that she had not been bitten. That threat, and all that went with it, put to one side for the moment, she focused her attention on what was going on outside in the corridor.

She listened as the group of biters shuffled past, the sounds they made were a mixture of animalistic growls, inhuman moans and almost human mutterings. There were other sounds too, the unthinkable moist, scraping, and dragging sounds of mutilated and detached body parts. She tried not to imagine what might be making these sounds. Through the tiny crack of light she could see their shadows passing her hiding place. She had no choice but to wait it out until it had gone quiet. There were too many. After what felt like thirty or forty minutes, her neck and back were aching and her left thigh was cramping. Most of the sounds had stopped but she could still hear shuffling right outside the door. Every time she tried to ease herself into a more comfortable position the dustpan under her left foot, slipped slightly. Ten minutes more and her whole body was screaming in pain. The shuffling continued. In desperation, she took the pressure off the dustpan for a fraction of a second. It immediately shot out from beneath her foot, throwing her sideways into the door, which burst open ejecting her into the corridor. She landed in a tangle of cleaning tools and products, hitting her hip on the edge of a bucket. She barely had time to register where she was and what had happened before the biter was on her, its smell suffocating, its hands holding her in a grip that belied its state of decay, its weight pinning her to the ground, as she struggled to break free, its deadly brown teeth tearing into the soft flesh of her belly…….

## They'll Never Find Me Here

## by

## Michael Andrews

"They'll never find me here!" I thought to myself as I climbed into the small, wooden cabinet at the top of the winding staircase. Pulling my legs in tight, I squeezed my twelve year old body into the cramped space, pulling the door closed, well, as closed as I could without trapping my fingers.

Minutes passed, or was it years?

I listened to the groans and creaks of the old house as I kept my breathing shallow and silent. Desperate to remain quiet, I held my breath as I heard light footsteps run past, before pausing at the end of the landing. A door creaked open before I heard a shout and scream from downstairs.

"They've found Sally," I whispered, thinking about how my thirteen year old cousin had chosen to hide under the dining room table. Resplendent with a large, white tablecloth, she had argued it was a perfect place to hide, but I disagreed. Now, my argument had proven correct and she was caught.

The staircase creaked and footsteps broke my thoughts. One pair, two pairs... no, now three pairs of footsteps climbing to the landing. A bead of sweat trickled down my neck as the oppressive heat of the cramped, dark space began to take effect on my nervous body. Voices cackled right outside the cabinet.

"Little piggies... we're gonna get ya!"

I closed my eyes, expecting the inevitable discovery but, to my relief, the footsteps didn't stop as they split and went in different directions from the middle of the landing. Holding my breath, I heard the now familiar creak of the bathroom door and, within seconds, the cry of my younger brother, Adam. The nine year old had obviously not hidden himself away, relying on constant, stealthy movement rather than camouflage.

With Sally and Adam now in their hands, that left just me as the sole survivor. I twisted my right arm and pressed the small button on the side of my watch, illuminating the digital display. Twelve minutes past ten. It had been just seven minutes. Seven minutes and I was now on my own.

"Where's the little sod gone?" I froze as a deep voice echoed directly outside the cabinet. Footsteps slowly stepped away, the sounds of the old wooden floorboards groaning throughout the old house.

"He can't have gone far," a light, female voice replied. I heard a 'shush' but let out a little sigh of relief as footsteps pounded down the staircase. I was safe, for now. It wouldn't be long before I was safe, for sure.

Bright light blinded me as the cabinet door was pulled open and the light of a torch shone directly into my eyes. I cried out in shock as a hand grabbed my arm.

"Gotcha little brother!" my sixteen year old sister yelled as she tapped me on my arm. "You nearly made the fifteen minutes but... TAG! You're it!"

**Assignment Three -** You have just been stood up on a potential date. It turns out to be the best night ever

4th August 2015

Again, S.J. had hand written her work, and no copy was kept at that point. This was the first time that Michael's critiquing stepped up a level as he tried to help the group along and S.J. did get a little upset with the "Nick Nick Nick" comment as he pointed out the continued use of the characters name.

AJ's twelve year old boy alter ego reappeared with a new take on the opening chapter of Max and the Marbles and her new catchphrase "Anyway I digress" which was some relief as it replaced her query of J.M.'s Scottish/Zimbabwean accent.

J.M. had taken on board the conversation from the previous meeting regarding S.J.'s descriptive use of words and went smutty, so please be aware when reading.

Michael offered a little insight into the background of

one of his vampire character's so again, please be aware that there are some spoilers from his Alex Hayden Chronicles series.

This was also the first homework where we increased the word count to one thousand words as we felt we needed longer pieces to achieve the improvement in skills.

# You have just been stood up on a potential date. It turns out to be the best night ever

## by

## AJ Jones

'Course, it's not a date! I'm just going to the pictures with my mate, Alex. Who just happens to be a girl!

I've known her since we were born - in fact, before we were born! Our Mums met at ante-natal classes so we're practically brother and sister. Neither of us has a real brother or sister, you see.

And no, I don't fancy her! Perish the thought! (As Granddad's always saying!)

She's pretty enough - but she doesn't think so. She's always telling me that she feels like an ugly toad, and then she chases me round the playground going "croaaaaaak, croaaaaaak" and we end up falling over on top of each other and laughing our heads off.

Mum always knows when we've been playing the Toad Game, because I come home with a button missing or a hole in my shirt. She moans at me all the time for not looking after my clothes, especially nowadays. Things have never been the same since Dad went, but that was ages ago and we've got used to it just being the two of us now.

It was funny the way he left. He went to buy ice creams while we were out on my birthday at my favourite place in the whole wide world, Monkey Town, but he didn't come back. We searched everywhere for him and the Police came to see Mum and asked her loads of questions, but she couldn't give them any answers that would help them to bring him back. So we've been on our own ever since.

I miss Monkey Town. The monkeys are so funny. They pull each other's tails and chase each other round their compounds, shrieking and chattering at each other - the naughty babies giving the quieter adult monkeys all sorts of grief. They all usually join in the fun, except for Shizaru, the wise old Japanese macaque who's been my friend forever.

Anyway, I digress! (As my Granddad Ron is always saying when he rambles on about something completely different - and when he sees Nanny Jojo roll her eyes and give him "the look", as he calls it.)

We were talking about my date - or actually non-date - with Alex.

She's a fan of monkeys too - maybe it's because we were born in the Year of the Monkey - so when a new film comes out and it's got anything to do with monkeys, the Mums get their heads together and plan a trip to the cinema.

It's weird but they decided this time that Alex and I could see the film on our own. They said they'd take us and meet us outside afterwards so that we'd be safe. But my Mum decided to drop me off and pop to the shops before they close to get a present for one of her other friends whose birthday is tomorrow, so I'm here all alone at the moment.

(Actually, we think they might be popping to the posh new bar that's opened a couple of streets away from the cinema, but we like the idea that they're doing something nice together because they haven't seen so much of each other lately, probably because they're both working full-time now.)

So here I am, standing outside the cinema, waiting for Alex and her Mum to arrive.

Where on earth is Alex?

If only we had mobile phones, I could phone her and find out where she is. But the Mums have decided we're far too young to have of one of those.

The film's about to start, but she's still not turned up. Should I go in without her? I've got enough money to go in - and to buy us a coke - but I don't think I want to watch the film on my own.

A car suddenly screeches to a halt right by my side.

My Dad gets out; he shouts at me to get into the passenger seat and I do as he says, even though I'm so scared that my kneecaps are shaking and my legs have turned to jelly.

"Dad! What on earth are you doing here? Where did you go? Why did you go? Why didn't you come back?"

I have so many questions that need answers, but all I can think of is how pleased Mum's going to be to have Dad back.

Dad takes me to our local burger place and buys me our favourite burger and fries - to make up for being "stood up" by Alex, he says.

We have the best night ever together, Dad and me, catching up on everything that's happened since he went away. He tells me he was kept in a cave where there were loads of monkeys, just like Monkey Town. There was no satellite coverage there though, so no way of contacting Mum or me. He only managed to escape with the help of Shizaru, who just appeared there, "out of the blue".

Mum is so shocked to see him when we get home that she bursts into tears and gives him the biggest hug I've ever seen her give anyone. I can still hear them talking downstairs as I fall asleep.

As I fall though, I wonder why he didn't try to escape sooner. And how does he know about Alex not turning up this evening?

But then the dream kicks in, so I find myself in that

creepy place again.

The next morning, Alex's Mum rings to say she's disappeared now. Mum tries to calm her down, but I can hear her sobbing loudly at the other end of the line.

Has she sacrificed her freedom so that I can have my Dad back? But why on earth would she do that?

Dad says it's all to do with a curse that's been put on my family because my Great Granddad stole something mysterious when he was a young man. But that's a whole other story . . .

# You have just been stood up on a potential date. It turns out to be the best night ever

## by

## J.M. McKenzie

He had waited long enough. He'd sat at the table nursing a gin and tonic until the ice had long since melted and the drink was lukewarm, staled by the slice of lemon gradually disintegrating into the dregs. He was desperate for a piss and desperate for a fag but reluctant to leave the table in case he lost it before she turned up. The bar was noisy and crowded, most of the drinkers were in couples or small groups all laughing and chatting, oblivious to him and his building mix of disappointment and frustration. He checked his phone again and looked around once more just in case she was in there somewhere waiting for him, although he knew that wasn't realistically likely, he'd scanned the bar at least hundred times.

There was one woman sitting alone at the bar but he was sure it wasn't her. She was tall, slim and brunette with a stern angular face made more severe by the square dark rimmed glasses she wore. Her hair was twisted up and held in place by a big clip that looked like a seashell. She was drinking a long glass of something gold and sparkling and she was talking, very seriously, to the bar tender, who was frowning slightly and nodding in agreement. They were not flirting. She didn't look like the sort of woman that would drink alone in a bar and flirt with the bar tender. When he first arrived he had thought that she might be his date simply because she was alone. He had made eye contact and started to walk towards her but she had looked away making it clear she was not waiting for anyone, or anyone unknown at least. She looked prim and professional, not the sort of person who would go on a blind date and nothing like the girl who had described herself as a bubbly blond with ample boobs and buttocks. Fuck it! A mental image of him and his supposed date rolling around in his tousled bed in a sweaty tangle of ample boobs, buttocks and long blond hair flashed through his head. Fuck her, or maybe not as it turned out!

He stood quickly and headed out to the smoking area. One quick fag, a piss and he was leaving. If she had been delayed or something she could have phoned. Bitch! She wasn't coming and he was going.

He finished his cigarette alone, hopping from one foot to the other partly to keep warm and partly to ease the pressure from his bladder, then headed to the toilets cursing his miserable luck as he pushed the door open unzipping his fly as he stepped towards the urinal. He had barely finished when the door burst open suddenly and he turned to see the brunette from the bar standing in the doorway. She closed the door behind her, unclipping her hair which tumbled down in long soft waves around her neck and shoulders. She removed her glasses and walked towards him, breathing heavily, small beads of sweat glistening between her breasts. He was instantly hard. What happened next could only be described as the most mind blowing sexual encounter he had ever had. He could literally feel his head exploding as she knelt before him and took him in her mouth. His neck and back arched, throwing his head back in a spasm of pleasure, and he closed his eyes, coming quickly in an orgasm that was so intense it was painful, leaving him shuddering and gasping. While he was recovering, she rose and without saying a word left as abruptly as she had arrived. As the door closed quietly and he was alone again, he found himself wondering if it had really happened or if he had had a strange daydream or a hallucination. He gathered himself together and went back into the bar. She was sitting at the bar appearing as cool and unruffled as she had before, sipping her drink and chatting to the bar tender. He then seriously wondered if he was going mad. He walked over to the bar, standing close to her as he ordered another gin and tonic. When the bar tender turned away to fix his drink he turned to look directly at her. She stared straight ahead refusing to acknowledge him, he turned away and paid for his drink, walking back to his seat, which was still free, but not before he noticed the small drip of creamy mucus clinging to the front of her otherwise pristine black blouse.

## You have just been stood up on a potential date. It turns out to be the best night ever

**by**

**Michael Andrews**

"So tell me, Eirwen... how did it happen?" the blonde detective asked. "How were you turned?"

"Gosh Vanessa, it seems so long ago now," I replied. "But it all started off with my marriage. I was supposed to meet the man who my father had arranged for me to marry."

■■■■■■■■■■■■■■■■■■■■■■■■■■■■■■■■■■■■■■■

As I pushed the wooden, tavern door open, my eyes were stung by the heavy fog of smoke billowing out of the open fire in the corner. I coughed, several times, to clear my throat which unfortunately drew attention to myself. Cursing slightly, I drew my hood over my platinum blonde hair and made my way to the bar.

"Whiskey," I ordered, garnering a strange look from the bartender. His thick, hairy arms reminded me of Harold, the village bully. I put my left hand on my scabbard as I tossed a copper onto the bar.

"It's two coppers for whiskey," he stated gruffly.

"Since when?" I spat back. "Unless Gwilim has started a robber's nest, you'll get the same that I paid last week."

"I wouldn't mess with her," chuckled a swordsman sat just three stools down. "Eirwen is as likely to slit your throat as kiss you."

I flashed him a smile as I quickly drank the shot. I clenched my teeth as the malt liquor burned the inside of my throat before slamming the wooden shot back on the bar. "Again!"

"In need of courage?" Idnerth asked as he indicated he'd pick up the cost. "Who's the lucky man?"

"Kidivor Bongam," I hissed. "My father believes that it's time that I settled down and got myself with child." I cringed at the thought of giving up my warrior lifestyle, but fathers are fathers and must be obeyed.

"That bandy legged brigand?" the dark haired swordsman laughed. "Surely your father could come up with a better suitor?"

"I think that is to punish me," I moaned as the third shot of whiskey hit my brain. "But he is rich enough to court my father's favour so here I am."

"Well, if you decide to run away, I've just signed up for a trader who wants good swords to protect his wares. He's going through Lancastrian territory and we all know how dangerous that can be," he whispered to me. "But the pay is good."

"I might take you up on that offer, if Kidivor doesn't show." The thought of spending my life as his wife, being forced to share the pock-faced man's bed, was only being considered as I dared not go against my father's wishes.

I watched as Idnerth left the tavern and I grabbed the bottle of whiskey from the hands of the hairy bartender, settling myself onto a table away from the fire. The last thing that I wanted was the smell of smoke in my hair. I sighed several times to myself over the next hour as I had to forcibly move on man after drunken man who thought that I was there as a bar whore. Hairy bartender calmed down as soon as I patched up the only man whom forced me to draw blood.

"This is ridiculous," I muttered as I drank the dregs of the whiskey straight from the bottle. I stood, swaying slightly as the effects of the liquor hit my body. I tossed ten coppers onto the bar and bade a goodnight at Gwilim who had finally surfaced for the evening's business.

Staggering outside, I looked at the muddy road and wished that I had brought my horse. The pale moonlight lit enough of the trail so that I could make my way, albeit it slowly. As I passed into the dark woods, I felt a stillness in the air. It was quiet. Too quiet. I put my hand on the hilt of my sword, ready to draw it if I was attacked. I cast my mind back but couldn't remember being followed out of the tavern.

A twig snapped off to the side and I spun, drawing my sword. The world continued to revolve as my vision swam and the whiskey reminded me how much I had drunk. I leaned over a tree as my stomach emptied its contents, the liquor burning my throat on the way up, just as it had done on the way down.

"I told thee to be more stealthy, my young bodyguard," I heard a deep voice, that seemed to be full of humour.

"Forgive me sire, but I thought that I had lost our prey," the voice of a teenage boy replied.

I held my sword ready as footsteps approached. The head of a blonde boy, maybe thirteen summers old appeared from behind a bush, a smile spreading across his face.

"There she is, my Lord," he announced, pointing at me. He was unarmed but carried himself with the confidence of a warrior.

"Ah, my Lady, it is good to find thee well." The man was tall. His dark hair was slicked back and, like the boy, he was unarmed. However, his aura shone with strength and I knew that if a fight broke out, I would surely lose despite my skill with the sword.

"Who are you?" I demanded. "And why have you been stalking me?"

"Stalk is a little unfair, my lady," the boy answered with a grin. "That makes us sound like wolves."

"And wolves we are not. I understand that your father wishes for you to marry. I come to offer you an alternative to the slouch who is in bed with his sister. I offer you a warrior's life, one that will be fulfilling and rich."

"Sounds too good to be true," I replied, but found my resolve faltering as I stared into his deep eyes. "Who do I have to marry?"

"Thou wilt become my wife, my lady, and mother to Alexander," the man replied. The boy bowed as I enquired who Alexander was.

"It'll be fun, I promise," the boy flashed me a grin. The whiskey seemed to be affecting my vision as I could swear that he had fangs instead of teeth.

My eyes returned to the man's face and I saw the same. I had already nodded my agreement when suddenly he was by my side, his teeth sinking into my neck. Pain coarsed through my body and, for a moment, I thought I would die.

"Don't worry, mother. The pain will pass," the boy patted my hand. "Then you will be like us."

"Like you how?" I croaked.

"A vampire!"

**Assignment Four -** Write a story about anything.  It must be 26 sentences long.  Each sentence must start with the next letter of the alphabet.  You can choose your starting point but must follow the rule

9th September 2015

S.J. was not present for this assignment and therefore it was just AJ, J.M. and Michael.  Everyone found this demanding but enjoyable as it was the first real test of structured writing which we wouldn't normally have to follow.

The biggest challenge found by the authors was to find a word for the letter X and each went in different ways.

Michael's anti-bullying stance came to the fore with his tale, while AJ's. science fiction tale within the House of Commons brought some interesting new words to the group.

Reading back through as we compile this anthology, J.M. remarked that this piece was her least favourite as she had concentrated more on the structure of the story rather than the plot itself.

## Write a story about anything. It must be 26 sentences long. Each sentence must start with the next letter of the alphabet. You can choose your starting point but must follow the rule

by

**AJ. Jones**

"Order! O-o-o-ORDER!" stuttered the Speaker of the House in an effort to regain some sense of decorum in the Chamber.

Pandemonium had just broken out in response to a question asked by the new Labour MP for Birmingham East.

"Question Time isn't quite the same when you're sitting in the Chamber, almost within touching distance of the PM and his cronies", she thought. "Roaring lions in the circus have got nothing on this lot."

Sweat was beginning to bead on her forehead as she waited impatiently for the PM to respond, expecting a sarcastic comment designed to belittle and humiliate her. To her surprise though, he actually looked a little sheepish and almost lost for words.

Up until this moment, the questions and answers had

to her been mostly banal and boring: one about the badger cull in West Yorkshire; and another relating to the HS2 debacle. Verity's question, which she'd spent most of the night composing and re-composing so that she got the wording just right, had certainly thrown the cat amongst the pigeons.

"Who knows what this could lead to?" she thought. "Xenophobia against aliens might even have the positive result of uniting all the earth's races into one – the human race."

Yes, the news that had rocked her world was certain to change things on this earthly planet, but why had no-one else picked up on it, she wondered. "Zooinism is one thing, but that's about animals passing diseases onto humans – not aliens!"

All sorts of unsettling and upsetting  ideas had been springing into her mind since hearing that a member of the team who'd been part of the Kepler mission to find life on other planets had died two weeks ago of a mystery illness, and, worse still, that another member of the team was now showing the same symptoms. By chance, she'd heard the story in a tiny news item late one night last week as it had just been leaked by someone working in the Queen Elizabeth Hospital in Birmingham where the second victim had been taken to try and save his life because they needed to use a special scanner that was only available there.

Claims had been made that the illness could be restricted only to the Kepler mission team, but what if that's not true, Verity had wondered – and so this was what had prompted the question that she'd asked the PM on that momentous Wednesday morning at Prime Minister's Question Time.

"Does the House believe that the mysterious illness probably being passed from aliens to humans which has already killed one member of the Kepler mission and which has now put another person's life in jeopardy could become the earth's next Black Plague or Ebola?", she'd asked in as matter of fact way as she could possibly muster, given the enormity of the potential consequences of the situation.

Everyone's eyes darted in panic towards her in the moment following her question. For the future of the human race, though, she knew that raising it in the House at that moment in time, before the rest of the world was put at risk, was the right thing to do.

"God", she thought, "even if He does exist, (which she personally doubted) can't be expected to have a cure for an alien disease up His sleeve; so we need to find a way to nip this thing in the bud before it escalates into something potentially catastrophic."

Her attention was brought back to the PM, as he cleared his throat and began his reply.

"I'd like to thank Miss Small for bringing this news item to the attention of the House. Just before I respond, however, I must point out that there is a news embargo that we must all be aware of here. Kepler's mission to find alien life on other planets has to be, by its very nature, a top secret venture. Losing control of the security situation surrounding the activities being undertaken by this team could have dire consequences, not only for the United Kingdom, but also for the human race on a global scale. My main aim, therefore, is obviously to quell any panic that may arise as a result of this news and, for this reason, I shall not be answering this question today, but will bring back an informed response when I have had a chance to consult with other key aliens – er, er, I mean experts - who have a much better knowledge than myself of the field of human biology."

Next, he quickly packed up his things and left the Chamber in a flash, his hurried footsteps echoing in the stunned silence that was left behind in that prestigious home of UK Government, where everyone was left wondering whether that day's session of PMQs may, just may, have been hosted by an alien!

# Write a story about anything.  It must be 26 sentences long.  Each sentence must start with the next letter of the alphabet.  You can choose your starting point but must follow the rule

by

**J.M. McKenzie**

"X-Ray?" she cried. "You think I need an X-Ray?"

Zara hobbled back to the grubby blue wheelchair collapsing into it with a sigh. As she did, the chair rolled backwards colliding heavily with an elderly man holding a bloody wad of tissue to the bridge of his nose.

"Bloody Hell!" he roared nasally, staggering sideways into the reception desk. "Can't you be more careful?"

"Do you think I meant to do that?" Zara snapped back at him. Even he could surely see the state he was in from behind his bloody tissue. "For God's sake!"

"God isn't going to help you, Darling" He shook his head and turned away to talk to the nurse surrounded by a hoard of other walking wounded crowded around the desk in various stages of bloody distress. It was almost six hours since it had happened and most of the people that had arrived in the same wave as her were still waiting to be seen. John, who was more badly injured, had been taken away quickly to another part of the hospital and she assumed they were dealing with others like him before moving on to the less seriously injured.

Kicking away the blanket that was covering her injured leg with her good foot, she examined her injury properly for the first time. Long grazes and darkening bruises covered the whole of her shin. More worrying was the large swelling just above her ankle.

"Nasty" a voice to her left sympathised.

"Oh, I suppose so but it could have been worse."

Perching on the edge of the chair, Zara wheeled around to face the owner of the voice, a middle aged woman, as bloodies and dirty as the rest of them, with her arm in a sling and a collar around her neck.

"Quite a day all things considered," Zara added.

Really, like no other I can ever remember and one I'll never forget," the woman murmered. She began to weep quietly. "Tried to help him...couldn't do anything...so much blood."

Uncomfortably, because of the lacerations on her

hands, Zara reached out and touched her shoulder.

"Very sorry…" she mumbled, and looked away.

Walking quickly into the room, a porter called her name.

"Zara Fisher for X-Ray."

⸭

# Write a story about anything. It must be 26 sentences long. Each sentence must start with the next letter of the alphabet. You can choose your starting point but must follow the rule

### by

### Michael Andrews

"Man, it must be great being that good!" Matty whispered as he watched the older boys playing football in the park. Normally, he'd hide himself away by the bushes so that there was no chance of the teenagers catching him watching them. Obviously they wouldn't want him anywhere near them, having been outed by his former friend, Freddie, but the lure of watching the older boys play was far too much of a temptation.

Plenty of times over the last month, the twelve year old had been punched, kicked and tripped at school. Quietly suffering the bullying to try to lessen it hadn't worked, but he knew better than to speak out against the kids who threatened him. Rather than risk an escalation of his pain, Matty chose to keep his mouth shut, lying about walking into doors or tripping up steps as an explanation as to how his new bruises appeared.

Stevie Harris, the object of Matty's fantasies, came into his view as the fourteen year old soccer god danced around three challenges. Tackles came in but the boy easily skipped over them before firing a shot past Jimmy Clarke and into the top corner.

"Urgh!" Matty groaned as he felt himself roughly pulled backwards, sprawling onto the grass. Very quickly, he realised that he had fallen into the hands of his main perpetrators of pain, his former best friend Freddie, Freddie's older brother Callum and three of the other year nine boys.

"What are you doing hiding here, pervert?" Callum kicked the boy as he tried to roll into a ball to protect himself. Xander Philips followed the older boy's example and quickly kicked Matty twice in the groin, causing the twelve year old to scream out in agony.

"You really nailed him good," Freddie laughed at his former friend's pain.

"Zip it, perv," Callum hissed as he glanced around, worried that an adult may overhear.

Any hope that Matty had for a peaceful afternoon vanished as Xander and Denny Fellows picked him up by his legs and dragged him further into the bushes. Bullied at school, and now at the weekend, life was becoming intolerable for the young boy. Crying more in frustration than in pain, Matty tried to stifle his sobs as his head bounced on the hardened grass, sun-baked throughout the mini heat wave of the last fortnight.

"Don't be such as wuss, you pansy," Freddie sneered at him. Eager to inflict more pain on the boy he had trusted, only for him to make a pass at him, the twelve year old glanced around before bending down and punching the helpless lad in the groin once more. Freddie grinned at his brother as he thought about what further torment they could devise.

"Get away from him," a harsh voice broke the bullies' entertainment.

"Help, please!" Matty cried out to whoever his potential saviour was, not caring, just praying that he wouldn't be hurt any further.

"I said, let him go," Stevie demanded, rolling his hands into fists as he approached the boys. Jimmy had thrown his gloves to the ground and jumped onto the nearest boy and, as fists flew, Matty crawled into a ball once more.

"Keep away from him... I won't tell you again," Stevie hissed as the bullies ran, leaving the park as quickly as they could.

"Look Matty, they've gone now and they won't hurt you again, I promise" the older boy said as he helped the twelve year old back to his feet, and with a feeling that he needed to make the boy's life a better one, he kissed the bloodied lips, bringing a smile of hope back into Matty's life.

**Assignment Five -** <u>As you are opening your birthday presents, there is a box which everybody swears they didn't put there.</u>

<u>7<sup>th</sup> October 2015</u>

This assignment will introduce S.J. to the book as it is the first digital copy of her work. We all found very different takes on quite a narrow subject and it was during this homework that we found out about S.J.'s darkness, something that will show up in her novel Ixagion.

Michael was very pleased with his work, to the point that it is one of his backburner projects as he wants to take it further and write into a full novel.

AJ's boy alter ego popped up once more, while J.M. was inspired by a scene from Love Actually with Emma Thompson and Alan Rickman regarding the Christmas gift.

S.J.'s piece though dominated the evening.

# As you are opening your birthday presents, there is a box which everybody swears they didn't put there

**by**

**AJ. Jones**

Don't you just hate it when you've opened all your birthday presents and, even though you love them all – well almost all – you get that empty feeling like a great big bubble has burst inside you because you know you're going to have to wait till Christmas before you get the same feeling again? So, when, Mum came over carrying another box wrapped in birthday paper, it's no wonder I gave an excited "Whoop" and began shaking the box, wondering what could possibly be in there.

"Where did you find that, Mum?" asked my brother, Tom.

"That's what I was going to say," I screeched excitedly.

"In the cupboard under the stairs," she said. "I presume your Dad left it for you before . . ."

She didn't need to finish the sentence. I looked away so as not to notice the slight 'tear-ing up' showing in her eyes. I knew she was trying hard to hide it because all my friends were there.

"Unless anyone else put it in there and forgot all about it, of course," she added with a cheeky smile.

We all looked at each other with question marks in our eyes but everyone shrugged their shoulders and giggled nervously. "It wasn't me," piped up Zoe, my best friend. "Nor me," shouted loads of the other girls in my class. Mum had invited every one of them. It was the same when any of the girls had a birthday party. You couldn't leave anyone out.

"Open it, open it," they all shouted, although, glancing over at Tom, I noticed him staring at the ceiling, not at the present like everybody else was.

After a bit of excited shaking and prodding, I began ripping off the paper. It was a shoe box shape so I was expecting a new pair of trainers or slippers, but what I saw when I opened the box completely took my breath away.

*2 days earlier:*

"A gun! What am I supposed to do with that?" whispered Tom as his mate, George, handed him the real-looking 9 mm Glock handgun wrapped in a tatty old cushion cover.

"Is it loaded?" asked Tom, trying to hide the fact that his stomach wasn't just doing cartwheels, it was more like a full-on gymnastic routine.

"Course not, Dick'ead!" sneered George. "The ammo's always kept separate. For safety reasons! If you wanna be in our gang, you gotta prove yourself. Surely you can think of somewhere to hide it for a few days, bein' so clever an' all."

Tom thought he could detect another put down coming, but George must've had second thoughts because he just started walking down the dark alleyway, leaving Tom alone holding the heavy metal object in his unwelcoming hands.

Walking through the front door, he looked around for hiding places that would pass his Mum's Snooping Test. He knew she'd be horrified if she saw the handgun, especially with what had happened to his Dad, but now that he was the Man of the House, he had to be tough enough to make sure nothing happened to her or his baby sister.

Wait a minute! What if he wrapped it in birthday paper and hid it in the cupboard under the stairs? Then, even if she found it, she wouldn't open it. She'd just put it with the other presents and he'd be able to hide it again before Abi got to open it.

In his bedroom, he found the box his school shoes had come in. He carefully laid the gun still wrapped in the cushion cover in it and then put the lid on. He tried shaking it to see whether it made a gun-like noise, but it just sounded like a surprise present inside a shoe box to him. So he wrapped it in the spare piece of birthday wrap that was left over from the real present he was giving Abi and hid it as well as he could underneath a pile of shoes in the corner of the cupboard. "Perfect," he thought, feeling quietly proud of himself.

*Back to Abi's Party Day:*

Just before the party started, Tom was relieved to discover that the "secret present" was still in its hiding place.

So, when he saw his Mum carrying it into the party room, the gymnastic routine in his stomach started all over again. He just had to keep his cool, or else his Mum was sure to guess it was all down to him.

"Poor Abi," he thought. "She looks so excited. But she won't be quite so pleased when she sees what's in there."

As he watched her tearing off the strips of paper and throwing them on top of all the other rubbish that had accumulated on the floor, the pangs of guilt hit him like a hurtling bullet. He just had to hold his head up as high as he could and look as shocked as everyone else was going to be when his pretty little sister opened up her extra special birthday present.

Uh-oh! Wait for it! She's unwrapping the cushion cover now, but what's that inside it?

Now he really did look shocked!

Instead of the horrid, filthy handgun, inside the cover was the box the Army had given his Mum to hold his Dad's medals.

"Your Dad would have wanted you to have some of these," his Mum said, again trying her best to stop the tears. "I've kept the others for you, Tom, but they won't be a surprise now. Hope you don't mind."

She looked over at her son, who wasn't as good as her at holding back his feelings. As he fled from the room, she could hear the gulp of air and the muted sobbing coming from his achingly raw throat.

"Who's for a game of Pin the Tail on the Donkey? Abi, you know what to do," she called over her shoulder as she left the room and went to find her precious Tom.

# As you are opening your birthday presents, there is a box which everybody swears they didn't put there

## by

## J.M. McKenzie

Emma was down, really down. Desolate in fact. After fifteen years together she knew her marriage to Rob was seriously in trouble for the first time. She was happy. He seemed happy too but what she had discovered told her otherwise. She couldn't believe it. She couldn't believe that he was hiding such a big secret and that she didn't know. The one thing she treasured the most about her relationship with him was the deep trust and honesty that she believed they had together. He had been her soulmate and best friend for as long as she could remember. They did everything together. They had hardly spent a night apart since they met and when they did they couldn't wait to get back into each other's arms. Their lovemaking, after only a short time apart, was urgent and intense. Every night she would cuddle up to his broad smooth back and lightly kiss the spot between his shoulder blades. She would slip her hand around his waist and he would pull it against his chest, holding it there as they fell asleep. Her heart was breaking.

She was sat alone in her bedroom on the evening of

her fortieth birthday. The curtains were drawn and the room was warm and dim. The party was going on downstairs and she could hear laughter, champagne corks popping and glasses clinking. She had crept upstairs when she realised what had happened. That morning, unable to resist trying to work out what Rob had bought her, she had a sneaky rummage round while he was at work. He had been very mysterious about her present. They had got to that stage in their relationship when they tended to buy each other practical gifts, little luxuries for the home that they wanted but didn't really need. Things that were too expensive to go out and buy on a whim. In the months leading up to her birthday she had had conversations about things like an expresso coffee machine, a good ice cream maker and a beautiful set of wall lights that were like a spray of blossom.

She only had herself to blame for snooping. She had searched in all the usual places, at the back of the wardrobe, the cupboards in the garage where he kept his tools, even the loft. Eventually she had found it tucked away in his jacket pocket. It was an old tweed jacket that he didn't wear often. It was hanging over the chair in the bedroom, which was odd in itself as she couldn't remember him wearing it recently. She found the small packet in the inside pocket. It was a small black box containing a small black velvet drawstring bag. The packaging looked expensive. She opened the drawstring bag with fumbling fingers, unconsciously holding her breath. She gasped. The necklace was the most beautiful thing she had ever seen. It was a delicate diamond and tanzanite pendant on a white gold chain. She was stunned. He had never bought her anything like this before. It must have cost a fortune. She was confused and a little cross that he had obviously spent so much money without discussing it with her first. However, her overwhelming emotion was absolute delight. She smiled to herself as she quickly put it back.

Earlier that evening, when she opened her presents in front of all the family and he presented her with a red shiny Nespresso machine, grinning from ear to ear, the truth hit her so hard she almost physically crumbled. She was stunned, a jumble of thoughts rushing through her mind. It wasn't for her! Who was it for? A fixed smile on her face, she fought back the tears that threatened to tell another story tears as she realised the implications. She made her excuses and ran upstairs, jaw clenched and throat aching with a deep and painful sob fighting to burst from deep inside.

"Emma you haven't opened all your presents!" her mother called upstairs. "Where are you, what are you doing?"

She was sure she had, as she had saved Rob's until last, but she took a deep breath and smiled into the mirror as naturally as she could, checking her mascara at the same time. As she walked downstairs she remembered that she had seen another small package on the coffee table by the TV. It was in a folded brown envelope, sealed with parcel tape. There was nothing written on it to indicate it was for her or who it was from. No one had taken ownership of it and It was so innocuously and badly wrapped she had not taken any notice of it. She had been so shocked and disappointed when she had opened the coffee machine she had forgotten all about it.

She walked into the room and her mother handed her the brown envelope. "You forgot this one. We don't know who it's from."

She tore open the package and a small black box fell onto the floor. She looked at Rob. "I love you," he said quietly.

That night as she cuddled up to his back lightly kissing the spot between his shoulders she fingered the necklace that she could not bear to take off. She slipped her other hand around his waist and he pulled it against his chest, holding it there as they fell asleep.

# As you are opening your birthday presents, there is a box which everybody swears they didn't put there

### by

### Michael Andrews

Jimmy sat back and looked at the collection of presents that he had received. Surrounded by his family and his three best friends, the twelve year old couldn't keep the grin off his face as he checked out the new Aston Villa kit that his parents had bought him, the model of a silver dragon, as well as the three new X-box games from Charlie, Bobby and Jake, his friends.

"Thanks guys, this is brilliant," the lad gushed as he hugged everyone in the room.

"Hold on, Jimmy," Bobby said. "There's still one more present that you haven't opened." He pointed at the brown paper covered box that no-one had noticed before.

"What's that?" Jimmy's dad, Patrick, asked as he picked up the final gift. "There's no tag on it."

"Who's it from?" Jimmy questioned as took the offered box.

"We didn't put it there," Charlie said, looking at the other two boys who shook their heads in agreement.

"Well, someone must have," Jimmy mother frowned. "It's not from us either."

"Maybe it's from Santa," Jake offered, only to have Bobby grab him and give him a nuggie.

"It's not Christmas, dummy," the boy giggled.

"Well, I'm going to open it anyway," the birthday boy said and carefully unwrapped the tightly sealed paper. Once uncovered, the boy looked at the intricately carved mahogany box. The lid had his name inlaid in gold letters and there was a catch that kept the lid shut.

"That's really nice," Jimmy's mother said, wondering who would have spent the amount of money that it would have cost. "Let me have a look."

As Jimmy held the box out, he felt a small vibration and watched as the catch turned. Fascinated, he opened the lid and saw a small piece of paper inside. Written in clear, neat writing was a message.

*Don't give the box to anyone else. It will negate its power.*

Shutting the lid, he pulled it to his side and said, "I think I'll go and put this on the shelf in my bedroom."

He quickly ran up the stairs to his room and hid the box in the bottom of his closet. "I wonder who sent you?" he muttered before rejoining his parents and friends downstairs.

After an enjoyable evening of pizza and the Minions, Jimmy was getting undressed for bed when he suddenly remembered the mysterious box. Fishing it out of the closet, he opened it only to find that it was empty. He looked in his closet for the piece of paper, wanting to know if he could recognise the writing, but he couldn't find it. Shrugging to himself, he put the box on his bedside table and drifted off into a sleep filled with dreams of girls and dragons.

He awoke to a strange buzzing sound. Looking at his alarm clock, it was still fifteen minutes before it was due to go off and he noticed the strange box shaking slightly. The catch slowly turned and, with shaking hands, he nervously picked up the box and opened it. Sure enough, there was another piece of paper inside. The same neat handwriting spelled out a message.

*When you get to old man Robbins house, count to twenty before continuing.*

"What does that mean?" Jimmy asked himself. Shaking his head, he got ready for school, eating his breakfast before kissing his mother goodbye. Getting on his bike, he pedalled quickly around the corner, calling on Bobby and Charlie who lived on the next street. Joking back and forth, the three twelve year olds didn't seem to have a care in the world as they rode towards another day of school.

As they approached the tight corner which they loved racing their bikes around, Jimmy suddenly screeched his bike to a stop. His two friends pulled up as well, wondering what was wrong with him.

"What wrong Jimmy?" Charlie asked but could see his friend's lips moving, as if he was counting silently.

"Come on, we'll be late," Bobby moaned and started to push his bike forwards just as the squeal of rubber halted him in his tracks. Jumping from his bike, the boy rolled onto the pavement just as a blue car sped past on the wrong side of the road, crushing his bike underneath its wheels.

"Wow!" Charlie said. "If we'd have ridden on as normal, we'd have been wiped out!"

"My bike!" Bobby moaned as he looked at the crumpled mess of metal.

"It could have been you," Charlie poked his friend as he helped pick up the pieces of now scrap metal.

"Are you boys alright?" an elderly voice echoed in the street.

They turned and saw the figure of Mr Robbins, hobbling down his path.

"Come inside and have a drink while I call your parents," he said. "That must have been very scary for you."

"I've gotta go home," Jimmy announced suddenly, breaking his silence. "I don't feel very well."

Without a word, he turned and pedalled home as quickly as he could. Explaining to his mother about the near miss, she phoned the school and told them that she was keeping him at home for the day.

Back in the safety of his room, he flopped onto his bed before turning and picking up the box.

"How did you know?" he asked the wooden ornament and felt it vibrate.  Opening it, he saw a new piece of paper.

*Trust me Jimmy.  I am here to help you fulfil your destiny.*

"What destiny?  Who are you?" the boy asked warily.  He jumped as the lid snapped shut before it vibrated once more.  Opening it carefully, he gasped as a new message had appeared.

*You will save the world, Jimmy Hardy.*

"How?  How do you know?"  Jimmy avoided his fingers being trapped as the box shut and reopened.

*Because I am you.  I am here to guide you.  I am James Patrick Hardy*

# As you are opening your birthday presents, there is a box which everybody swears they didn't put there

## by

## S.J. Gibbs

I pulled back my black hair and tied it loosely in a ponytail, highlighted my cheekbones with bronze blusher and admired my strong jawline in the mirror.

I threw on my little black dress and took the stairs down to the dining room where my guests were waiting to celebrate my fortieth birthday. I could hear them all laughing like eighteen year olds. My husband, Rudy, a small dark- faced man like the villains you see in films moved towards me and draped his arm around my shoulders. He had a glassy coolness about him and I felt his eyes inspecting me and piercing right through me at the same time.

I knew that he did not exactly idolize me.

The small party of six guests, Rudy, and myself moved outside to the swimming pool terrace.

I looked hard into Rudy's eyes, trying to calculate his mood. I looked around at the other six guests who had been our friends since forever and immediately began to relax. Status Quo drifted into my ears and I turned to Rudy and said, " the music's too loud, I can hardly hear myself think." Rudy adjusted the volume and the track continued at a level where we could engage in conversation.

Rudy led me to the table where ten or more presents lay awaiting my opening.

The first present, which caught my attention, was wrapped in beautiful homemade hand - painted wrapping paper. I knew this would be from Aidan and Daniela my friends' who are both artists as I recognized their style.

I was touched by their thoughtful gift. It was a poetry book we had discussed together and I had commented I would like to own it.

After opening all of the other presents, none of which, including Rudy's had given me much pleasure, there was one box left on the table, which had intrigued me from first glance.

I picked up the wooden box which held no wrapping paper and no gift tag and turning to the group said, "so who is this from?"

I found the gift even more intriguing when everyone swore they hadn't put it there.

The wooden box was sturdy and Rudy produced a crowbar to assist me with the opening. I peeped inside, excited to find out what secret the box held. I reeled with horror at the sight before me. My beautiful Yorkshire Terrier, Lazar, lay inside quite definitely dead.

I knew at this point my marriage to Rudy was over. His cruelty towards me had reached well beyond its limits.

## **Assignment Six -** You have been hexed by a gypsy with the most ridiculous curse ever. Describe the next hour.

### 25th November 2015

The inspiration for AJ's homework came from a dream where she had sleep paralysis and had scared not only herself, but also her husband who was jolted awake.

S.J. took the title too literally and thought that she had to write in the first person, and has since spotted the continued use of "I". This is certainly not her favoured writing style, much preferring a third person point of view.

J.M. enjoyed writing this piece and felt it is one of her better works, something completely different to her normal style.

Michael tried his hand at gross out humour with a little twist of romance.

# You have been hexed by a gypsy with the most ridiculous curse ever. Describe the next hour.

## by

## AJ. Jones

The party was in full swing and everyone seemed to be having a great time. Most of the guests were in the living room, being both bamboozled and awestruck in equal measure, by the weird little man that I'd hired as a magician for the evening.

The big, old house I'd found on the internet was turning out to be the ideal venue for Alan's 50th birthday party. It came with a reputation of being 'a little bit haunted', which added to the excitement of the occasion.

"Anyone want more drinks?" I shouted as I wandered into the living room, carelessly interrupting the flow of the magician's previously flawless routine. The look he gave me could have killed a lion, let alone little ol' me. His piercing blue eyes glimmered menacingly as he stared straight at me and so I left the room as quickly as I could, leaving him to wow the audience with the rest of his act.

Half an hour later, I noticed that people were drifting out of the living room, holding their empty glasses, so I realised he'd finished and went to find some full bottles to top them up with.

Someone at work had mentioned that they'd played children's party games at a 40th birthday party they'd been to recently and so, continuing my efforts to be 'the hostess with mostest', I shouted, "Who's for a game of Sardines?"

The whoops of delight told me that this was a great idea, especially because it gave everyone a chance to have a proper look around the beautifully renovated old house and to see whether they would encounter any of the gentle spirits that allegedly inhabited it. My research had revealed that it had been a schoolhouse in the early 1900s and it was also used to house orphans and other displaced children during the two World Wars. However, the lady I'd rented it from had assured me that none of the lost souls who'd currently made it their home were malevolent.

Anyway, that had happened earlier this evening and now, here I am, hidden in the wardrobe on the top floor landing, waiting nervously for someone to find me and pack him or herself in there with me.

Suddenly, the wardrobe door opens and who else but Alan gets in. I suppress a giggle as he squeezes himself awkwardly into the remaining space, although it's weird that he doesn't appear to notice me. I put it down to the amount of alcohol he's consumed.

"You're squashing me." I try to say, but I can't make a

sound.

The door opens again and, this time, Andy gets in. The two men start pushing and shoving each other playfully in a vain effort to make themselves comfortable.

"I wonder where Nita is," Alan says. "Knowing her, she's hiding under one of those huge old beds. She's not stupid enough to try cramming herself into a tiny space like this."

What's he talking about? I'm right here next to him. I try to manoeuvre myself into a more comfortable position but I can't. Hang on! I'm not only invisible, I'm paralysed as well.

Suddenly, that menacing look the magician gave me earlier springs to mind, along with a magazine article I read the other day. It was about a gypsy and the way he'd put hexes on people who'd upset him. Could the magician have been a gypsy? He did look a bit like one with his shiny, black, curly hair and his dazzling blue eyes.

So, what if he has hexed me? What exactly can I do about it? I can't stay like this all night. After all, who's going to clear up all the mess after the party? Certainly not Alan. That would be ridiculous. I can't just disappear into thin air. I need to find a way to unhex myself – right now!

The wardrobe door opens again and a giggling Jackie

tries to get in. Luckily, as they all fight for space, I get pushed out.

"So there you are," the magician says. "I wondered where I'd find you."

I'm lying on the floor and I still can't move or speak, but it's nice to know I'm not completely invisible. Well, he can see me, anyway.

He picks me up using a fireman's lift – he's obviously stronger than he looks – and he carries me into one of the bedrooms.

Bloody hell, is he going to rape me? Oh God, please no!

No, it's ok. He just stands there holding me like a rag doll.

Slowly, a shape begins to form in front of us. It looks like a young girl with shiny, black, curly hair and dazzling blue eyes, just like his.

"My little sister, Mary!" he says. "You look exactly the same as I remember."

"I'm sorry, Mary, but I've put the family hex on her. I know you'll understand because the same thing happened to you, remember."

"Mary, Mary, quite contrary, I used to call you," he

says, smiling lovingly at her. "Of course you remember. How could you forget that night when you called me a demon and threw water over me? You made me really angry, you know."

"But I'm so sorry now. I just want to put things right. That's why I took this gig tonight."

Mary opens her mouth like she's about to speak, but I notice it's turned down at the corners. Something tells me she's not keen to renew her acquaintance with her older brother.

The magician puts me down on the floor and walks towards his sister, his arms outstretched.

Suddenly, I feel a surge working its way from my stomach, right up through my chest and into my voice box. And I scream the most blood-curdling scream I can possibly muster.

"Aaaaaaaaaaaaaaaaaaaaaaaaaaaaaaaaaaaaaaaaaaaaaa aaaaaaaaaaaaaaaaaaaaaarrrrrrrrrrrrrrrrrrrrrrgh!"

"What the hell was that?" shouts Alan, as I wake up lying next to him.

"Really sorry," I say, as I snuggle gratefully down under the plush covers of our lovely comfy bed.

# You have been hexed by a gypsy with the most ridiculous curse ever. Describe the next hour.

## by

## J.M. McKenzie

"So you think it's funny do you?" The old woman cackled. Her small dark eyes took on a malicious glint and I instantly regretted my fit of the giggles. I was a total sceptic about fortune telling and had been on the verge of laughter as soon as I entered the room. It was a preposterous cliché, dark and draped all around with deep red and rust coloured fabrics. In the gloom I could only just see the woman hunched over the table, her severe features illuminated by an actual glowing crystal ball. I started laughing quietly when, with a much rehearsed flourish, she whisked away the lace cloth that was covering the orb. It was when she had said that I would meet the man of my dreams before the end of the day that I lost it completely, the pent up hilarity erupting from me in a startling combination of a snort and a loud moan.

"I'm so sorry," I spluttered, blowing my nose and wiping the tears from my eyes.

"You will be my dear," she said slowly, smoothing the cloth again over the orb again and placing her hands in her lap, before fixing me in her uncomfortable gaze..

It was clear the encounter was over and I rose quickly from the chair bursting back outside into the sunlight where Liz was waiting for me. She had made me do it. She had broken up with her boyfriend, lost her job and written her car off in the space of the last 3 weeks and was struggling to decide what to do next. She wanted to have her fortune told but would only do it if I came with her.

"What did she say?" she asked.

Her words evoked another uncontrollable bout of laughter.
"She.....said....I..would....meetthemanofmydreams.....by the endoftheday..." I managed to get out, breathless and bent double with irrepressible mirth.

Liz stood and watched me as I tried to regain control. Every time I looked at her it started again. It was only when I stopped trying to explain and avoided looking at her at all, that I began to recover. We walked in silence back down the seafront for a while until I had managed to calm down. The tide was in and it was a blustery day. Waves were crashing against the sea wall.

"She told me that I should think about immigrating to Australia..." Liz began.

I instantly exploded into piercing peals of laughter so intense and overpowering that I was forced to sit on the low wall at the side of the promenade. I couldn't breathe and the muscles in my throat began to tighten and ache. Liz looked hurt and confused. As I threw my head back again and roared with uncontained abandon her expression changed to one of concern and then fear.

"Are you OK?" she asked tentatively.

I nodded trying to take some deep breathes. After a few minutes I was able to get up and continue walking. It was almost a full ten minutes before Liz tried again.

"Anyway, she said it might be good for me to have a new start..."

The moment she spoke I was instantly overcome again by wild peals of laughter. Now I was afraid. I couldn't get my breath. I seemed to have no control over what my body was doing. I was shaking and choking, my eyes and nose were running freely now and I was aware that long strings of mucous were drooling from my chin.

Liz grabbed me by the shoulders. She shook me hard. Black spots began to float in front of my eyes and her face swam in front of me. Tears blurred my vision. I felt a sharp sting across my face as Liz slapped me. Knocked off balance by the blow, I staggered backwards groping for the low wall behind me, now completely paralysed with a mix of anguish and hysteria. I managed a genuine scream as I tumbled backwards over the wall.  The shock as the cold water hit me stopped the laughter for an instant but it resumed almost immediately.   My laughing mouth was wide open and I drew the salt water deep into my lungs as I fought to breath.  I was still laughing as I sank below the surface, chortling softly as the violent thrashing, foam and froth gave way to quiet, calm stillness.  A few large final bubbles escaped from my mouth with the last few gurgling chuckles.   You could say I died happy.

## You have been hexed by a gypsy with the most ridiculous curse ever. Describe the next hour.

### by

### Michael Andrews

As I staggered away from the old woman, my head was throbbing as though a migraine was about to set in. If it wasn't for the dull pain behind my skull, I would've been chuckling to myself at the ridiculousness of the situation.

I'd been walking down High Street, minding my own business, looking for the old bookshop that Jackie had told me about when this ugly, raggedy old woman accosted me. Shoving a lucky heather under my nose, she near demanded that I cross her palm with gold, to which I told the ugly old toad to go away, or words to that effect.

"Curse thee, old Haggie will," she crowed. "Ne'er will thee mutter such words again! In fact, ne'er will thee mutter words again until thee shows respect."

I started to laugh but that's when the headache started. As I looked up, with the rain starting to drizzle a little heavier, I was relieved to see that I was standing outside 'Corianders'. I ducked inside the shop just as a thunderclap of lightning echoed down the street.

The shop smelled wonderfully musky, the scent of ancient books. I wandered down aisle after aisle, looking for nothing in particular but waiting for something to grab my attention.

"Can I help you, sir?" a young voice asked from behind, startling me out of my browsing.

I turned to see a young woman of infinite beauty standing in front of me. It was as if the gods themselves had placed Aphrodite in front of me. I stood, transfixed for a moment, before realising that I must look a fool to her, and opened my mouth to ask for a book about the ancient gods. However, as I tried to speak , only a loud burp came out of my mouth.

I saw her scrunch her nose up in disgust but, as I tried to speak again, another wet, squelchy belch erupted my mouth. She turned away from me and headed back for the safety of her counter. I must have turned the colour of scarlet and decided to do a runner to save any further embarrassment.

The rain was falling heavily so I headed across the street and into the cover of The White Swan. It was a bit dingy inside and a lot of screaming kids, which made me frown. I remember the days of sitting outside the pub on my best behaviour with my bottle of pop, while my parents talked inside with the other adults. Walking up to the bar, my eyes were drawn to the small, petite blonde barmaid who had a disarming smile. She reminded me of pictures of Venus, the Roman goddess.

"What can I get you, love?" she asked.

I was about to use one of my famous chat up lines, when "BUUUUURRRRRRRRRPPPPPPPPPPP!" came out before I covered up my mouth with my hand. Starting to apologise, I could only look on in shock as more squelchy belches flew out.

A deep, booming voice echoed from behind me. "I think you've had enough already," a big, burly bouncer told me as he put a heavy hand on my shoulder.

"BUUUUUURRRRRRRRPPPPPPPPPP!" I argued before he practically pushed me out of the door and back out into the pouring rain.

I shivered and felt sick at the sudden belching that I had been doing. Looking at my reflection in the pub window, I thought that I must be getting ill because there was a definite twinge of green to my complexion. My nose also looked weird, as if it was flattening and widening but I shook my head, trying to push away the growing headache.

I staggered up the road, wondering my legs were getting a strange bowing to them. Walking felt weird as though I wanted to leap rather than put one foot in front of another. The rain was getting heavier, although it now felt quite comforting as it pitter pattered against my face. I could see people looking at me strangely to the point where I had to stop and confront a pretty mother who had pulled her two children behind her.

Wanting to tell her to stop being rude, I opened my mouth to castigate her.

"BBBBEEEEEEELLLLLLLLLLLLLCCCCCCCCCCHHHHH HHHHHHH!" Oh God, not again I thought as she recoiled in disgust. What was wrong with me? I never had a problem attracting the women and charming them off their feet. Always happy to be seen with a trophy girlfriend on my arm, I was a legend amongst my friends. Yet here I was, not even able to speak.

Misery set in as I kept my head down and walked away from her, hearing her harsh words echoing past the dull pain in my skull. I sat down on a bench, letting the rain soak through my clothes when I heard a frustrated sigh. Looking up, I saw a woman who I immediately recognised from my school days. 'Plain Jane McGrain' we had nicknamed her and had fun taking the mickey out of her drab clothes. She was struggling with an arm full of bags while trying to keep hold of a cute toddler, who was trying his hardest to jump into every puddle. I heard her stifle a sob as the bottom of one of the bags gave out, spilling cans of food all over the pavement.

Not knowing where the emotion came from, sadness swept through me as I watched the single mother look around hopelessly. Jumping from the bench, I quickly pulled out the bag which I had in my pocket and gathered up the tins which were rolling in every direction. Handing them to her, I caught her gaze. It was one of surprise and recollection.

"Here you go, Jane," I said, surprising myself that I could speak once more.

"Thank you, Keith," she replied with a faint smile.

"You remember me?" I asked, kicking myself for dragging up the past. "Do you want to go for a coffee?"

# You have been hexed by a gypsy with the most ridiculous curse ever. Describe the next hour.

## by

## S.J. Gibbs

The gypsy is not happy with my refusal to buy a piece of heather from her. She hisses and curses at me saying, "you don't realize the great deal of power I have, I curse you."

Foolishly I laugh in her face.

Suddenly I'm aware I am dancing in a yellow light but it all feels rather strange. I have no legs or arms and my body is no longer present, I'm flying, I'm a fly.

I'm sad at the loss of my body but this is so exciting, I'm a fly.

I land on a lady's face and she swats me away, this is fun.

I fly to my office and listen to my colleague's intense discussion they don't even glance up at me on the ceiling.

Davena Cotterill, an overwrought woman with a puffed up view of her own importance is discussing me, in my absence, only I'm not absent I'm on the ceiling.

Spotting the mirror on the wall, I fly towards it and take a look at my self this is whimsical.

The comments Davena is making about me will take time to heal,

I never liked her anyway. "She's a pain in the ass", she continues about me. I buzz down and land on her nose. I'd like to punch it. I jump up and down on her stupid long nose as if it's my own bouncy castle. Irritated she tries to swipe at me but I'm too fast for her slow reaction.

I am having great fun, flying off and then landing on her small, pale spotty face.

I am ubiquitous in her surroundings and am now probably more of a "pain in the ass" to her as a fly than I was as a human.

I land on the desk in front of her and her fist comes down with a satisfying thud but yet again I am too fast for her action.

I notice the piece of paper in front of her, written in my hand and observe her reel off my hard work as if it is her own to my colleagues. She has stolen my information and is using it to her own advantage.

I jump up and down all over my own paperwork and she becomes distracted by this annoying fly, trying to swat me continually with her right hand as she divulges my thoughts as her own.

My colleague's heads turn and they stare at her in disbelief that she has finally managed to put something of interest together which actually warrants their attention.

Her voice is shrill as she outlines my objectives to the group.

I am now frustrated at being a fly, " that stupid gypsy," I think, " how long is this curse going to last, I need to be human again to defend my position."

The office door opens and I buzz off through it, finding an open window to the bathroom, I enter.

As I observe myself in the bathroom mirror, I watch with relief as I suddenly transform back into my human body.

Brushing myself down, I head back towards my office to confront Davena Cotterill, once and for all.

**Assignment Seven -** The pregnancy test kit in the bathroom proves what you thought.

15th December 2015

For the first time, we found two of the writers with the similar themes. It was commented on as this is something that normally did not happen.

Both AJ and J.M. took on board that it was nearly Christmas at the time of writing and took on new spins of the Virgin Birth.

As we were reviewing the pieces, S.J. noticed that each line of her work was a separate sentence and had no paragraphs at all. Since she started her writing course, she has picked on this point and has improved her formatting. S.J. also used the opportunity to explore the erotic genre.

Michael turned his hand to a more moral story, aiming advice at parents and teenagers alike.

# The pregnancy test kit in the bathroom proves what you thought.

## by

## AJ. Jones

Extracts from The Secret Diary of Mohammed Aslam, aged 15¾

*Friday, 20 March (Week 0)*

Strangest thing ever happened on my way to the Mosque today. Bumped into a weirdo standing at the end of our alleyway. Told me I'm going to have a baby and she's going to be the Daughter of Allah! What a Wally! I'm a boy. Boys don't have babies. He told me that, when I was born, I was something called a Hermaphrodite. Just googled it. Weird shit, man! No way am I part woman!

*Monday, 18 May (Week 8)*

Was sick this morning. Yuk!

*Monday, 25 May (Week 9)*

Felt like shit every morning this past week. What's wrong with me?

*Sunday, 2 August (Week 19)*

Good job Ramadan's over. Found it a lot harder than usual to fast all day. Been feeling a spider crawling inside my belly for the past couple of days. Wonder what it feels like to be pregnant. Decided to buy a pregnancy testing kit. Had to get it from Boots in Brum City Centre so no-one asked any awkward questions. Got a few funny looks from the sales lady. Hid it under the loose floorboard in my bedroom where I keep my secret diary. But will I really use it?

*Wednesday, 26 August (Week 22)*

Been feeling really emosh lately. Burst into tears in front of the whole class the other day when we were talking about how girls get radicalised. Soooo embarrassed!

*Sunday, 20 September (Week 25)*

The creepy-crawly feeling inside my belly is getting stronger, especially when I'm in bed. Could that weirdo have been right? Can't stop thinking I might be pregnant. Googled it and I've deffo got all the symptoms.

*Sunday, 27 September (Week 26)*

Finally had the balls to pee on the pregnancy testing thing. Waited in the bathroom to see what would happen. Said PREGNANT! I knew it! Checked the booklet over and over. Says a positive result is 'rarely wrong'. Now what do I do? Thank Allah that my djellaba is hiding my bulging belly.

*Friday, 2 October (Week 27)*

Mum noticed my fat belly yesterday. Told Dad to stop buying me sweets. No way, man!

After Friday prayers, I decided to tell the Imam what's happening to me. Weirdly, he believed me. Told me the Christian Bible says the Prophet Jesus – Peace be upon Him – will be reborn after 2,000 years. Says the stars are saying that Allah has decided to switch it around and chosen a virgin man to bear his Daughter instead. Says I'm not to worry because he'll look after me.

*Monday, 5 October (Still Week 27)*

Dad told me the Imam came to see him today and told him I've been chosen by Allah for a very special task and that he must ask Mum to pack a bag for me because he's taking me to live with one of his oldest friends for a few months. Dad says he told him not to worry because the task is nothing to do with me being radicalised or anything. I've got to be packed and ready to travel first thing on Thursday morning and I'm to tell everybody that I'm going to Bangladesh to see my dying uncle who wants to leave me his farm so I need to go and see if I like the idea.

*Thursday, 8 October (Week 28)*

Didn't sleep at all last night. My baby girl was moving round all over the place. Made sure I packed my secret diary and the pregnancy testing kit in case Mum and Dad go snooping in my room while I'm away.

The Imam collected me in his tatty old Escort at 9am and drove me to his old friend's house. Turns out to be a bloody great mansion just outside London. His friend is something called a gynaecologist. Googled it and found out it's somebody who treats women. I am not a woman! How many times do I have to say this?

The doc's a really nice bloke, though. Made me feel ok about everything – treated me like a prince actually. He's even got me the latest Playstation and all my favourite games. My room's pretty cool too – like a palace compared with my room at home. Even got my own TV and the bed's enormous. Doc says I need to stay here for a few months and then I can go home. That's ok by me. All this luxury and no school. Praise be to Allah!

*Thursday, 24 December (Full term)*

Haven't written much lately. Too busy enjoying myself – food's great and playing on my Playstation all day has been awesome. Doc came to see me today though. Told me I'm going to have an operation tomorrow morning. Scared shitless!

## Friday, 25 December

I'm dying! Doc made me walk to the stables which he's converted into an operating theatre. Made me lie down and told me he was just going to scratch the back of my hand. Next thing I know, he's waking me up and I've got a really bad pain in my belly. Turns out he's cut me open and taken my baby girl out. Didn't even let me see her. Literally gutted!

## Saturday, 26 December

Back in my room again being waited on hand and foot. Even had a visit from three of the doc's rich Saudi friends this afternoon. Brought me some more games for my Playstation: Gold Fever; Castlevania (a game about Dr Frankenstein) and Murder on the Eurasia Express. Awesome!

## Sunday, 27 December

Woken up last night by a really bright light beaming into my room. Lots of shouting and screaming. Turns out an American SWAT team were raiding the house. Doc came to tell me my baby girl's been kidnapped. What'll happen to her now?

Oh well, time to go home!

*12 years later – News from The White House*

12 year old Girl turns Wine into Water in a Fit of Rage at White House Garden Party.

# The pregnancy test kit in the bathroom proves what you thought.

## by

## J.M. McKenzie

The Second Coming

Elizabeth sat on the toilet and looked at the clear blue line in the middle of the oval window on the small white plastic wand. She looked at it with a mixture of shock, fear and resignation. All the symptoms she had been experiencing for the last few months had suggested this, but it was still impossible. She was fifty-seven years old. She had left the menopause well behind her. She was a grandmother for God's sake. She was almost certainly not ovulating but, when you added in the fact that she had not had sex for at least two years since Robert died, it was nothing short of a miracle.

About three months ago she had noticed that her breasts had become swollen and tender. The feeling reminded her of how they had felt before a period, when she still had them. Around about the same time she had begun to experience nausea in the mornings and sometimes at night just after she went to bed. She had also had a longing for wine gums that took her back to the early days of her pregnancies (or should she say previous pregnancies), when they were all she could stomach for months on end. Her stomach had begun to swell when she felt as though she ought to be losing weight, and not gaining it, as a result of the nausea and her general lack of appetite. It was when, a few days ago, she had been awoken by a slight fluttering in her lower abdomen that she immediately understood. It was a feeling a mother never forgets. The first movements of a new life stirring deep within her. Tiny limbs and hands and feet pushing gently against the wall of her uterus, making his or her presence felt and marking the beginning of a shared journey of unconditional love.

She had though she was going mad at first. She refused to even acknowledge what she was thinking and feeling. It was insane. Worse than that, it could be a portent of something more sinister. She had heard that some cancers could mimic the signs of pregnancy. She had made an appointment to see her GP later that week. However, as the week went on she became more and more convinced that the things she was experiencing were real and identical to those she remembered from her pregnancies over thirty years ago. When she was shopping in Boots the previous day she had seen the aisle containing the home pregnancy tests and made a snap decision to discreetly pop one into her bag. It was crazy but what harm could it do. If it was negative she could put these ridiculous thoughts from her mind once and for all.

But it wasn't negative, it was positive! She shook her head slowly as she tried to take in what this meant. It was both frightening and exhilarating at the same time. She would have to keep her doctor's appointment for later in the week. If she recalled correctly, she felt movements at around four months in her previous pregnancies. That would mean she would be due around the end of December and she would be showing soon. She would need to tell the children. How would they react? They would not believe her story. Would they be shocked and angry? Would they think she had finally gone completely mad? They were getting frustrated enough with her these days anyway, since she had been on her one woman mission to save the world. They were worried that she was doing too much and getting involved with groups and individuals that they thought were weird.

All she had really been doing was getting involved in things that mattered to her. The past few years had begun to get to her. Terrorism, climate change and war. Flooding, drought, poverty, refugees, violence, intolerance and hatred. They were all things that were beginning to threaten the future of the world as she knew it for her children and grandchildren and she felt compelled to do her bit, however small, to make things better. She wasn't religious but she had become more spiritual. She had joined a group of like-minded people who met on a Sunday to talk about peace, harmony, meditation and mindfulness. She had read about, and bought into, ideas around there being one human consciousness that everyone could tap into to make a positive difference to their lives and the lives of others, if they would just take a moment to do so. She had become immersed in charity work. She did a shift as a volunteer at her local Charity Shop, she had organised a collection of clothing and camping equipment for the refugees at Calais and had driven the kit down there herself over a weekend at her own expense. She had set-up monthly direct debits for significant contributions to a range of different charities.

She went to bed that night with her mind spinning. She was barely able to believe what was happening to her. She was excited and afraid at the same time. It was late before she drifted off into a fitful sleep. She awoke again in the early hours suddenly aware of a soft rustling sound at the end of her bed. She opened her eyes and pushed herself up on one elbow as a small point of white light hovering at the end of the bed, about three feet from the ground, began to grow and build as the rustling grew louder. A light breeze seemed to emanate from the source of the light and sound. The sound got louder and the breeze became a roaring wind as the light began to form into a distinct a shape. The shape rose and grew until it resembled a human figure behind which were two huge arching structures. They looked like wings. They were moving gently and she realised it was them that were making the rustling sound and creating the wind. She was not afraid. As the figure clarified further she could hardly believe what she saw. She began to think that she must be dreaming. The figure at the end of her bed looked remarkably similar to all the pictures she had ever seen of a classic angel. It opened its mouth and began to speak.

# The pregnancy test kit in the bathroom proves what you thought.

## by

## Michael Andrews

"What the bloody hell is this?" I asked, picking out the thin, pencil shaped object from the bin. I had gone into the family bathroom to give it a once over before my mother-in-law descended on us for the two weeks leading up to Christmas. That was enough to test my patience in itself, but the way that my sixteen year old son, Harry, had been acting over the last three weeks was getting close to pushing me over the edge. The normally quiet and sensible boy that I loved had turned into a secretive lad who's attitude was changing daily. I guess that since my wife had died a few years ago, he had no mother figure to keep him in check and with my long working hours, he was lacking the discipline that I should have been providing.

I thought back to the previous evening when I had come home early from work, with a migraine the size of Rhode Island, only to find that he had bunked off school with his girlfriend. I had caught the pair of them in his room, with his door closed, and I initially thought that he had ignored all of my warnings about starting a sexual relationship with the girl just two weeks after he had asked her out.

I was surprised when the door opened and not only was Harry and Jessica in the room, but Jessica's friend Becky also came out. The three of them were red-faced, embarrassed I am sure at being caught by me, but Becky seemed to be taking it worse. I could see tears in the corner of her eyes and so I held my tongue lashing in check. I'll admit that a small part of me, the geezer part, felt slightly proud that my boy had two girls in his room, but the responsible parent in me kicked in. I saw a look on his face which seemed to plead for me to hold my questions so I nodded at him and watched him walk down the stairs with the two girls. I heard the front door close and Harry was being the gentlemen that I had raised him to be and was walking the girls home.

I had crashed out, my headache getting the better of me and when I awoke the following morning, Harry has already left for school. Now, here I was, cleaning the bathroom bin and I had discovered the pregnancy test kit underneath the cellophane wrapping of the toilet paper pack. I heard a noise behind me and turned, my eyes catching the horrified stare of my son.

"Dad... it's not what you think," he babbled out.

"What had I told you?" I asked, frustration evident in my voice. "I thought that we had talked about sex and protection, yet here I am holding this?"

"Please, let me explain but you've got to promise me that you'll keep it secret," Harry replied, a hint of desperation in his tone. He should be desperate, because he would be going over my knee... well, if he was younger. I pointed him to his bedroom and he took a seat on his bed while I sat down on his computer chair.

"Talk," I instructed.

"Firstly, I need you to swear that you will keep this secret," he repeated.

"You're in no position to demand that," I hissed at him, trying to keep the anger from my voice. "What are we going to say to Jessica's parents when it comes out? You can't ask me to keep something like this from them."

"What have Jessica's parents got to do with this?" Harry asked before a look of comprehension dawned on his face. He giggled at first before turning serious. "Dad, I promise you that the kit wasn't Jessica's... we've not got past kissing yet," he chuckled. "You told me to make sure that I felt that I was with the right girl before I did it for the first time and I promise you that's what I'm doing." I heard the sincerity in his voice and I believed him.

"Then what is this doing here?" I asked.

Harry sighed. "Becky had too much to drink at Mike's birthday party last month and she, ah, missed her period. She was embarrassed to get the kit herself so I went with Jessica to get it and we came here so that she could take it without her parents finding out."

"What did the test result say?" I asked, my parental concerns for the young girl kicking in.

"She isn't, but she still doesn't want her parents to find out that she had sex," he replied. "They don't like Mike and her Dad would kill him if he found out."

"I won't say anything, but make sure she knows to use protection next time," I said, breathing a sigh of relief for the girl. "By the way, you're a good friend to her," I clapped him on the shoulder as I stood up. "I'm proud of you wanting to be there for her."

"It's how you raised me, Dad," Harry shrugged. "You told me to always stand up for my friends and protect them."

I turned away before he could see the tear that welled up in my eye. I should never have doubted him. I knew all along that Harry was a son that any father would be proud to call his own.

# The pregnancy test kit in the bathroom proves what you thought.

## by

## S.J. Gibbs

More than twenty thousand pounds profit rested on the blue line appearing on the stick.

Life, in Fay's opinion was too short to struggle without enough money to spend on things she wanted.

In a minute or two she would know if she was going to have a baby to sell to the couple she had been dealing with.

She waited and watched the stick with anticipation.

A satisfied grin appeared on her face as the blue line appeared, she was pregnant.

Try as she might, she could find no fault with the plan.

The defining moment had come a few months before when she had answered a query in an internet chat room, from a couple asking for help in conceiving a baby.

She had sketched out a scenario in her own mind and arranged to meet the couple to discuss her plan in further detail.

She met Cameron and Ricki at a café for the first meeting.

Fay watched Cameron's eyes widen as she suggested her plan to them.

She watched the couple occasionally glance uneasily at one another as she furthered her idea.

As she concluded her plan, Cameron and Ricki just stared in silence for a while, both seemingly reluctant to accept or reject her idea.

Fay reached over to Cameron and with a gentle soft touch placed her hand on Cameron's.

Ricki edged himself up and keeping his voice low said, "Give us time to think t through and make a decision. We will be in touch."

The weight of her own suggestion made fay aware of her own breathing as she watched the couple exit the café.

Three days later an invitation arrived through Fay's letter box at home, from Cameron and Ricki inviting her to their home.

As Fay sat in their living room less than a week from their first meeting, sipping a glass of wine, she watched Cameron and Ricki and her body yearned for release.

The wine helped her to pluck up the courage to move next to Cameron and casually place her hand on the inside of Cameron's thigh.

Ricki moved over and rubbed his hands through Cameron's hair, tugging at it with excitement.

Fay made a pact with herself that what happened next would determine the rest of the story.

Fay brushed her hand very gently across the top button of Cameron's blouse and looking at Ricki, she said, "We can arrange for your bank to transfer funds from your account into the prearrangement trust account each month."

Fay knew that Ricki would agree, the power of the erotic movement of her fingers undoing Cameron's top button concluding the deal.

Cameron was her principal aide.

The power lay in Fay's hands as she continued to unbutton the rest of Cameron's blouse.

She rubbed her fingers slowly against the cotton fabric of Cameron's bra and felt Cameron's left nipple harden.

Ricki stood over them watching as Fay unclipped Cameron's bra, gently removing it and Cameron's breasts sprung free.

There was no way of escape for all three of them

now, the moment had become intensely erotic and the deal was sealed.

Ricki came alongside Fay and removed her jumper revealing her black bra and ample breasts bulging over the top, bursting to escape the confinements of her bra.

The emotional complications of what was occurring were far from Fay's thoughts as she rubbed her fingers across Cameron's nipples.

Fay removed the remainder of her own clothes revealing her slender legs and her breasts stood out in splendor.

She made eye contact with Ricki knowing the effect her long black hair, dark eyes and lashes, and her ripe body would be enough to turn his brain to a mushy mess.

She fancied him too, his face handsome classic and his curly hair.

He touched Fay now, gentle and softly.

They knew their roles, all Fay had to do was to ensure his sperm came inside of her in the hope of producing a baby which would result in the big payment when she handed it over to them as their own.

She closed her eyes as he came deep inside of her.

Not interested in small talk, Fay dressed quickly and left.

In the intervening weeks, the pattern repeated itself two or three times per week. During this time, Fay had started to formulate a different plan.

The pregnancy now confirmed by the blue line on the stick she could set the ball in motion.

Against the rules, which they had agreed at the beginning, she called Ricki and invited him over to her apartment on his own. She knew he would come, she had seen how he had fallen in love with her and his desires for her body were too great for him to resist.

Her heart was pumping hard now as she opened her front door to let him in, adrenalin pumping through her system.

That he was keen to be with her on his own, almost fantastically keen, was apparent immediately.

He was shaking, his left hand in particular as he started to undress her.

She knew he trusted her and the twenty thousand pounds was present inside of her no matter what, but she wanted more. She had observed their wealthy lifestyle and wanted it for herself.

As he came inside of her all she could hear was the wind outside and the sound of his harsh breathing.

She pulled her cashmere sweater over her head and leaving her slender legs and panties on display for him she made them both a coffee.

She felt nervous as she said," I'm pregnant, I'm carrying your baby."

Ricki leaned back in his chair, the cup of coffee cradled between his long fingers.

Fay could almost see the change of gears behind his face.

She laughed, a rich, throaty laugh.

Her words seemed lightweight and somehow ludicrous, "Leave Cameron, we will give her the baby, and you can have me."

"That is simplistic and unfair, I need breathing space," he retorted getting up from his chair, and left slamming the front door behind him.

A sensible fear grew within her, had she gone too far too quickly, she wondered.

**Assignment Eight -** You take a chance and pick up a hitch-hiker. It is either the best decision you have ever made, or the worst. You decide.

20th January 2016

Michael, taking on board the Virgin Births of the previous assignments, had lots of fun as he spun a humorous take on the Nativity. You need to watch out for the hidden meanings.

AJ went with a little twisted tale to show her ability to write something that wasn't a twelve year old boy.

S.J.'s learning curve continued as she tried to squeeze a complete novel inside a thousand words but was pleased with how it came out.

J.M. went back to her roots as a zombie fan and wrote a piece based on two characters from her debut novel "Wait For Me" so please be aware of spoilers.

# You take a chance and pick up a hitch-hiker. It is either the best decision you have ever made, or the worst. You decide.

### by

### AJ. Jones

To say the past year has been life-changing is to put it mildly. It all began on my husband, Alex's, 40th birthday, when I was driving us home from his birthday dinner at The Red Lion.

About a mile from our house, we noticed a young, very pregnant girl standing on the side of the road with her thumb pointing in the direction we were travelling.

Alex's medical instincts kicked in immediately – after all, he is the local GP – and without considering any of the warnings you see on Facebook, he asked me to stop the car. He rolled down the window and asked the girl where she was going. She went to answer but instead of words, a deep-throated groan emerged from her contorted mouth as she clutched at her swollen stomach with her beautifully manicured hands.

Alex glanced warily around the area but, not seeing anything threatening, he got out of the car, walked round to the boot and took out the medical bag that he always carries with him in case of emergency.

Before he could ask her any more questions, the girl lowered herself delicately onto the freezing cold ground and began hyperventilating.

"We need to take her home straight away, Philippa," Alex shouted.

"Are you sure it's safe?" I said. "Wouldn't it be better if we called an ambulance?"

"No!" the girl screamed. "The baby's coming. Now!"

"Get out of the car and help me lift her up, Darling," Alex urged. So, I did as he asked, and we managed to manoeuvre the girl carefully onto the back seat.

Alex took out his stethoscope and began to examine her. He quickly decided that there was enough time to get her to our house before the baby was born, so I drove us all, very gingerly, towards our comfortable home.

Baby Alexa was born just minutes after we got her mother onto the big double bed in our spare bedroom. After cleaning up, Alex and I left both mother and baby to rest after their tiring ordeal. It was 1 am before Alex and I had calmed down enough to go to bed ourselves, and, I can tell you, I didn't get much sleep that night.

Around 6 am, I heard the tap running in the kitchen and I went downstairs to find that the girl was making coffee for us all.

"I'll finish that. Sit down and tell me about yourself," I said. "What's your name and where have you come from? And why were you out hitch-hiking in that condition last night?"

"I'm Anya," she replied. "I live in London and I was on my way to visit my biological father."

"Where does he live?" I asked.

Her reply sent shivers down my spine. "Right here," she said, with a look of childlike menace spreading across her face.

At that exact moment, Alex came into the kitchen. "Wake up and smell the coffee," he said with an irritating smile.

Ignoring his flippant remark, I asked her, "What do you mean? Does he live in this village?"

"Yes!" was her only response, but she was staring directly at Alex.

"How are you this morning, er, er?" Alex mumbled, still half asleep.

"I'm Anya," she repeated. "I've come to see you because you're my biological father."

Alex looked at me in shock. "What do you mean, your biological father. I can assure you . . ."

"My mother worked at the clinic where you donated your sperm when you were a medical student," Anya interrupted. "She was the administrator there and she decided to use your sperm to make me. I only found out yesterday. I've always believed that her husband, Steve, was my real Dad but she says he couldn't have children, so he agreed to go along with it.

Mum said she was telling me all this now because my baby deserves to know who her real Grandfather is. She gave me your address. She's been keeping tabs on you all this time."

"So why are you here?" Alex asked suspiciously.

"Because I was totally disgusted with them both, so I left and walked around London for a while. Then I found the piece of paper she'd written your name and address on and decided to head here."

At that moment, the doorbell rang. I opened the door to an attractive dark-haired woman who shouted at me angrily, "Is my daughter here?"

Anya appeared behind me. "Mum! What are you doing here?"

"I knew you'd be here. He's delivered your baby, hasn't he? Where is she? There could be a problem with her. Steve and I have come to take you both home."

"You can't! It's too early for them to be travelling anywhere," said Alex, joining us at the front door.

Ignoring him completely, Anya's mother pleaded with her daughter. "You don't understand, Anya. If what you told me last night is true, your baby could be in big trouble."

"What are you on about, Mum?" shouted Anya, alarm draining the blood from her face.

"You told me that the baby's father is Scott Dawson. Well, I checked my old records and he's your half-brother. He was created using this man's sperm, too."

Alex's face froze in a look of complete panic. "I need to examine her thoroughly," was all he said as he bounded upstairs.

Well, that was twelve months ago and our lives have been turned upside down ever since.

Alexa is growing by the day. Anya, her mum and Steve have moved in with us, and life is all about Alexa.

She's a beautiful child – perfect face, perfect body – but her head is GIGANTIC – big enough to hold her superbrain. Everyone who sees her falls under her spell.

We're trying to teach her about good and evil but she

has her own ideas.

It's clear this child is capable of just about anything, which both delights me, and scares me to death. What does the future hold for us now?

# You take a chance and pick up a hitch-hiker. It is either the best decision you have ever made, or the worst. You decide.

by

## J.M. McKenzie

It was an eerie journey down the deserted motorway. They could have chosen either carriageway but, in true British style, stuck to the left hand side, despite the absence of oncoming traffic, or any traffic at all for that matter. It had been at least an hour since they left the city and so far it had proved to be the right decision. They had made steady progress and had not encountered any significant trouble from the living or the dead. They had had to negotiate the inevitable progression of wrecked and abandoned cars and the occasional snarled pile-up, but other than that the route had been surprisingly clear. They had seen evidence of other survivors in the form of disused camp-sites, decaying makeshift dwellings, graffiti, and tattered flags or banners, but had had no actual human contact whatsoever. Everyone left alive seemed to have gone to ground. The dead were still around of course, though not in the terrifying thronging hordes of the city, just occasional small groups of two or three, shuffling and stumbling in the carriageway. They had passed them by before they even noticed they were there. Lisa watched them disappear in the rear-view mirror as they lifted their heads and opened their mouths in a silent moan, before shambling fruitlessly in pursuit.

With each passing mile she felt herself relax little by little. The tension that had built up in her body from weeks of living in fear and uncertainty began to ease slowly but surely. With Neil driving beside her, his back straight and strong and his features clear and untroubled, she felt good for the first time in weeks. She had a sense of purpose and a glimmer of hope for the future, their future together. She reached out and quietly put her hand on his thigh and he turned to her and smiled as he covered it with his own. She sighed and closed her eyes.

She had no idea how long she had been asleep when she was awoken with a start as the car lurched to a stop. "What the fuck?" Neil growled.

She looked at him in confusion and then followed his gaze to the road ahead. A small figure in dark tattered clothing was standing only a few inches in front of the car, arms outstretched palms facing out. "He just walked right out! He came from no-where. I nearly hit him." Neil opened his door bristling with irritation and ready for a confrontation.

"Wait...be careful..." Lisa warned, but too late. He was out of the car facing up to the figure before she could get the words out. Glancing around nervously, she half watched the interaction. At first he was upright and aggressive, gesticulating and posturing, but he quickly softened and bent toward the figure nodding in a gesture of concern. Suddenly, there was movement on the left of the carriageway and two or three infected appeared from the undergrowth, shambling toward them. Neil hurriedly put his arm around the figure and guided it towards the car.

"What's happening?" Lisa asked, as he opened the rear door, her anxiety building as the undead steadily approached. The figure was girl of about sixteen. She was gaunt and pale.

"It's ok Lisa. She needs help. She's hurt and exhausted. She's not infected." He spoke quietly but firmly as he helped the girl into the back seat.

Seconds later they were driving again leaving Lisa speechless with shock and concern. She trusted Neil completely but was surprised by his apparent reckless disregard for their safety. The girl briefly explained that, like them, she was trying to get north of the city. She had been with a group but had been separated from them and had been alone and on foot since the previous evening. She had no food or water, had cut her leg on a metal fence and was desperate. With that, she stretched out across the back seat and was asleep within minutes, her breathing loud and laboured.

"Are you sure?" she whispered. "Are you sure she's not infected? How do you know she cut her leg?

What if she was bitten?"

"I think we can trust her Lisa, I believe her. We couldn't leave her. What if it had been you?" he whispered back. The girl stirred and he looked at Lisa pleadingly. Lisa nodded and they were quiet again, each lost in their own thoughts.

They had only been driving for another ten minutes or so when they had to stop again. A wrecked lorry and car were blocking both sides of the carriageway apart from a small section. It was big enough for them to get through but a loose tyre from the lorry was blocking their path. Neil got out and tried to move it. Lisa could see he was struggling. Warily she got out to help. The next few moments were a blur. As she walked towards him she saw an infected emerge from behind the lorry. She called out "Neil! Behind you!" He spun around but it was on him before he had time to reach for the machete that was slung over his back in its leather sling. It lurched at him knocking him backwards onto the ground and falling on top of him. He grabbed it by the throat straining to keep its gnashing teeth away from his face. Lisa was frozen with terror and indecision. Her own weapon was in the car. What had she been thinking? Her instincts were screaming at her just to launch herself at the creature but her head was telling her to go back for her weapon first.

It felt as though she was rooted on the spot for minutes but it could only have been a split second.

Whatever, it was enough time for the girl, awoken by Lisa's cry of alarm, to burst from the car, draw a crowbar from beneath her coat and devastate the creature's skull in two swift blows. It stopped thrashing and was still. Neil rolled it off him and got to his feet with an infuriating grin. Open mouthed in amazement Lisa looked at girl who just winked at her and hobbled back to car.

# You take a chance and pick up a hitch-hiker. It is either the best decision you have ever made, or the worst. You decide.

**by**

**Michael Andrews**

The rain was terrible. It was hammering against the window screen so fast that my wipers could barely keep up as I crawled along the winding, country lane that lead back to the small village where I lived. As I rounded a tight corner, slowing down to snail's pace, I swore as I narrowly avoided a car that was parked up on the verge.

Pulling to a stop, I peered through the pelting raindrops and could see two people, one huddled in the passenger seat while the second, a tall, rangy man was trying to undo the bonnet of his car. The old mother's warning about picking up strangers flashed through my mind, but I decided that the weather was no place for two people to be stranded so I wound down my window.

"Do you need a lift?" I shouted at the man, who looked up startled, having obviously missed my approach. "This storm is good for the rest of the night so you're going to get drenched."

"That would be great," he flashed me a smile. "Let me get the wife."

I watched as the man helped his wife from their car and into the back seat of my own. Where I had thought that she was just fat, now proved not to be the case.

"How far along is she?" I asked as the man got into the passenger seat.

"Mary is actually due any time now," he replied. "I'm Joe by the way. Joe Carpenter."

"Larry Shepherd," I shook his offered hand. "I doubt you'll get anyone out tonight so you are more than welcome to stay in my guest room."

With their grateful acceptance, I pulled off, leaving their car behind and carefully made my way home. I started to get a little concerned when Mary began to pant a little heavier, and having watched far too many episodes of 'ER', I was worried that she would actually have her baby in the back of my car. As we pulled into the driveway which I shared with my neighbour, she cried out in pain.

"Are you okay, dearest?" Joe asked, worry evident in his voice.

"I think he's coming... now!" Mary croaked.

"Oh crap!" her husband replied. "What are we going to do?"

"Don't worry, my neighbour is a doctor," I reassured them. "His wife is also a mid-wife so when we get in, I'll give them a call."

I hit the button on the remote to open the garage door and Joe looked up in surprise at my house.

"It's a converted barn and stable," I smiled at him. "Cost a small packet but it's nice and quiet, and big enough for what I want. Let's get you settled and I'll go and call Doctor Wiseman."

It took some time to help the now heavily panting Mary out of the car and into the guest bedroom and, once she was settled, I made the quick phone call to my neighbour.

It was mere minutes before the bell rang and I was surprised when all three of them entered.

"Hello Larry, where is she?" Balthasar asked, his concern for a patient cutting through the normal banalities.

"She's in the guest bedroom." I replied, nodding to his wife Mel.

"I thought I'd bring Casper along as he's just starting his student nursing placement," Mrs Wiseman answered my unspoken question.


It wasn't long before Joe and I were pushed to one side, letting the three Wisemen get to work, helping Mary through a very comfortable birth. The cry of a newborn rang throughout the house, just as the new father finished his cup of Nescafe Gold Blend. In the rush to be with his new family, he set his cup down on top of the remote control for my stereo and we were greeted with a blast of the latest Olly Murs record. In my haste to shut it off, I grabbed the wrong remote control and switched on my tv. Of course, I'd left in on the horror channel, being an avid fan of the Hammer House movies. Christopher Lee was just in the process of chasing Peter Cushing's Baron Frankenstein before I managed to shut down both entertainment systems.


"I have a boy!" Joe crowed, holding his new born son up. "I don't know what we would have done if you hadn't stopped for us, Larry."

"Think nothing of it," I told him as I pulled a face at the smiling baby boy.

"Thank you, Mr Shepherd," Mary added, tiredness in her voice.

"So what are you going to call him?" Mel asked, always happy when a new born baby arrives. I guess it was her motherly instinct.

"We've been discussing it for some time…" Joe said. "We've decided on… Brian!"

Just then, the baby let out one very loud fart… proving that Brian was indeed, a very naughty boy!

# You take a chance and pick up a hitch-hiker. It is either the best decision you have ever made, or the worst. You decide.

**by**

**S.J. Gibbs**

Beverley drove off without giving him the satisfaction of seeing her cry.

She tilted her head back to keep further tears at bay as she raced down the lanes away from her home of the last six years.

She tried to hold on to some degree of control, as she had no idea of where she was heading.

She passed the quaint old inn where they had eaten many times together and took the main road East.

As she drove across the bridge over the river she could hear the blustery cold wind outside and turned up the heater in her car to maximum.

As she slowed for the traffic lights, which had changed to red, she noticed the young woman with short, black hair standing hitchhiking at the side of the road.

Uncharacteristically Beverley pulled the car over, leant over opening the passenger side door and offered the young woman a lift.

Her gaze settled on the young woman as she gratefully jumped into the passenger seat. She could see the panic deep in the woman's eyes.

A deep and abiding fascination with this woman stirred within Beverley. Anxious to establish the reason the woman was hitchhiking, she started asking her questions, as she pulled off down the road.

She tried not to show delight as the woman explained her name was Clare and that she had walked out of her marriage with no thoughts or ideas of where her future plans were going to lead her, she just needed to get away.

Beverley felt she had an immediate ally they were in the same boat.

Clare explained that she had been in a violent relationship and she had escaped, but Beverley couldn't see any scars or bruises consistent with the story.

Beverley observed the faint rise and fall of Clare's chest as she started to relax beside her.

Beverley's thoughts swooped around as she tried to get a hold on something tangible.

As the journey progressed with neither of them clear of any direction, they discussed the disasters of their marriages.

The air cleared between them and they found themselves laughing together at some of their memories.

Recognizing Clare as a victim of domestic abuse and the danger she had been in, Beverley felt very protective towards her new companion although she did wonder whether the story was true.

Occasionally they both glanced uneasily towards each other but in the main they were both feeling more relaxed, in each other's company.

They drove along in silence for a while, both with there own thoughts.

She started to question herself if she had been foolish picking up a hitch- hiker and whether she was trying to rescue Clare in an attempt to rescue her self.

She observed Clare again and thought to her self, " she would have been pretty once, now she looks undernourished and ill."

She was in her thirties and wore jeans and a sweater, which looked cheap and were too big. Had she picked up a vagabond who had been loitering for a lift?

As she thought about it the air in her lungs seemed to condense.

As they approached the next junction, Clare opened the passenger door and jumped out quick as anything.

The movement threw Beverley and in her distraction she mounted the curb of the narrow road and ended up on the grass verge having lost control of the car.

She climbed out of the car and on examining the buckled wheel realized she was going nowhere with the car. She looked around but Clare was nowhere to be seen.

Fortunately she could see a pub further down the road and began to walk quickly towards it, trying not to entertain any of the horrendous possibilities flooding her mind.

The pub looked closed but she pushed the door anyway in the hope that some person was inside. She found a room with dirty magnolia paint on the walls, a dark wooden floor and the odd dark wooden table with stains all over.

A man sat smoking in the corner, barely lifting his head as she walked in. She called out behind the bar but there was no reply.

The man just sat drinking his pint, smoking and staring at Beverley.

He was not an attractive man, he had a pimply vulgar face and there was something mean and furtive in his expression.

The way he stared at her made Beverley feel grubby. She could almost see the demons skipping in his wake.

Apologetically she explained to the man that her car had broken down and whether there was a phone she could use to summons some assistance, thinking to herself that it had been sheer stupidity on her part to pick up a hitch- hiker, leaving her in this mess.

Suddenly, the man hurled himself at her and dragged her by her hair across the room and through a door into a dark back room.

She could smell his bad breath as he wiped his hand across his snotty nose. She had no defense against him, she was totally unprepared having led a very sheltered and privileged life.

He held her face against his as she watched him lick his teeth.

He fingered her face and she could smell his foul fingers touching her skin.

For a stupid second, she thought he was going to let her go but then he grabbed her even harder than he had before.

Every line of his body reeked and she was filled with disgust.

He pushed her down on the cold, hard ground.

Beverley screamed and as she did so she heard the door open and a warning gun shot echoed around the room as Clare appeared gun in hand and shouted, " Move away from her, or I will kill you."

**Assignment Nine -** You're in line at an unemployment office when someone comes up to you with an odd proposal.

26th February 2016

AJ turned her hand to romance, with a twist as she continued to push her boundaries, while Michael delved into his love of Star Wars with a small piece of fan fiction while mixing it with commentary on the real world.

J.M. went with her favourite theme of horror as she continued to practise writing tension and fear, while writing about gore without mentioning gore in detail.

S.J. looked into human nature with her story and feels looking back that this was written in a colloquial style, something again that she is working to improve.

# You're in line at an unemployment office when someone comes up to you with an odd proposal.

### by

### AJ. Jones

"Hello! Do you remember me? I'm Sue's friend, Jenny. We met last year at her retirement party. How are you?"

Jenny's voice shakes me to the core. Of course I remember her. How could I not? She's the reason I'm standing in this bloody unemployment line, and that I've been forced to stand in it every woeful week for the past 6 months.

"Hello. What a nice surprise!" I hear myself say, trying to turn the grimace that I know shows on my face every time I visit the unemployment office into a genuine-looking smile. "What brings you here?"

"Well you, actually!" Jenny purrs, employing her compellingly hypnotic voice to its full extent.

"Me! Why?" I ask, trying to hide the annoyance that's welling up inside me.

"Sue told me what you've been through when I rang her for a catchup at the weekend. She mentioned that you have to sign on here every week, so I thought I'd come and find you because I need to thank you for your part in what's happened to me since we met. You'd never believe it, but I'm a millionaire now."

Her mesmerising voice flows on like a sultry siren, explaining that, just after Sue's party, she'd won £100,000 on the lottery and she'd used it to start up a business that's going from strength to strength.

"And it was all down to you," she beamed.

Great, I thought. She's come to rub my nose in it. She just wants to gloat in my misfortune.

"And I've come to make you an offer I hope you can't refuse!" she continued.

I feel her voice captivating me all over again, just like at that fateful party. But can I really believe her words this time? I fell for it last time, remember, and look where it got me; well, right here, actually, with a broken marriage, a bankruptcy charge and a miserable future ahead of me.

"Don't bother signing on today. You won't need to when you've heard my offer," she buzzes excitedly.

"Oh, I can't do that!" I suddenly realise my voice is sounding far too loud. I'm not going to allow myself to be so gullible again, but who am I trying to convince here?

"Well, let me take you for a coffee afterwards, then. After all, I've come all this way to find you."

She's got a point, I suppose. "Ok, then. Meet me outside. I won't be long."

Half an hour later, we're walking towards her brand new silver Merc. "Nice car," I hear myself say, half under my breath.

"Yes, I've got a few nice ones now. I do love this one – but she's yours if you want her."

"Why on earth would you say that?" The words spill out before I can stop myself.

"Because I've come to ask you to marry me, that's why!"

What on earth! Did I hear right? Does she think I'm a lesbian or something? I mean, do I look like a lesbian?

"But I'm a woman." (What a ridiculous thing to say!)

"Yes. But I think we both know how happy we can make each other. I've been thinking about you ever since we met. We're old souls, you and I. I know you feel it too; I can see it in your eyes. I knew it as soon as we met at that fateful party."

We get into her fabulous car and she drives us to a smart coffee shop where she orders a cafetiere for two. Her voice drones on, dripping with honeyed tones. "When that money came into my life, I knew exactly what I had to do with it. Our chance meeting made me realise that the world needs an app that can recognise the type of love that lasts throughout time, so I found a guy who knows how to build apps and he helped me create 'Constant Craving'. It's amazing how many happy souls there are that have been reunited by my little app. But I couldn't have done it without bumping into you at that party."

I feel myself falling under her spell. She's right; I knew we had a special connection straight away, but I was a married woman when we met. And I still would be now if it wasn't for the terrible advice she'd given me that day – to remortgage my home and invest everything in my struggling business. The business had still failed and I'd lost everything, including my lovely husband. Was it all because she wanted me all to herself?

I lower my voice to a whisper, not wanting anyone else to overhear our strange conversation. "If you genuinely believe that we can have a happy future together, I want you to agree that you will never force me to do anything that I'm not comfortable with."

"Of course, I won't," she says, staring straight into my eyes. "I want you to be happy because, if you're happy, I will be too.

"Well, will you? Marry me, I mean?

"I haven't told you yet, but I'm living in a penthouse apartment in London now, and there's the flat in Monte Carlo, of course. And I nearly forgot the villa I'm having built in the Florida Keys."

Looking at the size of the sparkly rock sitting majestically in the middle of the fabulous engagement ring she's holding out towards me does enough to sway my misgivings. And checking out the name on the box quells my fears entirely.

I'd be a fool to let this opportunity go. She believes she loves me, so what have I got to lose? My life is going nowhere at this precise moment in time. And maybe she's right – maybe our souls are meant to be together in this life, and the next, and forever after. I've always believed that it's our souls that are our real selves, not the body we're inhabiting.

So goodbye Unemployment Office! I won't be standing in line ever again.

## You're in line at an unemployment office when someone comes up to you with an odd proposal.

### by

### J.M. McKenzie

I had a feeling something wasn't right as I walked out of the unemployment office, but I was pretty desperate after seven months without even a sniff of a job. In my hand was a crumpled piece of paper containing a handwritten address and list of instructions. The man who gave it to me had been well-dressed and well-spoken but there was something about the way he looked at me, or rather didn't look me in the eye, that made me feel uneasy. He was furtive and had been looking around him as we spoke. He had approached me as I stood in line and promised me one thousand pounds, cash in hand, if I just followed the instructions, no questions asked.

It seemed too good to be true and much too easy to be legitimate, but I had literally nothing to lose. I was behind with my rent and close to eviction. I had three pounds seventy six pence in my pocket and little else to my name.

The first instruction was to walk to the given address taking only the route directed. I was sure I knew the street and it was quite nearby but the instructions directed me to take a rather long way round through back streets and down deserted alleyways. What should have been a ten minute journey took me over twenty five minutes and I arrived at the building from a service lane at the back and not from the main street. It was a four story white Georgian townhouse. It looked smart and well maintained and, from the similarity of the décor and window dressings, appeared to be one dwelling, unlike the other houses in the area which were all divided into flats.

The next instruction was to enter the building from the basement door, down some steps and through a covered porch area. It explicitly stated I should ensure that I was not seen entering the building. Decidedly dodgy! Nevertheless, I looked around and sure that no-one was about, descended the steps towards the porch. Now I was curious, almost excited. Even without the prospect of the money, at this stage, I probably would have done it just for the hell of it.

Inside the porch was a solid black door. I tried the handle. True to the instructions it was unlocked. I pushed it open and stepped into the room. The door closed behind me. The first thing I noticed was the strong and acrid smell of a combination of ammonia and bleach. That was bad enough but what was worse was the unmistakable odour of rotting flesh that the strong smell of cleaning fluids failed to mask. Now my curiosity instantly changed to fear. I stepped back towards the door I had just come through and looked around, one hand reaching behind me groping for the handle.

The room was empty except for a large butchers hook hanging from the ceiling. It was well lit by celling lights and tiled neatly from ceiling to floor with oblong white tiles. It had a clinical look and feel to it. The floor seemed to slope gradually towards a drain in the middle of the floor beneath the butchers hook. There was another door, this time stainless steel on the opposite wall. The only other single feature I could see was a grill low on the wall to my left. Now I knew for sure that things were not right and my skin began to prickle with fear. Beads of sweat began to form on my forehead and my hands were clammy and began to tremble. Fuck the money! I spun around to leave the way I had come in. Shit! The back of this door was also smooth stainless steel like the one opposite. Also, like the one opposite, it had no handle.

I was trapped. I was panicking. I banged on the door shouting, "Let me out! Someone help me!"

As I was banging on the door and feeling round the edge of the frame for the slightest hint of a rim or a bit of purchase, I became aware of a gentle hissing sound. I saw a soft mist was beginning to form at my feet. I looked around the room again. A white gas was flowing steadily from the grill on the wall. It was quickly filling the room. The blanket of mist now reached my knees. I ran over to the other door and started banging on that. I was now screaming more than shouting. "Please, please let me out!"

When the gas reached my waist I began to feel its effects. The room began to swim and there was a strange buzzing in my head. My vision blurred so much that I had to close my eyes. I felt dizzy and weak, overcome by a sudden sense of fatigue. The last thing I properly remember was sinking to my knees into the swirling white mist.

After that there were flashes and images of the man at the unemployment office dressed now in surgical green. There was pain, terrible tearing sounds and more pain. There was red and wetness and more pain. In the middle of it all there was something monstrous, something terrible but undistinguishable. Then the pain became all I could think about. There were more sounds, more tearing, but now this was accompanied by crunching and growling. Pain. Red. Wetness. More pain. More red. More wetness. Then suddenly no pain, no sounds, no red, no feeling only dark quiet blackness.

# You're in line at an unemployment office when someone comes up to you with an odd proposal.

## by

## Michael Andrews

Oh God, here I am again! Signing on day. Having to stand in line with the great unwashed masses who are queuing for their sign off with no intention of actually trying to get a job. It's so frustrating when I am out there, applying for job after job, going for interview after interview and I am getting the same amount of dole money as the lazy arses who sit around all day watching Jeremy Kyle and Loose Women.

At least there are only three people in front of me this week. The bloke at the front of the queue looks like he's already spent the morning down Wetherspoons. He's actually swaying on the spot and I could imagine him stumbling over at any moment. I'm glad I'm actually not next in line because his clothes reek of cigarettes. Then there's the stereotypical mother of five, with all five kids in tow. Looking at them, there's at least three different fathers as one is black, two are ginger and the two babies are screaming the place down. I wish I'd remembered my i-Pod. The man in front of me actually looks half decent. Well, he isn't drunk anyway and he's dressed in decent clothes, although they may be lifted from the local market for all I know!

Jesus! How long is this going to take? Oh, I see... there are only two work coaches on today. I feel like getting into the same state as the bloke at the front. I think it's happy hour at the pub at the moment.

FINALLY! Movement. This should be funny, as Mr Drunk is going to try to explain what he's done. I remember him from last time. At least the lady he shouted at before isn't working today. I suppose I should check that I've filled in all the boxes in my book. I swear it takes longer to write up what I've been doing than actually applying for jobs in the first place.

Oh blimey... the bloke in front of me has just gone outside to answer his mobile. The good news is that it bumps me up the queue. The bad news is that I am now directly behind the screaming brats. I think after I'm done here, I'm going to chill for a couple of hours on my X-box. I've just bought myself that latest shoot 'em up that everyone is raving about. You know the one... it's set in space and you are in control of either an X-Wing or a Tie-Fighter. I've got quite good at blasting the First Order to smithereens.

Hurrah! The screaming brats and their mother have sat down as well. That means I'm next in line. The drunken man doesn't seem to be getting on very well with his work coach. I can hear him beginning to raise his voice, just like last time. He'll soon be on his feet shouting... oh there he goes. I'm going to take a step back, I think!

"Sorry mate," I say to the man behind me. I didn't notice that he'd come back inside from his phone call and I bumped into him.

"That's okay, I should have told you I was standing here," he replied with a faint smile. His eyes were a piercing green and I found myself unable to break eye contact with him. "Alex isn't it?" he asked me.

"Yeah, have we met before?" I queried. I couldn't place him.

"Not in person, but I have been monitoring your progress," he answered. "You've become quite adept with the new ship."

"Pardon?" I asked, wondering what he was going on about.

"The X5 fighter... you handle it better than any pilot in the ranks at the moment."

I looked at him. He didn't seem to be drunk or on drugs.

"I am here to offer you a job, and we are desperate for

you to take it," he smiled faltered. "We lost Commander Dameron in the last battle, and with General Solo dead, we need a new impetus in the fight against the First Order."

"Okay, I'd love some of what you're on, but I'm afraid you're going to have to wake up to the real world," I chuckled at his fantasy.

"Actually, it's you who needs to join the world around you," he came back. "I'm Colonel Datoo, and I want to recruit you to Red Wing. Do you accept?"

"Heck, it'll be a laugh to see what you do if I say yes!" I sniggered.

He placed his hand on my shoulder and the world went fuzzy...

# You're in line at an unemployment office when someone comes up to you with an odd proposal.

## by

## S.J. Gibbs

Dave Langdon stood in the queue at the employment office wondering how one of the finest salvage experts in the country was now standing in line looking for employment.

More than a million pounds profit had rested on his latest deal and yet it had ended with him having lost everything.

He had a high opinion of his own capabilities and was annoyed at finding himself stood in this queue looking for any type of employment.

He had stood in line for over half an hour now and the line seemed to be standing still.

He fixed his eye on the canvas on the wall of a tree stump and a rainbow, he felt like the tree stump but where was his rainbow?

The thought of being homeless was just too awful to contemplate and yet this is what he was facing if he didn't find some work.

It was raining and windy and his mood felt the same

as the weather.

He knew he couldn't just sit and wait for things to happen, he needed work.

He had specialized in airline salvage but it had all gone terribly wrong.

His fiery nature was struggling with the slowness of the queue.

A woman approached him. The first thing he noticed was her full mouth and lips.

He almost ignored her welcoming smile but then thought better of it.

She offered her hand to shake his and whispered in his ear, "I have a proposition for you, can we go for a coffee?"

Taking a seat opposite her in the coffee house, she introduced herself as Gina Garnet and explained she ran a private member's house, providing society with entertainment and the higher things in life and how it was impossible to obtain the staff needed to run the place properly.

Dave was unaware of his good looks and with his 6 foot 4 inch heavy frame and wearing his black suit had little idea of the effect he had on women.

It took less than a minute for him to decide that whatever position she was offering he would take it, a job was a job and he needed the money.

She suggested he go with her to see the house and as she swung her Range Rover out of the car park, he tried to keep his eyes on the road. He abandoned reason, and decided to just go with the flow.

As they entered the house, Gina explained, the more we charge, the more exclusive " The Code" becomes.

She explained more about the trade and Dave told her he thought she was insane offering him the position of manager, as he knew nothing about the trade whatsoever.

She laughed as she stated, " your looks fit the bill, all you have to do is act in a pleasant manner, especially with the women members. Your attitude and behavior, towards the women, is all that will matter."

They exited into the courtyard and as the river rushed past. Dave was starting to understand why people might want to pay large club membership to be sat in such an amazing setting. The place was stunning. A huge oak tree provided some shaded seating for hot summer days.

After Gina introduced him to the staff, she kissed him on the cheek and said, "start tomorrow, have fun, all you need to do is mix particularly with the women," and she promptly left.

Dave bit this finger to see if he was dreaming, and

laughed thinking to himself, "from salvage expert, to employment queue, to gigolo."

He felt like he was starring in a Hollywood epic, in his world, the real world, things like this didn't happen.

The next day, he chose his clothes carefully and headed to " The Code". The first woman he spoke to looked him up and down and then walked right past him, as if he wasn't there. This wasn't going to be as easy as he had imagined.

Another woman caught his look and he leaned forward to whisper in her ear. He walked beside her, out into the courtyard and led her to the edge of the riverbank. He stood there for a minute or two, a little bemused at the role he was playing and found himself wondering how much money she had.

She took him by the hand and led him back inside to the roulette table.

She sniffed at the claret he had poured her and made him pour one for himself. He felt a little foolish and embarrassed but he smiled and sipped the wine anyway, thinking to himself " it beats sweeping the streets, digging ditches or salvage work for that matter."

He had relied on his salvage business to earn hundreds of thousands of pounds, but maybe there was more to be earned in human commodities.

He improvised the best he could, smiling and chatting politely.

In a bizarre way, he suddenly recognized this woman's stupidity could be fooled by the illusion he was creating for her. It was becoming very clear to him just how he would be able to keep the standard of life he was accustomed to, these women had money.

She had finished off the bottle of claret with Dave' help and now requested a whisky but Dave opted for a water to keep his head clear.

She wanted to eat now and headed to the dining room asking Dave to join her for dinner. She was becoming rambunctious as the alcohol took effect. Dave observed her as she chopped her steak into delicate bite-sized pieces.

She was crude and vulgar with her conversation but all Dave could see was her money and his future.

**Assignment Ten -** Write about anything. However, the last line from your character must be: "It was then that I discovered I could not die".

14th April 2016

AJ spent hours researching the topics in her story to ensure accuracy as it touched heavily on science facts and the group were loving it right up to the last couple of sentences. However, instead of rewriting, it was decided to leave it in its original format.

J.M. based her story on the song "Ghost in this House" by Alison Krauss, about the love of a married couple.

Michael's political side and humanity shone through as the lead up to Brexit had stoked up a lot of anti-immigration feelings throughout the country. He wanted to put a human face to the issue and feels to this day that this is his best piece of flash fiction work.

S.J. enjoyed this assignment developing the thriller

aspect of her writing style, something which has been taken on with her novel, Ixagion.

The group feel that topics of the day can often lead to a good idea for plot lines.

# Write about anything. However, the last line from your character must be: "It was then that I discovered I could not die".

## by

## AJ. Jones

Over and over, I've asked myself this question. But I've never actually come up with an answer that satisfies both my sense of justice and also my own personal perception of human experience. As the Moody Blues can attest to, there are always "more questions than answers".

What's the question, you may well ask?

Well here's the thing: Why on earth have we, the sensible majority, allowed the minority of so-called "Leaders of Men" to make this beautiful world we live in one full of hatred, power-struggles and corruption just by making up stories that we can't actually prove? To the majority of us, it's all just Chinese Whispers. Why, then, have we allowed ourselves to be brainwashed into believing every word they've either said or written down, as if only they have the true insight into how we should all live our lives?

When I say "leaders", I'm not just talking about dictators, like Hitler and Kim Jong-Il, and politicians, like Tony Blair and Donald Trump, I also mean religious leaders - prophets, like Jesus and Mohammed - who have influenced people in more subtle ways to get them to believe in their doctrines and, ultimately, to do their bidding.

Why have we, as rational beings, fallen for their stories? Is it just because most of us can't be bothered to think for ourselves? Have we all been coerced into a false sense of security because all we really want is to live a long and happy life with our loved ones around us, not having to worry about anything or anyone that might threaten our very existence on this earth? And is this just because we're all selfish, lazy bastards who don't actually give a shit?

Well, my thirst for the answer to this question has led me inextricably into the world of quantum physics, also known as quantum mechanics or quantum theory. This, on the surface, is about the behaviour of atoms and their interaction with energy, but it can also explain how and why we work as human beings in that, apparently, we are all, along with everything else in the universe, made up of a collection of atoms and subatomic particles that exploded out of a single, pea-sized entity a very long time ago and have continued to expand ever since - "to infinity and beyond", as Buzz Lightyear put it. All these atoms are held together by light, by the way. That could explain why so many of us love a nice holiday in Benidorm every now and again.

Anyway, continuing on the quantum physics theme,

"the entanglement theory" tells us that all these atoms react together and all that activity is synchronised into what could be termed the Dance of Life. The entanglement theory means that the atoms in our brains are constantly changing due to their reaction with the atoms in the environment, so we are a different person at every given moment in time and there is actually nothing about us that is truly "individual". In fact, time doesn't even exist - that, along with space and everything else disappears into "nothingness".

Still on the topic of our brains, we have a left brain that deals with logic and fact (the male side) and a right brain which deals with intuition, philosophy and religion (the female side) - that explains a lot. The right side of the brain continually challenges the left side so that a "fact" becomes merely a perception; nothing is actually real, meaning there are no longer any certainties, only probabilities. The atoms in our brains have evolved in such a way as to help us survive not only as an individual, but also as part of a group, so our reactions to the so-called "Leaders of Men" are just a way of us coping and staying alive for as long as possible. That's all right then, isn't it?

But does this explain why they did the things they've done? I suppose it all depends on the reaction between their own set of brain and environmental atoms. Or, anyway, is it all just hearsay?

As you can imagine, this has caused much snarling

and gnashing of teeth in the scientific arena. Even to the scientists who believe in it, it's all very confusing, but they do agree that they don't, and probably never will, know everything. This is because of what they're calling "the measurement problem", which is the inability to assess how or whether the waves that were generated at the time of the original "big bang" are affecting the atoms during the reaction process.

I told you there were more questions than answers, didn't I? After all, even the cleverest person on this planet can only ever have a limited perception of what is actually real. It has been said that we are all like ants staring at the moon - they can see it, but they'll never be able to touch it.

Quantum physics has somehow led to the belief in a "parallel universe". ("And why not?" your left brain is probably asking - only your right brain is saying, "Only a male could have thought up this pile of poo!") Some people are even trying to tell us that life is but a dream and there is no such thing as death.

But, this has now led me to another question: Can quantum physics provide an explanation for the "fact" that I was standing in a queue at Brussels airport the other day, when I heard a very loud bang right next to me and the next thing I knew I was hurtling towards an intensely bright light, inside of which I could just make out my Nan waving to me, shouting at me to float towards her.

Or was that the precise moment that I discovered I could not die?

# Write about anything. However, the last line from your character must be: "It was then that I discovered I could not die".

by

## J.M. McKenzie

We spent most of our evenings now sitting in silence, she on one sofa and I on the other. Sometimes she would read or watch TV, other times she would sew or knit with the radio on, but most of the time she would just sit in silence staring into space. She kept the lights low and when she moved it was so silently and softly that it was hard to distinguish between her and her own shadow on the wall in the gloom. But, she moved very rarely. When she got in from work around six she would quietly slip off her shoes in the hall and deliberately hang up her coat before going straight to the kitchen to fix herself some dinner. I had no appetite these days so she would eat alone. Even she seemed to have lost her enjoyment of food. It had become a necessary evil rather than a pleasure. More often than not she would settle for toast and jam and a cup of tea and even this usually ended up congealed and untouched on the plate. Around seven she would rise and take the plate and cup back into the kitchen, washing and drying them and putting them away before returning to her place on the sofa.

Around nine she would rise again and slowly climb

the stairs to bed. Each step seemed like a huge effort. She moved as if she was perpetually exhausted. I suspected she wanted to take to her bed long before then every night but that nine was probably the earliest time that she saw as acceptable. She had become thin and gaunt, her hair straggly and often unwashed, her clothes baggy and crumpled.

She would use the bathroom before stepping out of her clothes and getting into bed, leaving her them in a heap on the floor. She no longer brushed her teeth or washed her face before she went to sleep. The light would be out minutes after she reached the top of the stairs and a few minutes after that her deep and slow breathing would indicate that she was asleep. I would follow her into the bedroom easing myself onto the bed beside her, afraid to wake her. Her utter pain and misery was more than I could bear but I felt powerless to help her. I somehow knew I was the reason she was so unhappy but could not specifically recall what I had done. For some reason I knew could not leave her and yet that my being with her was making her suffering more severe. At the end of more and more nights like this I came to the conclusion that the only way to help her was for me to die.

I couldn't recall when it became like this. It hadn't always been this way. It must have been gradual because I couldn't remember when or why it changed.

I did know that it had been different. There was a time when she had been full of life, a whirlwind of energy, plans and ideas. She would burst in the door at night after work, calling out to me about her day, as she kicked off her shoes and hurried in to ask me about mine. She would kiss the top of my head before she rushed into the kitchen where the sound of opening cupboards, rustling packets and rattling saucepans would precede the delicious odours of her latest culinary adventure. All the time she would be chatting and laughing, occasionally sticking her head round the door to emphasise or illustrate a point with an elaborate gesture or comical facial expression.

She was beautiful. She was soft and curvaceous. Her skin glowed and her hair was thick and glossy. She was always smiling and even when she wasn't her eyes sparkled with warmth and love.

After dinner, which we usually ate at the small dining table in the bay window, most evenings were the same. We would wash-up together then, if we weren't going out, sit and talk. How we talked. We could talk all evening, snuggled together on the sofa, touching and stroking as we planned the rest of our lives together. We would plan our next holiday, weekends away, trips to the theatre, ideas for the house and the garden, our careers, our families, our plans for a family of our own one day.

When it got late we would climb the stairs together. Before she came to bed she would scrub her teeth and meticulously cleanse and moisturise her lovely face before carefully folding her clothes over a chair and settling in beside me. Most nights we made love.

Yesterday night something different happened. As she sat on the sofa staring into space and I sat on the other contemplating my death, she suddenly put her head in her hands. A small sob escaped her and when she looked up tears were streaming down her face. Now we were getting somewhere. Now she was showing some emotion. Maybe now we could talk. She rose and went to the little desk in the corner of the room where the computer sat. She opened the desk drawer and took out a crumpled photograph. She looked at it for a long time. She stroked it and held it to her breast as she wept, before looking at it again through her tears. She was whispering the same word over and over again but I couldn't make it out. Confused, I stood up and went over to her. As I stood behind her, I looked over her shoulder and I saw the photograph for the first time. I instantly went cold. The photograph she was holding was of me. The word she was whispering was my name. It was then I realised I could not die.

# Write about anything. However, the last line from your character must be: "It was then that I discovered I could not die".

by

## Michael Andrews

"Sami? Sami?" The anguished cry of Amira's voice echoed around the small cove as the young mother dragged herself out of the rolling surf. Clawing her way to the beach, she looked around at the bodies strewn along the beach. She felt a warm trickle down her cheek and raised a hand to wipe away the salty sea water, only to discover that it was her blood flowing down her face.

Fumbling in her pocket, she pulled out a sodden handkerchief and dabbed at the small cut on her forehead and unsteadily got to her feet. Waves of nausea washed over her and she stumbled back down, sitting heavily in the wet sand.

Her gaze settled on the smashed wooden boat that was supposed to have been her salvation. The journey across the sea had been fraught with danger, but it was a danger worth risking as opposed to staying in her small town on the edge of the Mediterranean Sea, waiting for the extremists to find them and do whatever it was that they were doing to her people. She had packed a small bag of personal possessions and made her way to where she had been told men where ferrying survivors across into Europe. It had been a long walk and her two year old son Sami had barely made it.

'Sami!' she thought, as she struggled to stand once again. Her legs nearly buckled as she made it to her feet but her stomach betrayed her. Clenching her mid-section tightly, Amira bent over as she heaved, trying to hold back the vomit but, unable to do so, she sank back to the ground, crying in agony and frustration.

"SAMI!" she shouted, trying to attract her son's attention, hoping against hope that he had made it to shore safely. She remembered the large waves as they tossed the small boat around before it was hit by the biggest wave she had ever seen. It had turned the boat over, smashing it on an unseen rock and splintered into pieces. She had tried to grab her small boy but the strong, swirling current of the sea had pulled him from her despairing clutches and the memory of his cries would haunt her until she found him.

Finally, she felt steady enough to stand and started a slow walk to her left. Tears were already flooding her eyes as she saw the lifeless bodies of the two youths who had been playing with Sami during the calm waters at the start of the crossing. Up and down the beach she walked, sadness and fear taking hold of her heart as she failed to find a single survivor amongst the twenty odd bodies that the sea was threatening to reclaim with its insistent crashing of waves.

"What have I done?" she cried out to the sky. "I thought we'd be safe, that we would have a life, but now... you have taken my whole life from me!"

As Amira began a slow walk back down the beach, she noticed that the captain of the boat wasn't among the dead. Nor were that couple who she had taken an instant dislike to on the boat when they snapped at her son to be quiet. A faint sliver of hope pierced her despair and she noticed a small stretch of sand that crept around the rocks at the southern end of the beach.

She hurried down, tripping on the wet sand as she ran past the dead, pausing as she rounded the craggy rocks. Her eyes lit up with delight as she saw more bodies, some of them moving and she rushed to the nearest figure.

"Have you seen my son?" she begged the old man, who's gaze was befuddled in shock and pain. Amira looked down and saw a large splinter of wood had pierced his calf and she could only hold the old man's hand as his eyes rolled back in his head and he gasped out his last breath of life. Holding back tears, she patted his grey cheek, and stood once again. She studied the bodies of the dead, breathing a sigh of relief as she saw no sign of her Sami before making her way to a young woman who was holding the body of a dead man.

"Excuse me," Amira started, not wanting to interrupt the woman's grief but needing to find her son. "Did you see a young boy, dark curly hair, wearing a red shirt, about this high?" she held a hand to the approximate height of her son.

"Sami?" the woman asked. "He was crying and wanting his Mama."

"He's alive?" Amira cried. "Where is he?

"They tried looking for you, but they thought you were dead," the woman replied. "They went off in that direction to look for help."

Amira turned and saw a winding path, leading away from the beach into the rocky countryside. Relief and hope caused her emotions to swirl and all thoughts of the previous despair vanished.

'My boy is alive and scared,' she thought to herself. It was at that point that Amira discovered, for the sake of her son, that she could not die.

# Write about anything. However, the last line from your character must be: "It was then that I discovered I could not die".

**by**

**S.J. Gibbs**

Roxanne Norris didn't want to think about the damage Kat had done to her.

The reward she had offered for any information leading to her arrest was substantial.

She drove past the monotony of green fields towards her sister's home.

Her recovery was going to demand more of her than she could imagine.

Finally, she saw the dull grey waters of the bay and took the lane left towards her sister's cottage.

As she pulled the car on to the driver the air was cold and dry, a typical English, February day.

She felt scared as though she was no longer in control, as she knocked the door to the cottage.

Gabby, her sister, answered the door and taking Roxanne by the hand led her into her lounge.

As they sat down on the sofa, they eyed each other in

silence for a moment, but Roxanne caught the grimace in Gabby's face although it was so brief.

Gabby left for the kitchen and returned with a tray of tea and cakes.

A high – pitched squeal left Roxanne's mouth, as the pain shuddered through her, but it was gone as quickly as it came.

"It's a relief to have you here," Gabby said, " away from London."

Roxanne replied, "I want her dead, but I know I have no right to kill her."

The television was blaring out, and Gabby got up to switch it off.

Gabby sat down on the sofa and placed her arm around Roxanne," we all want Kat dead, but she will be found and serve many years behind bars, which will punish her more than a quick death."

"It would be a good feeling to chop off her fingers one by one though," Roxanne retorted.

The next two days, the sisters spent cleaning, cooking and chatting, the weather outside too cold to entice them outdoors.

The power cuts at the cottage were numerous and the candlelit dinner they ate in front of the fire with a bottle of Chianti relaxed them as they reminisced about their childhood and their parents whom they had lost in a car crash six years ago.

Roxanne looked at Gabby "I always had the odd feeling that Kat was trying to tell me something."

"Shall we listen to some music?" Gabby asked getting up from her position on the floor, by the fire.

Gabby ventured," You trusted her too easily." She watched Roxanne as she continued "your interaction emotionally with people has always been your downfall."

Gabby placed her hand on Roxanne's as she cried, " she tied me to a chair before she threw the acid in my face, you know."

Before Gabby could offer a reply, Roxanne ran to her bedroom and slammed the door behind her.

Roxanne lay on the bed, blinking away the tears as she thought about the forensics teams at her house, which all seemed pointless, she knew who her attacker was it was Kat, and she hadn't even tried to disguise the fact she wanted her to know how much she hated her.

She should have stood up to her and thrown her out before she had gotten the upper hand.

She pulled the quilt tight around her to try and get warm. This cottage had always been cold.

She hadn't been sleeping properly and with the help of the wine she had consumed earlier, she suddenly felt very tired and drifted off into a deep slumber.

After the initial shock of finding out about Roxanne's attack, Gabby had felt quite clear about how her sister would convalesce with her at the cottage, but now she was here she didn't really know what to do.

She cleaned up in the kitchen before retiring to her bedroom, where she brushed her hair with the brush from the beautiful dressing table set which Roxanne had bought her for her birthday, touching her own face as she thought about Roxanne's disfigured face.

They took breakfast together the following morning and Roxanne felt calmer than she had the night before, a good night's sleep had helped.

Kat checked she had enough fuel in the car she had hired and set off towards grey seas.

Roxanne examined her face in the bathroom mirror, the doctors had told her it would take time to heal, but she knew it was beyond much more repair.

Kat parked the car a short distance from the cottage, and looking through her binoculars she could see that the windows were very small.

Smiling to herself she observed Roxanne's car on the driveway, she had guessed correctly, Roxanne was here.

The time seemed to slow as she carefully picked her way towards the cottage, sneaking behind the hedgerow and the low walling. She had been in awe of Roxanne and now she hated her. At six feet tall she could easily just break Roxanne's neck, now there was a thought.

She lit a cigarette and thought about Roxanne's fine, solid legs and her pearly skin, which she now wished to see dead.

Roxanne gave her self a dim, watery smile in the mirror and the headed back to the kitchen to Gabby.

The misty air gave Kat some cover as she ran across the last stretch of garden to the cottage. She could feel the excitement growing within.

Of course, there were a number of ways to get to Roxanne but she wanted her to die at her hands, knowing it was her who had killed her.

As she was about to knock the cottage door something hit her and the force of the blow knocked her off balance.

She felt nauseated as she realized the man now had her hands behind her back and was placing them in handcuffs.

Roxanne heard the commotion and saw the private detective she had hired place the handcuffs on Kat's wrists.

She explained to Gabby later, "it was then that I discovered, I could not die."

**Assignment Eleven -** Write a letter to yourself from one of your characters (or from another novel) revealing something about themselves that you didn't know.

28th April 2016

The group really enjoyed the subject of this assignment as it allowed us to delve deeper into the characters we were developing.

AJ had an angry letter from Max, while J.M. found out that while Lisa seemed to be a strong woman, she was actually driven by fear.

Michael's goddaughter Petra thanked him for her new crossbow whilst admitting her feelings that she had kept secret.

As S.J. was still outlining her novels, she took a

character from a previous homework and went with her.

As these letters are mainly to do with characters from books written or in process by the authors, please be aware that they all contain spoilers from the books either already published or still in progress. Therefore be aware that there are spoilers from the following books:-

AJ – Max and the Mystery of the Marbles

J.M. – Wait For Me

Michael – the letter is set partway through Dragonfire, book four of the Alex Hayden Chronicles, and therefore refers to history within books one to three as well.

# Write a letter to yourself from one of your characters (or from another novel) revealing something about themselves that you didn't know.

## by

## AJ. Jones

Dear Mrs Jones,

I just can't hold my anger in any longer. I need to let you know how hacked off I am with you for putting my story on hold for such a long time. It needs to be "out there" so that people can read about what happened to me when I was a little boy.

So I've decided that, if you're not going to do it, I'm going to write it myself!

You might know all the facts about my great adventure, but you didn't live it like I did. You can't get into my brain and see the sights, hear the sounds, smell the smells, feel the excitement, like I did. Only I can do that! So it makes sense for me to tell it like it was instead of you.

You can tell the readers about how I found the first "marble", but you can't tell them about the wonder I felt when I found it and the butterflies that flew around in every nook and cranny of my stomach when I discovered the story behind it. I yearned to go out and find the rest of them, but I had school and my

Mum to contend with. She, of course, hated the idea of my going off on any kind of adventure, especially such a dangerous one. She kept telling me I "shouldn't go near the silly marble again" - she even tried to ban me from visiting my Nan and Grandad in Cornwall. But I knew I had to do it, especially when Great Great Grandad Robert kept talking to me, using all those strange old-fashioned words that I'd never heard before. The first time I heard him, I remember, I nearly jumped out of my skin, his voice was so loud. I felt sure that everyone else could hear him too, but, of course, they couldn't.

I'm not angry with Mum for wanting to wrap me up in cotton wool; she told me afterwards that she thought I'd got some sort of mental disorder that had been caused by the disappearance of my Dad. But I knew it wasn't that. GGG, as I started calling him, was just a lost soul who needed someone to put right all the wrongs that he'd inadvertently caused by his naivety when he was a young man. And I was the only person who could do that for him. I'm so grateful that he gave me the opportunity to put the world back on track. Who knows where we'd be today if I hadn't?

So, let's get back to you. I'm a reasonable adult now, and I understand that you have other priorities - and, of course, other books to write, but . . .

"IT'S IMPERATIVE THAT THIS STORY IS TOLD!"

"Yes, okay, GGG! That's the reason I'm writing this

letter."

You see, he still pops into my head occasionally, usually when I'm sitting here all alone in my hospital room contemplating what it would've been like to have had a normal childhood.

I did ask him once, "Why me?  Why did I have to be the one to become your puppet?"

He told me that he had tried to use my Dad before me - that's why he disappeared for a while - but he was "too weak", as he put it.  He said that Dad had had me and my Mum to think about so he wouldn't agree to do the dangerous things that I did without even a backwards glance, because I couldn't see the danger at that age.  I just got caught up in the great adventure of it all.

It's hard to get that feeling back now, though.  I've tried everything I can to feel the hit I felt every time I found a new "marble" - legal highs to begin with, and then literally anything I could get my hands on.  They all worked for a while, but then you have to keep taking more and more of the stuff to get just a couple of flashes of "euphoria", when everything glows with amazing colours you've never ever seen before and the world is full of marvellous things to see and do.

I even killed a girl once - only as an experiment, of course.  She was just someone I'd met on Facebook and, after a few months of messaging each other, I arranged to take her out for dinner at a nice posh restaurant.  We were chatting away quite happily when she suddenly came out with the words, "Anyway, I digress!" and I knew right there and then that GGG was giving me a sign.

Afterwards, I took her back to my flat and, once we'd got high on some top notch coke I'd bought from my dealer earlier that day, I slit her throat with a kitchen knife. I don't remember too much about it really, but I do remember the great buzz it gave me.

So, that's why I'm locked up in this hospital room, getting more and more frustrated with you. The doctors can't decide what to do with me. I just need my story to be told, so that they - and the rest of the world - can see why I'm not to blame for my actions.

I'm not a killer; I'm just a product of my unique family history. And you're the one with all the facts, so, if you're not going to tell humankind how I saved them all, then I will - and it won't take me long.

I can see it now - it'll be a #1 Best Seller! And after all my heroic deeds are revealed, I'll be released so that I can go back to living my normal life.

And then I'll be free to come and kill you too, so that the story will end, as all good stories do, with a paradoxically shocking twist.

See you very soon then.

From your dear friend,

Max

xxxxxxxxxxxxxxxxx

# Write a letter to yourself from one of your characters (or from another novel) revealing something about themselves that you didn't know.

## by

## J.M. McKenzie

Dear J.M.,

I just wanted to write to you as I think you may have got some things wrong about me and why I was so driven to get back to Neal, in in the way that I was, when the Zombie Apocalypse first broke out.

I know that you think I was driven entirely by my love for Neal and that it was this, and this alone, that gave me the strength to fight to get back to him whatever happened, and whatever got in my way.

Actually, although I know you like to think that I was, and still am, an incredibly brave and strong woman, the real thing that drove me to do what I did, and still drives me to this day, was fear.

I was then, and am now, full of fear. Each morning when I wake the first true emotion I feel is fear. Like everyone who has survived this so far, I have those first few blissful moments at the start of each day when I wake and forget to remember what has happened. For a few drowsy moments I believe the world is still the same, and today will be just a normal day like every other, until I remember and the fear comes flooding in.

I'm not saying fear is always a bad thing. It does get you moving and makes you do things that you might have never have thought yourself capable of. It fires up your adrenaline and makes you fast and strong and feel no pain. It is ever present and makes you alert and quick thinking. In short, it is essential to survival.

At the same time you need to manage and control your fear. It can be exhausting and draining and make you incapable of thinking clearly. It can make you impulsive and take risks, that if you sat down and contemplated for very long, you would never take. It can make you stupid and foolish just as easily as it can make you smart and clever.

I think it was my ability to learn to control my fear early on in the days after the apocalypse, which has helped me survive so far. Even in the first hours on the train, when I was so afraid my body felt completely out of my control, I knew I had to somehow regain control or I was certain to die. My knees were like jelly, my hands were shaking and my heart was racing so fast I could barely breathe. My overwhelming desire was just to curl into a ball on the floor and wait until it all went away. But I didn't did I? I got back some control and it was that that enabled me to use my fear to get away from the train, and that which drove every other lifesaving action or decision I have made from there on in.

So what I am afraid of you might ask?  There again you might not, because that probably seems pretty obvious.  Of course, I'm afraid of being caught and eaten by one of the infected; anyone who says they're not is a liar.  I'm afraid of being killed but, even more than that, I'm afraid of becoming one of them.  I'm afraid of being doomed to roam the earth trapped between death and life.  I'm afraid of living forever in a rotting body, driven only by an all-consuming urge to eat the living, driven to tear them to shreds with my teeth, to bury my face in their soft wet flesh and feast.

But I have other fears that drive me J.M.. I'm afraid of losing the people I love.  I'm afraid of losing Neal and my family and friends, new and old.  I'm afraid of being alone in this terrible new world.  I'm afraid of what this is doing to some of the people I know.  I'm afraid of what they are becoming, or have already become.  I'm afraid that we will become like them.  Hard and cold. Ready to steal or kill to ensure our own survival, ready to take advantage of the weak and vulnerable in order to make ourselves strong.

Most of all J.M., I'm afraid of the future.  Where is this all going to end?  What will the future hold for us and our children?  Will we have any children? Would it be the right thing to do?  What will happen to the world if people don't have children?  How will it end? Who will win?  These are the questions that fill me with real terror and the questions that sometimes, in my darkest moments, make me wonder whether there is any point in surviving at all? These thoughts make me more afraid than ever. The thought that I might even consider not surviving, is enough to start me sweating and trembling and drives me to get up and do something, rather than think about what this all really means for the future of the human race.

So J.M., don't think I'm brave and strong all the time. I'm a real person, not a fantasy. I am driven by fear and fear alone. Whatever I do and say, and however I may appear, underneath it all I am an ordinary woman that is sick to my stomach with fear.

Please remember that when you are writing about me. It will help you understand my character and help you to tell my story in a way that other ordinary women can identify with.

Lots of Love

Lisa xxx

# Write a letter to yourself from one of your characters (or from another novel) revealing something about themselves that you didn't know.

## by

## Michael Andrews

Dear Michael,

Thanks so much for the lovely birthday present that you sent me. How did you know that I wanted the Majinsky six stake automatic single handed crossbow? You must have been talking with Uncle Bill. I know that he was very eager for me to have added protection, especially now that I seem to be seeing a lot more of the world with Alex. I'll be honest with you, I did nearly mess myself when his old captain turned up at Harry's house. I could feel the raw power emanating from him. Alex's old master, Chlothar, is rumoured to be even more powerful and it really scared me when Alex didn't come home straight away after the fight at the Shadow Castle.

I've been training hard, putting in the work, because Alex and Harry reckon there is going to be some big battle coming up soon. Even my mother has talked quietly about it. Thing is, she seems to be more on the side of picking a fight with Lord Chlothar, rather than trying to keep the peace between everyone, like Uncle Bill was trying to do before he died. I'm a bit confused as to where to place myself. My obvious loyalty is to the Comitia, I am a sworn protector of humanity after all, but since I met Alex and spent time with him, my assumptions about vamps have been totally altered.

I think it's Alex who's confusing me. I mean, to look at him, he's just a kid. He's fourteen in body, but in reality he's a lot older. But he can still act like a kid as well. Does that make sense? When we first met, I used to be horrible to him, and we'd argue like teenagers do, but I've stopped recently. He seems to be changing as well. From what I have read about him while he was still in service to his Lord, he was a vicious killer. Now though, he goes out of his way to protect people, and that's what confuses me about Mother. It seems that she wants to wipe all vampires from the face of the Earth, but looking into what some of them do, they have done a lot of good for humans, and the Earth. Did you know that they have funded some of the biggest science research projects, including space exploration? Thinking about it thought, it would suit them down to the ground, being able to control the sunlight inside a spaceship.

Alex is saying that we have to go to Rome. By we, I mean Harry, myself, and another vamp called Jonathan. He's very handsome and charming but there is definitely that killer edge to him. I know I said that I'd stopped winding Alex up, but he seems very jealous when Jonathan shows me any attention. I have to say that I kind of like that. As I get to know Alex better, I think that I am really getting to, you know, like him in THAT way. It's totally wrong isn't it? A Comitia hunter being in love with a vampire

Crumbs... I've actually said it! I admit it! I love Alex Hayden. He's so cute that it sometimes just makes me stop and stare at him while we are sparring. He has a very dry sense of humour, and he can fly! Do you know what it's like? He's taken me up on a few occasions, although he has threatened to leave me at the top of Blackpool Tower. I think he was joking :-o

I guess it would never work out between us though, even if you ignore the fact that I am a hunter. After all, I would age and he'd stay the same. It would be very weird in twenty years time wouldn't it? Me being thirty six and him still looking fourteen?

Harry reckns that we should live in the moment, but he's lucky because he's got Y'cart to snuggle with. All I have is my Sumpter Crossbow... although George the bear does still live on the bedside table. Yes, I still have him. He was my Christening present from you after all.

Well, I'd better finish this and try to get it emailed to you. I'm not sure whether this place has wifi or not, and I think we are going to busy over the next couple of days tracking down this mage.

I promise to come and see you when we get back. I

might even try to bring Alex along because I think you two would get on really well.

Fondest regards

Your Goddaughter

Petra xxxx

# Write a letter to yourself from one of your characters (or from another novel) revealing something about themselves that you didn't know.

## by

## S.J. Gibbs

Dear S.J.,

I am writing this letter to you to try and explain more about my life than you seem to understand in your story about me.

My name is Kat Jephson and you have only told one side of the story and that is from Roxanne's point of view.

Firstly, I am twenty-seven years old and am now locked up in prison for my crimes against Roxanne Norris.

I have lived my life completely foreign to yours and Roxanne's way of life.

I grew up as a child in Australia.

I had no living relatives who wanted me and I was brought up in an orphanage having been abandoned as a baby.

I moved to England when I was eighteen and lived on

a barge with a guy I met.

I understood nothing and was a gullible fool.

Would any revenge I took against anyone be too cruel to consider?

I had witnessed rape, drugs and prostitution in the orphanage and had experienced all of these myself from a very early age until my escape to England.

My nature could either be very jealous of people or at other times indifferent.

Childhood memories are not easy to erase.

I stick out like a sore thumb with my accent and my height of 6 feet.

I suppose you could describe me as malfunctioning.

At the orphanage I was scorned for being conceited.

I have obsessions with certain people I meet and become total obsessed with their lives.

Although you may find it hard to believe, I lived in cheerful chaos most of the time and am honorable to the point of foolishness.

I am passionate but this turns to fury, I am joyful but cruel.

You can publish this letter if you want, I don't care.

I am reckless. I guess I am what people would consider of the lowest possible level.

I am all of the names the orphanage threw at me, a

liar, devious and treacherous.

The cold sterility of my childhood has made me all of these.

I grew up in fear of my elders, belittled by many.

I feel foolish and inadequate, and am unable to trust anyone.

I have no plans to terminate my existence but maybe I should?

I specialize in the murders of women. If I had killed Roxanne she would not have been my first.

I am a bad, horrible person and I am deeply ashamed of myself.

I could be careful and fine-tune my writing here, but I won't, if you are to tell my story, you need to know the truth.

I am stubborn. The demons skip in my wake.

I am a nobody who has made myself a somebody by taking the lives of those stupid women.

I hope I am giving you the full picture so you can tell my side of the story.

Such a devil should not be allowed to roam this earth, and I guess that is why I am behind locked bars, institutionalized again.

The first one I killed, I let her walk a long way ahead until I could only just make her out and then I set out after her. I felt more excited than I had ever felt before and it made me cheerful. It was a matter of wonder to me, to stick the knife in her chest.

It was hard to resist the impulse after that first one, and I caught my second in the shadow of some trees. There she had been pretty and alluring and then by my hand she was dead.

Sometimes I used to get aggressive at the orphanage but it was beaten out of me , or so they thought.

I thought I wasn't capable of hurting anyone until that first one.

The killings seemed to invigorate me rather than depress me.

I wonder now how you are going to unveil this story?

The world became a dangerous playground to me and I became increasingly reckless.

I liked them to be wearing silk. Roxanne wore silk often.

I am one of society's misfits.

I am nothing like Roxanne, she was carefree, and confident. Why should she be allowed those privileges of life when I had nothing?

That is why I should have killed her and why I killed the others.

KAT JEPHSON

**Assignment Twelve -** Getting caught trespassing. Where, by whom and in what circumstance is up to you.

19th May 2016

AJ's story gripped the group with the starting act and set the scene nicely for revenge.

J.M. addressed the secrecy of the Freemasons, looking into their history.

S.J. took on the alter ego of the young boy who was definitely troubled by his father's death, breaking into the morgue while Michael's love of horror popped back up as he continues to develop his writing style with his main character in his novels being a fourteen year old boy.

## Getting caught trespassing. Where, by whom and in what circumstance is up to you.

### by

### AJ. Jones

She'd woken up feeling excited about the day ahead. It was Saturday and her new puppy, Bobby, was yelping at the back door waiting impatiently for his first walk of the day. She got dressed hurriedly and went downstairs where her Mum had left a note saying she'd popped to the village to buy some milk.

Laura's Mum had rented the cottage near Exmouth for a week while her Dad visited his terminally-ill brother. He'd decided it was better to go alone this time as his brother was close to the end, but, before he left, he'd brought Bobby home, telling her, "He'll protect you while I'm away."

Laura decided that she'd have time to take Bobby for a run before her Mum got back so she attached his lead and went outside into the glorious sunshine.

Half-way across the field at the back of the cottage, Bobby, a boxer puppy, managed to wrench the leash from Laura's hand and raced away triumphantly. She tried in vain to catch him up, and was out of breath by the time she discovered a hole in the field's high, important-looking fence, so she ducked through it shouting out Bobby's name as she made her way intrepidly through the overgrown copse on the other side. She walked in the direction of Bobby's barking and suddenly saw him being dragged along by two boys who looked a little older than herself.

One of the boys saw her and yelled, "What are you doing here? You're trespassing on our grandfather's property!"

"I was following Bobby", Laura shouted nervously. "Thanks for catching him for me."

"Well, come over and get him then," one boy summonsed, but she noticed a glint in his piercing pale blue eyes.

She felt a little scared as she walked over to them, but she could see Bobby was pleased to see her, so she tried not to show her alarm. As she neared the shorter boy, though, the other one, who had the same weird eyes, grabbed her arm and forced it up her back, making her cry out in pain.

"If you want your dog back, you've got to do something for us first," the shorter boy said menacingly as he began undoing his belt . . .


Afterwards, as she and Bobby walked calmly back to the cottage, she worked hard on controlling her feelings of revulsion and violation at what they'd done. She decided to block out the whole disgusting episode for ever, but she somehow knew their sickening pale blue eyes would haunt the rest of her life.

Her Mum was in the kitchen preparing breakfast when she got back, so she shouted something about being pulled over by Bobby into a puddle and went upstairs for a long soak in the bathtub to wash away as much of the dirt as she could.

Growing up, Laura became obsessed with self-defence. She joined several women's-only martial arts groups - Jujitsu, Karate and the like. She avoided men wherever possible and never dated anyone - EVER! She was sure her Mum suspected she was gay, but she knew she wasn't. She just didn't want THAT sort of a relationship with anyone.

At the age of 34, the company she worked for decided to open an office in Devon and they asked her to manage it. After discussing the move with her Mum and Dad, she decided that the salary increase was far too good to miss out on - "especially if I'm going to remain single all my life," she thought to herself.

She settled into her new home and job in Exeter and, after a few months, decided to look for a martial arts club where she could continue her Karate training. The only group she could find, however, was mixed, so she reluctantly signed up. They met every Tuesday evening and she began to look forward to the classes as they gave her an opportunity to show off the skills she'd acquired at her London club. She even began to admire the Sensei, Steve, who showed respect to everyone - even her.

One evening, as they were packing away, Steve asked her if she'd like to go for a coffee with him afterwards. After a long pause, she decided that the coffee house was far too public a place for him to entrap her, so she accepted. As they chatted enthusiastically about each other's Karate experiences, she realised she felt comfortable in his company.

After that, they'd go for a coffee every week and Laura's mistrust of all men gradually melted away. Two years later, they were married and Laura's life became conventional for the first time since "the incident".

Steve was a junior doctor at Exeter General Hospital and, despite the long hours, he enjoyed his work enormously. Eventually, the time came for him to look for a position in his chosen specialty of paediatrics.

"I've invited Johnny Charlwood and his wife over to dinner on Friday evening," he announced one rainy Saturday morning. "He's the senior paediatrician over at Taunton Hospital and he's looking for an intern. I'll cook, if you like."

They arrived at 7pm and she recognised his pale blue eyes immediately. However, he didn't seem to realise she was the little girl whose life had been torn apart by him and his brother that fateful day when they'd caught her trespassing.

What would she do? What could she do? "He's a paediatrician now, and apparently very well respected - and he's about to become Steve's new boss," she told herself.

"Why did you go into paediatrics?" Steve asked him as they chatted after the meal.

"Well, it's common knowledge that my brother hung himself aged 18 after it was discovered he'd been abusing local kids," he explained openly, "so I wanted to pay something back to society."

As he spoke, Laura noticed the pain behind those disturbing eyes of his and she knew there was nothing more she needed to do.

# Getting caught trespassing. Where, by whom and in what circumstance is up to you.

## by

## J.M. McKenzie

In a day and age when science and technology have rendered nothing scared or mysterious any more, as a young woman, the idea of the Freemasons was profoundly intriguing to me. But, it was both intriguing and irritating at the same time. I am the sort of person who likes to know everything there is to know about everything I touch, so it was deeply frustrating to think that men I knew had secrets that they would never share with anyone, including their own wives. As someone who could never keep a secret, especially from my partner, something about this was fundamentally disturbing. Part of me felt that the concept of an exclusive fraternity was a direct and blatant expression of sexism that should not be tolerated, but another part believed that only men would be childish enough to want to belong to a "boys only" club renowned for secret handshakes, phrases of recognition, initiation ceremonies and undisclosed rituals.

On the surface I accepted the positive explanations of the organisation being about like-minded groups of honest god-fearing men, choosing to live by a shared spiritual and moral code based on brotherly love, relief and truth. I understood that on a practical level Masonic Lodges were essentially business networks and charitable organisations benefiting members, their communities and individuals. At the same time though, the cynic in me felt that there must be more to it than this, and it was probably more likely to be about corruption and conspiracy and "old boys networks" that conferred certain financial and political advantages to members. However, the deepest intuitive and instinctive part of me could not shake off the thought that this might be some sort of pagan or satanic sect with evil aspirations and intentions to the world.

I could never speak to or look at any of the men I knew who were members of the Masons without these thoughts swirling around in the back of my mind. They might seem like normal decent guys on the outside, but how could they be? What was hiding behind that big smile, firm handshake or jovial manner? They attended meetings with their fellow members inside dark masonic lodges, dressed in peculiar symbolic garments and took part in strange and ancient ceremonies. They never spoke about what went on at these meetings. They were identifiable to each other in normal society through hidden signs and covert signals and you never knew when they would be surreptitiously working together in the business world for competitive advantage over unsuspecting non-members.

Harold was the husband of woman I knew through

the school. We occasionally went to the same dinner parties and on a couple of occasions Harold took my husband to one side engaging him in a private, murmured conversation. My husband later confided that he had indeed asked him if was interested in joining the Masons and that we had both been invited to attend a forthcoming Ladies Night. While my husband had no intention of joining the Masons, he held similar views to my own; we thought it would be a laugh to attend the event, which would be held inside the main Masonic Hall in the city. This was a building that had long fascinated me. I had worked in an office across the road for a time and often gazed out of the window at the windowless structure wondering what went on behind those walls.

So at last I had a chance to find out. On the night of the event everything was disappointingly normal. We ate dinner and drank wine. There were formal speeches and gifts for the "ladies". It was stuffy and old-fashioned. The whole thing was a slightly cloying gesture of appreciation and gratitude towards the long suffering ladies. For most of the night I was on my best behaviour and fought against the internal cries of rebellion trying to force their way to the surface. I slipped for just a moment when I received my gift of an enamelled pen in a soft velvet presentation case. "Why thank you darling." I smiled at my husband who could read me like a book and quickly turned away. "This will be *perfect* for writing my daily shopping lists."

After dinner, fuelled by wine I decided to go exploring. I made the excuse that I needed to use the ladies room and stepped out into the wide cool hallway. To my right were the toilets, to my left a long dark corridor. I went left. I tiptoed along the tiled floor trying to be as quiet and quick as I could in my high heels, rehearsing my explanation. Taken a tipsy wrong turn on the way to the toilet tried a few doors, all of which were locked, until I came across an ornate set of double doors with a crack of light shining from within. I pushed them open and slipped inside.

The room was large and open and dimly lit. The floor in the middle of the room was laid out in black and white tiles like a chess board. There was an alter, candles and a lectern, or was it a pulpit? Basic seating lined the room interspersed with larger ornate throne-like chairs. The first impression was that of a cross between a chapel and a court room. But, there was no sign of cross only symbols, sun moon and stars, square and ?,

I was about to examine some of the imagery in more detail when I heard a noise behind me. I turned to see Harold standing in the doorway

# Getting caught trespassing. Where, by whom and in what circumstance is up to you.

## by

## Michael Andrews

"You're not chicken are you?" Billy Makepeace giggled.

"Bwark, bwark!" Jordan stared making wings with his arms.

"Sod off!" I hissed at them and climbed over the wall.

That's how I'd ended up inside the rundown house on the edge of town.  As a teenager, image was everything and with the threat of Billy telling everyone that I had bottled it, I'd swallowed my nerves and scaled the wall.  We had been warned at school not to go into the house, warnings echoed by our parents.

For years, schoolkids had told stories about the creepy house and the ghosts that haunted it.  No-one really believed in ghosts, really, but ever since the death of Vinny Deschamps six years ago, the place was avoided like the plague.

Poor Vinny.  I can just about remember him.  He used

to live in the next street to mine, but his family moved away soon after his body was found in the basement of this very house.  Apparently he'd stepped onto a rotten floorboard which collapsed and he fell to his death.  My Dad said that he'd broken his neck when he fell and that a bone must have snagged through the skin because his friend in the police department said that there was blood everywhere.

So why was I here?  Some stupid bet.  Some stupid argument with Billy about who was the bravest in our class.  Various challenges had been set, and I thought I'd win when I dared him to climb the eighty foot water tower, knowing that he hates being up high.  But he did and now, here I am, in the abandoned house.  No-one has lived here for years, decades, but it is still owned by someone and any attempt to knock it down has always been challenged and beaten.

"So where are the stairs?" I asked myself.  I fished my i-phone out of my pocket and hit the flashlight app.  Immediately the hallway lit it.  I shivered as I saw spider webs galore.  I can't stand spiders, so there had better not be any big ones.  Or hairy ones.  Or small ones for that matter.  Did I say that I hated spiders?  Ever since I had woken up to one crawling across my face when I was, like, eight years old or something.

A floorboard creaked as I stepped on it and I froze.  Not wanting to take the shortcut down to the basement, I moved backwards and my gaze caught sight of the stairs. Breathing a sigh of relief, I quickly ran up them and, after opening several doors, found what looked like was the master bedroom. Turning on the camera, I stood next to the bed and took several selfies, my eyes squiniting against the flash. I quickly looked through the pictures, satisfied that I could prove that I had been in the room.

"Just got to do the basement now," I smiled to myself. Honestly, I didn't know why I had been so afraid of the old house. It was just that, simply a house that was old, I thought as I walked back out onto the landing. There must be a window open somewhere because I felt a cold breeze down the back of my neck, so I turned up the collar of my jacket and headed back down the stairs onto the ground floor.

"I guess that the basement door must be in the kitchen," I mused, thinking back to our old house, which was similar to this one. We'd moved when I was younger into one of the new estates that had been built by Acula Housing, which I always thought was a funny name for a building company. I guess that Doctor Acula had made enough money through his doctor's business and looked to invest.

I found the kitchen and, sure enough, there was a door on an inside wall. I tried to open it but it seemed to be jammed. Not wanting to be labelled chicken, I put my phone back in my pocket and gripped the door with both hands. Bracing myself, I pulled hard and, with a loud creak of rusty hinges, the door opened wide enough for me to be able to squeeze through.

Another cold breeze brushed past me and I looked behind me for a moment, wondering which window was open but I couldn't see one. Shrugging to myself and wanting to get the hell out of the house before I found any spiders I tried to find the light switch but there wasn't one. I took my phone back out and turned on the flashlight. I shone the light down the stairs and I could see the switch at the bottom. Why did people do that? Creepy old movies came back to my min, but I shook them away and headed down carefully, trying each step in turn.

I reached the bottom and turned on the light. The basement, unlike the rest of the house, was tidy and well kept. There was a weird box over to one side. It looked like... no it couldn't be... but I'm sure it looked like a coffin! That would be the perfect image to get in the selfie.

I hurried over and stood next to it, taking several pictures. Scanning through them to make sure that at least one was passable proof of my trip, my mouth dropped in horror at the sight of a man behind me. I spun around.

"Who are you to trespass in my lair?" the old man's deep voice echoed around the basement.

"I'm sorry... I'm just here as a dare," I babbled as he

walked towards. I found that I couldn't teat my gaze from his yellow eyes, a look of pure evil within them.

"Dare or not, you are now mine."

"Who are you?" I asked, as if conversation could get me out of this situation.

"My name is Dracula."

I felt dampness in my shorts as I saw fangs in his mouth. I couldn't move as he bent my head to one side. Pain pierced my skin and I went limp as my life was drained from my body. I guess that Vinny didn't fall after all.

# Getting caught trespassing. Where, by whom and in what circumstance is up to you.

## by

## Shelly Gibbs

Bernadette knew her son Josh was sullen and violent. Thirteen was a difficult age for a lot of boys, but he just seemed to always be the one to go that step further.

Josh had been drinking sneakily from the vodka bottle for over a year now and still he knew he had not been, detected by his mother.

He knew he was his mother's blue- eyed boy and although he was often in trouble, she was weak and forgave him very quickly.

He spent hours in the paddock at the bottom of their garden and enjoyed the peace and solitude the place held for him, sitting quietly, contemplating his young life.

His mother played bad music, too loudly, constantly and it drove him insane.

His solitude today in the paddock was broken by his mother shouting, "dinner is ready."

He jumped over the wooden fence, which divided the

paddock from the more formal garden and ran towards the house. Josh grunted as his mother placed the food in front of him " not this crap again, we had spag bol only the other day."

His mother's tolerance and patience to his rudeness infuriated him, " why didn't she ever stand up to him", he pondered.

The pastel shades of the walls, the carpet tiling, the strip lighting and the smell of this kitchen he hated with a vengeance. In fact, there wasn't much in this life he didn't hate.

"Nobody seems to understand me," he thought, as he pushed the spaghetti around the plate with his fork," even my violent outbursts seem to have no effect on anyone."

He hoped she wouldn't talk. It only led to questions, which always led to explanations or lies.

Bernadette started asking him questions with distrust written all over her face. She had other things to worry about and these thoughts distracted her from pushing Josh too much with any more questions.

"I'm going to redecorate your bedroom, which colours would you like?" she ventured, trying to diffuse the look of hatred on his face.

Josh glared at her in defiant silence.

He pushed his chair back noisily from the table and went to his bedroom slamming the door behind him. He removed the vodka from its' hiding place which was on the top of the wardrobe and slugged a few sips from it before replacing it inside a shoebox. Carefully he pushed the box to the rear of the wardrobe, where he knew his mother wouldn't look.

He climbed into bed and fell into a deep sleep.

Bernadette knew she should reprimand his behavior but it was easier to ignore it as it only led to a shouting match between them or even worse.

Instead she sat at the kitchen table and prayed for him.

She would not allow any thought that would cloud her love for him to take root in her mind.

The following morning the atmosphere was lighter between them as they ate breakfast together, and Bernadette found herself laughing at her son as his mood seemed brighter.

Josh's face was burning brightly at the thought of what he was going to do today.

Uncharacteristically, he kissed his mother as he set off for school, only he had no plans to go to school today.

It was a plan he had long coveted and today he was going to make it happen.

He was soon at his destination and he entered the stone building and walked down one of its' long corridors.

He wasn't afraid of dying and he didn't feel frightened as he pushed the door open to the morgue.

The idea of looking inside a morgue had fascinated him for months, and now here he was inside of one.

His eyes came to rest on the first dead body he had ever seen, and the air around him made him tremble.

He looked up and saw the mortician hurtling towards him.

As the mortician grabbed hold of him Josh cried, "I didn't do anyone any harm, I just wanted to look."

The police were called and Josh was arrested for trespassing. He was taken to the police station where thy summoned Bernadette immediately.

She sat in the chair they offered her at the side of Josh, lifted her chin, closed her eyes and absorbed the information the policewoman was divulging about her son. She forgave him instantly but now was shocked into the realization that Josh really did need some professional help so that he may come to terms with his father's death.

**Assignment Thirteen -** Somewhere in your story must be the phrase: "If we do this, we both have to commit to it.  There's no turning back."

30th June 2016

AJ went dark once more with a horror based human interest story.

Michael went completely out of character, writing a family story.

J.M. delved into a fantasy political world based on true characters, something mildly prophetic and it must be stated these actions are purely fantasy.

S.J. used this assignment to try to put more detail into her writing but she felt she gave too much focus on the descriptions while ignoring the basic plot.

# Somewhere in your story must be the phrase: "If we do this, we both have to commit to it. There's no turning back."

by

## AJ. Jones

THE DAUGHTERS OF LYSETTE LYNAM

The two women sat diagonally opposite each other trying not to catch each other's eye.

As she looked around the room, Maureen couldn't help but notice that her younger sister was still as beautiful as she remembered her. Her large brown eyes smouldered with skilfully applied makeup and her skin glowed with the golden tan she'd carefully built over the last few weeks at her house in San Tropez. It was obvious to Maureen that Marilyn had been able to put the past behind her. Why, then, had she found it so hard to do the same?

Marilyn smiled nervously as she finally got the courage to look over at her older sister. She looks so much like Nanna, she thought. She could do so much more with herself but I don't think she's ever cared what people think. I'd love to be like that - happy in my own skin, just taking every day as it comes.

After a couple of minutes, the solicitor entered the room followed by his entourage of young, eager trainees. Nick Rosenberg had been appointed the Lynam family solicitor on joining the firm of Samuel & Blackstone in 1998. He'd met the mother of the two ladies sitting uncomfortably at the large oval glass table on only a couple of occasions but he knew her back story very well.

"Hello, Ladies. How nice to see you again after all this time?" He smiled across at them as he settled his paperwork in neat piles on the table.

"You must be wondering why I asked you to come into the office today," he continued. "Well, before I tell you that, I need to explain a few things to you about your mother."

Our mother, thought Maureen. The woman the whole world hates!

She tried to stay calm as she raised her eyes to look at the solicitor. "What more can you tell us that we don't already know?" A feeling of dread was beginning to build inside her as she thought about her own daughter, Amber, who was studying Psychology at Cambridge. What would she think of her if she knew the truth?

"I don't think anyone will ever condone her actions," Nicky interjected. "What she did was pure evil and no one could, or should, ever forget that."

The old, familiar feeling began to well up in Marilyn's stomach so she quickly got up and left the room saying she needed a toilet break. Maureen almost ran after her, but instead stuck her nails into the palms of her hands to stop herself from thinking about "that night" - the night all their lives had changed for ever.

As Marilyn re-entered the room a few minutes later, Maureen could tell from her demeanour that she hadn't been able to completely erase the memory after all. Maybe the confident woman that she outwardly portrayed was a sham and she did actually remember that brutal night in the same way as Maureen did.

Nick began his long speech by telling them that their mother had been diagnosed with terminal breast cancer and she only had a few weeks to live.

His words started whooshing around in Marilyn's head. She began to feel sick again, but this time decided to control it by closing her eyes and thinking of a sunny beach, the sea rippling lazily onto the sand while she lay dozing dreamily on her sunbed.

"Blue sky, blue sky," she repeated over and over to herself. "Think of nothing but lovely blue sky."

But, suddenly, she was a child again and the blue sky was beginning to darken ...

"Maureen, Marilyn, I need you for a moment." Marilyn heard her mother's voice calling her from her baby brother's bedroom so she went running upstairs to see what she wanted. Maureen was already there but the look on her face sent shivers down Marilyn's spine.

"Mum, stop, you're hurting him," Maureen shouted.

"It's alright, Darling. He's going to have to go and live with Jesus," crooned their mother in a voice she'd never heard her use before.

"Get me a clean nappy from the wardrobe, please. We don't want him meeting his maker in a dirty one, do we, Dear?"

What happened next was too terrifying for Maureen and Marilyn's minds to take in. But, by the end of it, their baby brother lay quietly on his changing mat, his eyes closed as if he were asleep.

The girls' mother looked over at her two young daughters and saw the shock on their faces. "Let's go downstairs and have a cup of tea and we'll talk about all this, shall we?"

Down in the warmth of the kitchen, with the dark night closing in around their cosy home, their mother explained that their brother was "evil, pure evil!" She knew this because she'd noticed the face of the devil growing on his back. She'd asked God what to do and He'd told her that "he must go and live with Jesus so he can be forgiven for killing lots of little girls in his previous life".

"He couldn't be allowed to grow up under the same roof as my precious daughters, could he?" she pleaded. "I did it for you, Darlings," she concluded with a sickly-sweet smile.

That night in bed, the girls made a pact that they would never, ever speak about that terrible night. "If we do this, we both have to commit to it. There's no turning back," said Maureen, the bossier of the two. Marilyn nodded submissively. Their covenant was sealed.

Nick closed by telling them that their mother wanted to see them before she died.

Maureen looked over at her precious sister. Were they about to break the vow they'd made all those years ago? Would they admit that it was all their fault? That their mother loved them so much she'd sacrificed her only son.

"We have to go, Marilyn," she whispered, large tears beginning to well in her eyes.

# Somewhere in your story must be the phrase: "If we do this, we both have to commit to it. There's no turning back."

## by

## J.M. McKenzie

The first formal meeting had taken place in the backroom of a dingy wine bar in Lambeth about a year before the referendum. However, they had bumped into each other on several occasions over the past few years, and more frequently still when Boris had been Mayor of London. Truth be told, although he was a bit rough around the edges, Boris quite liked the man. Back in 2013 he had even referred to him in his column in the Telegraph as a "rather engaging geezer" whose beer swilling cigar smoking image held a certain appeal for a specific sub-group of the electorate. A sub-group that, as old "Etonians", they could not easily win over themselves. After a particularly nasty clash between Nigel and Ken Clarke, he had worked hard to reassure his fellow Tories that the man was "essentially a conservative" just like them and that his anti-EU and anti-immigration policies were not necessarily a bad thing. Ever since then they had developed a kind of twisted mutual respect for each other. But it was only when Cameron called the EU Referendum that Boris recognised the potential opportunity for them to work together to support each other to achieve their personal goals.

For Boris it was simple, he wanted to be Prime Minister, always had, always would. There was nothing else that would satisfy him. Nigel was more complicated. Initially, Boris thought he wanted power at any cost too and that he could be a dangerous competitor. He believed his ideology was constructed specifically to generate a following among the growing section of the population who were stifling deeply held racist and nationalistic beliefs. By giving this group a voice and essentially legitimising their views in a day and age when political correctness had gone mad, he was sure to gather a small but strong body of support. However, as Boris got to know him, he realised he was not interested in constructing complex Machiavellian plots and manoeuvres to secure a position of power. He actually believed everything he said. In many ways that was more disturbing than someone who simply wanted power. Boris could identify with that. That he could understand. This he could not. This was frightening. Nigel had a chilling vision and ambition for Britain that was destructive and divisive. There was something in his eyes that glinted with malice. Something about his leering grin that made Boris's skin crawl. Sometimes, during the small hours, a tossing and turning Boris was haunted by the niggling thought that Nigel might be the closest thing to pure evil that he had ever encountered.

However, his desire to realise his own ambitions was stronger than his fear. In the light of day his "night niggles" seemed silly and over-dramatic, Nigel couldn't be evil. He was just an ignorant bigot. A clever and ambitious ignorant bigot for sure, but still just an ignorant bigot, nothing more. So he happily sat down with him , over a pint of bitter, at a grimy table in a dimly lit room, to plot how they could dupe the unsuspecting British public into voting to leave the EU to achieve their own unscrupulous ends.

Later that night they as each folded away their own scribbled version of the first draft of the barrage of lies they had concocted to tell the voters, they made their pact. Nigel agreed that after the vote, when Cameron had been forced to resign and the Tory party were in chaos, he would support Boris's campaign to replace him as Prime Minister. In return Boris would ensure that Nigel received a peerage in recognition of his role in bringing about the referendum in the first place, enabling him to enter the government and continue to pursue his ambitions. As they parted with a furtive handshake, both with their lists of actions to deliver before they met again, Boris held Nigel's hand for longer than he should and looked him square in the face. He spoke in a voice that was quiet but clear, articulating each word slowly and deliberately, "If we do this, we both have to commit to it. There's no turning back."

# Somewhere in your story must be the phrase: "If we do this, we both have to commit to it. There's no turning back."

### by

### Michael Andrews

"If we do this, we both have to commit to it. There is no turning back."

That is what my wife of twenty years told me. We'd fallen in love as teenagers, too young really I suppose. How could a boy of fourteen know what his life would pan out like?

As a kid, the world is your oyster. You could be a fireman, an astronaut, a doctor or a warehouseman. The latter was me. Someone who's dreams disappeared as quickly as England's chances at Euro 96 when Gazza missed that sitter and Gareth Southgate fluffed his spot kick.

So I got a job and I was happy, earning a wage and with a girlfriend to boot. She was fine. We had our ups and downs as any couple does, but she knew that I was there for her. All in all, life was good.

Four years in, I had been promoted to a supervisor at the warehouse. It was an extra two thousand pounds a year and with Gemma now earning as well, we went to the bank and got ourselves a mortgage. We'd worked out the money and we were confident we could afford it, as long as things stayed the same.

We talked about having kids, and at the time, we decided that we needed to concentrate on getting ourselves on the property ladder so that wasn't on the cards.

Life was good. We went out with friends, we got drunk, and we enjoyed life. It was good until Gemma dropped the bombshell on me.

"I'm pregnant," she said over a steak meal at the local restaurant. It was as if she expected me to react badly and make a scene, so she had picked a neutral venue. I have to say that I was annoyed to say the least. We'd agreed that we weren't going to have kids as it didn't fit into our plans. How would I retire at fifty if we had kids?

"What?" I muttered out. I knew it wasn't the most coherent of replied but it was the best that I could come out with.

"We're going to have a baby," Gemma proudly announced.

I looked at her, the shock and adrenaline running

through my body. How could she be so stupid? How could we afford to bring a baby into the world? Did I want to be a father? All of these thoughts crashed onto my mind, into my brain.

"Don't be bloody stupid!" I cried out. "How can we afford it?" I begged her.

"We'll manage," she smiled. "Mike, it's our boy," she grinned. I looked at her and couldn't help but to smile back. She had already found out the sex.

Yes it would be hard, especially with all of the Government cuts but could we survive without handouts? This was my son we were talking about.

So we bit the bullet. We cut our cloth as it was known and for fifteen years, we struggled through. Baby David grew up into teenager David and we couldn't have been prouder of him. He wasn't the best sportsman, or the most intellectual kid, but he was a good boy, a friend to his friends and somebody that, as a parent, I could stand by and say that I am proud he is my son.

So when a son, a boy, makes a mistake in life, you stand by him. It's not like he's killed anyone, in fact it's the opposite. So he got too involved with Harriet, but she's a nice girl. We know her parents. They've lived down the street from us for ten years for God's sake. Was it any surprise when they started dating? Probably not.

However, when Harriet and David called us parents together yesterday to tell us the news, it was still a shock. At sixteen, they'd 'made a mistake' as they called it. They'd forgotten to take care and now, Harriet was pregnant.

Gemma's first though was, of course, 'I'm too young to be a granny!' but once we settled down, we took stock. Talking with Harriet's parents. Did we want the stigma of an abortion to ruin our children's lives? I argued against it, and so did Gemma and Melissa, Harriet's mother. I could understand Frank wanting to inflict pain on David, because if it was a reverse of roles, I'm sure I'd be the same, but we talked it out.

Finally we came to an arrangement where we would let the kids complete their education, even going to university if they could, but as parents, we would be there to support them.

I love my wife, and still believe that she should have been a politician because she was the one who told us, "If we do this, we both have to commit to it. There's no turning back."

And to this day, I have a wonderful granddaughter, and a wonderful family that I can be proud of.

## Somewhere in your story must be the phrase: "If we do this, we both have to commit to it. There's no turning back."

### by

### S.J. Gibbs

Marianne West had not brought an umbrella out with her today as the forecast had been for sun, so as she crossed the plaza in Malaga to begin her sightseeing for the day, she was shocked when a sudden downpour caught her by surprise. She darted to the nearest café with an outside canopy and taking a seat, she ordered a hot chocolate from the passing waiter.

She consulted her guide- book to try and assess the distance between the café and the cathedral where she had been heading. It didn't seem more than a five minute walk but she decided to 'sit it out', here under the canopy until the rain became, at least, a little lighter.

Sipping her hot chocolate, she glanced around her, and although feeling fairly annoyed that it was raining, she began to relax as she watched people running for cover or strolling past, umbrellas high, those who had the foresight to bring one out with them.

The rain stopped almost as quickly as it had started

and throwing enough change into the silver dish to cover the cost of the hot chocolate and a small tip, she continued her journey, down a narrow alleyway lined with fascinating shop windows towards the cathedral.

As she turned the corner, the cathedral stood in all its' glory, before her. She grabbed her camera from around her neck and began snapping as many shots as she could.

She climbed the few steps, where a beggar woman rattled a pot in front of her nose, and gesticulating her indifference to the beggar, she approached the huge, magnificent, wooden doorway. A guard informed her, that they were not allowing tourists inside until 1'o' clock. Glancing at her watch, which showed ten past ten, she wondered what else she could do now. As she pulled out her guide-book from her bag, she heard a woman's voice shout, " Marianne, Marianne West, I don't believe it." Looking up, she met the eyes of an old school friend, Katy Womack, from their boarding school days.

Kissing each other on the cheeks, and exclaiming how amazing this was to bump into each other, in Malaga, of all places, they found the nearest café to catch up on each other's news. Both now in their early thirties, they were both still single and both travelling alone.

They chatted for a while and then decided they would meet up at six 'o' clock for tapas and wine in the main plaza. Marianne watched as her friend walked away, admiring her smart outfit, she clearly was a city girl.

Marianne was more of a country girl, with more casual looks than Katy but their differences had never interfered with their friendship.

Marianne paid the bill and ventured off to some antique shops, which she wanted to visit. She was particularly looking for a, Lladro piece to add to her collection.

Six 'o'clock, soon came around and the two women were relaxing with a selection of tapas dishes before them and their first bottle of white wine. By 9 'o' clock, they were nearing the end of their fourth bottle of wine and were becoming jollier and louder by the minute.

Katy laughed and said to Marianne," I have a suggestion, but if we do this we both have to commit to it. There's no turning back. You said how much you hate your job, and I hate mine. We have no ties other than jobs back in England. Let's not go back. Let's travel together, now, on a huge adventure for twelve months. We will make a list of the places we most want to travel to." Marianne, astounded at her self, found herself agreeing to Katy's suggestion.

Katy pulled out a notebook from her bag and started to make the list. "I will go first," she said, jotting down, "Israel; The Dead Sea, Jerusalem and Bethlehem."

"Mexico," Marianne shouted and this went next on the list.

Five minutes later, the list read:

ISRAEL – THE DEAD SEA, JERUSALEM AND BETHLEHEM

MEXICO – RIVIERA MAYA, MEXICO CITY, PUERTO VELLARTA

ITALY – ROME, VATICAN, VENICE, FLORENCE, PISA, AMALFI COAST, POMPEII, CAPRI, LUCCA, SIENNA, SAN GUINAMANO, LAKE GARDA, LAKE COMO, VERONA

AUSTRIA – SALZBURG, VIENNA

SPAIN – ALL OF IT!!!!

EGYPT – LUXOR, SHARM EL SHEIKH, CAIRO, HURGHADA, TABA

AUSTRALIA – ALL OF IT! !!!!!!

They both fell about laughing. They were going to have a fun – filled, massive adventure for the next twelve months.

**Assignment Fourteen -** A mobile phone in your cabin starts ringing. You don't own a mobile phone.

31st August 2016

With J.M. having been on a writing retreat, Michael ran with that theme and tried his hand at suspense.

AJ actually swears for one of the few times in her writing. Despite the shortness of the story, she manages to complete a plot and adds in her usual twist.

J.M. turned to the world of espionage with a different take on the meaning of the word cabin. Looking back, she is concerned that the ending was a little weak but still enjoyed the process. With her novel partly set on the canal network, she used the exercise to explore the setting and atmosphere of Britain's waterway.

S.J. was quite pleased with this one as she felt she was growing her descriptive writing alongside a plot development and even managed to add a twist to her ending.

# A mobile phone in your cabin starts ringing. You don't own a mobile phone.

### by

### AJ. Jones

As I open the door to the cabin I'd rented as a place to de-stress for the weekend, I can hear the sound of a mobile phone ringing. It's that Nokia tune that all the old cell phones used to play when a call was coming through.

As I don't actually own a mobile at the moment, I pull that face that says, "What the fuck?"

I play 'hunt the thimble' for a few minutes. Then I realise it's coming from inside the wardrobe. I open the door and there it is, large as life - and I mean LARGE!

It's one of those brick-sized mobiles that everybody who wanted to impress had glued to their ear in the eighties. You know, the ones with the great big aerial on the side that you had to pull out to be able to hear the person at the other end.

I pick it up, extend the aerial, press the answer button and put it to my ear. "Hello," I say, feeling like a complete numpty. A voice says, "Connecting you," and I hear a load of clicks and buzzing noises while I wait to see what happens next.

"Hello, is that you Matt?"

I drop the phone on the floor! It lands with a bang and I think I've broken it. But then I hear his voice again.

"Matt, don't hang up. It's me, Dad."

I pick it up very gingerly and hold it again to my ear. "Hello, are you there?" my Dad's voice says again.

"Dad. Where are you? I thought you were dead. We all thought you were dead. How can this be happening?"

"I am dead, Son," he says, sadness showing unmistakably in his voice. "And so are you! Just take a look outside and you'll see."

I go to the window and outside I see someone swimming in the pool, except he's not swimming. In fact, he's not actually moving, he's just floating on the surface.

"You've had a heart attack, Son, and you've drowned. You're ok, though. You're with us now."

I see lots of people gathering at the side of the pool. There's my Grandpops and Nanna holding hands, and then I see my Dad holding something to his ear.

"Don't be scared, Matt," he says. "You're going to be very happy here."

I put the phone down and go outside. I feel all light and floaty but it's actually quite a nice feeling.

"Hello, Matt," they all shout. "Let's go and play."

# A mobile phone in your cabin starts ringing. You don't own a mobile phone.

## by

## J.M. McKenzie

He sat, in a low deck chair, wrapped in a blanket, on the roof of the narrow boat. He nursed a steaming cup of coffee, letting the heat warm his face and hands, savouring the tranquillity of the moment. The water lapped gently against the side of the boat in the light breeze. The other only sounds were the calls of night birds and the rustling of small creatures rooting in the undergrowth. He was unusually relaxed, his pistol resting loosely on his lap under the blanket. It felt glorious to be outside and alone in the dead of night and not feel nervous. Nevertheless he was still alert, his senses ready to pick up on anything that didn't look, sound or feel right.

The canal network was one of the few places he felt safe these days and he returned here again and again. Of course, he used different boat hire firms and different identities each time and travelled different routes in different directions at different times of year. Sometimes, when he found a spot like this, he'd stay in the same place for a few days. Moor up beside the tow path and just stop for a while. Generally, he slept during the day and moved around at night and it was hard to break that pattern. His body had functioned like this for so many years now that he could not make himself sleep at night even if he wanted to.

Over the years he'd covered the length and breadth of the country like this, chugging slowly down shady, silent waterways, slipping unnoticed through small towns and villages. He used other forms of transport too. Sometimes he'd hire a small camper van and drive the back roads of deserted parts of the country, the Highlands and Islands of Scotland, Wales, or the South West, for a few weeks. When he found a particularly remote and deserted place he'd sometimes return on foot with a tent and a backpack and stay for a while. He never stayed anywhere longer than a week. He avoided large towns and cities. He travelled light. He had virtually no possessions. At any given time all he would be carrying was a change of clothes, food and water for a few days and some cash. He carried no electronic devices of any kind. He couldn't take the risk of being traced.

There was no telling where or when they would find him. He had to be ready and able to move, and move quickly, at all times. He had small network of trusted friends and family who supported him, who he could turn to if he ever needed help. He tried to keep face to face encounters to a minimum, in part to protect himself from their well-intentioned attempts to persuade him to stop, but in the main to protect them from dangers they could never even imagine. His sister kept his money and when she received a postcard from him containing a coded message, would send cash to the name and address concealed within the message. If he could, he would have preferred to have no contact at all with friends and family, but he had to eat and he couldn't work, other than short-term casual labour which was increasingly hard to find, and he couldn't have a bank account.

At moments like these, when he had time to sit and think he wondered if it was worth it. He played with the idea of ending it all, examining it in his mind from different angles, weighing up the pros and cons. He was lonely. He was weary. He was afraid. He was sad, sad to his very core. But he was alive. He was breathing. His heart was beating and his blood was coursing through his veins. That was what they wanted. To stop him breathing, stop his heart beating, remove all trace of him from the face of the earth. He could not allow that to happen. Then they would have won and it would all have been for nothing. That could not happen. He would never let them win, NEVER. It was that that kept him going. It was that that got him out of bed each day. It was that that kept him focused and alert, sheer hatred and bloody minded determination.

A pink hue on the horizon signalled that dawn was near. He rose and made his way inside the boat, swilling out his coffee cup and drying it carefully with a bit of kitchen towel, he placed it in the cupboard closing the door with his elbow. He moved around the boat, wiping everything he had touched, securing the doors and windows and closing the curtains. He made his way into the cabin. He did not undress but removed his slip on trainers placed them by his rucksack on the floor. He lay back on the bed. He lay flat on his back, with his right hand resting lightly on the pistol by his side. He closed his eyes.

He was in that strange place on the edge of sleep when a ringing sound suddenly jolted him awake. He sat bolt upright. A phone! He leapt to his feet shoving his feet into his shoes, both hands holding the gun out in front of him. He spun around the tiny cabin. The ringing got louder. It was coming from the bed. He kicked at the mattress and bedding with his feet, gun pointing at the source of the sound. The phone fell to the floor from its hiding place just under the mattress, flashing and vibrating. He looked at it for a second before stamping on it with his heel several times until the ringing stopped. He picked up his bag, turned and left the cabin, sprinting through the boat and out onto the tow path. A second later he was gone, a couple of swaying branches the only indication that he had ever been there.

# A mobile phone in your cabin starts ringing. You don't own a mobile phone.

### by

### Michael Andrews

The setting couldn't be more perfect. My agent had come up with the idea after I had admitted to her that I was being distracted by the lights of the city and I was struggling to put the finishing touches to my latest vampire novel. Breaking away from the current vein of the creatures of the dead who can walk around in the sunlight and live on the blood of animals, my vampire characters would burn to a crisp and were a blood thirsty, human feeding lot, so I was veering back more to the true horror lore rather than the tween fiction of the past decade.

And so, with deadlines already passed, my agent physically dragged me into her car, armed only with a MacBook and enough clothes for a week, and left me abandoned in the wood cabin, miles from anywhere. I looked around the cabin, happy to see that she had, at least, filled the fridge and cupboards with food and drink, and that the bed looked comfortable enough.

There was no television, and my initial scout around found no radio either. It was literally going to be Mother Nature and my cast of vampires to keep me occupied. I started to unpack my bag when I noticed that my iPhone was missing. I cursed her light fingered approached for a few moments before deciding that maybe not owning a phone for a week could be beneficial, as it would mean that I have no access to Facebook, Twitter or the internet to distract me. I was truly alone with just my thoughts.

I cooked up a quick pot of chicken curry and rice and booted up my MacBook. Pulling up the latest chapter, I quickly re-read it to familiarise myself with the state of the storyline before my fingers became a blur on the keys.

Four deaths, an invasion of the Vatican and the main characters getting their required information to plot their next move led me to the end of several chapters and when I looked up and out of the window, darkness had fallen. With no music playing in the cabin and my concentration now away from my story, I could hear the hooting of owls and the rustle of the leaves of the surrounding woods.

I stood and walked to the window to close the curtain. The woods were as black as the bottom of a coal pit, and I would be lying if I didn't admit to a small shiver running down my spine as I realised how alone I actually was. I quickly closed all of the flimsy curtains and, with a yawn, headed for bed.

For three days, I settled into a routine. I'd awake to the sound of the dawn chorus and, after eating a hearty breakfast, go for an hour's hike in the woods.

Each day, I'd wander in a different direction, exploring the surrounding area, storing ideas for when the werewolves reappear later in the series. I'd settle down to a review of my previous day's scribing before cracking on with the next part of the story, interrupted only by lunch and dinner. Finally, I'd head back to bed for a restful sleep to start over again the following day.

By Thursday however, the isolation was starting to set in. As much as I claim to like being independent, living on my own, doing what I want, when I want, I am quite a social person and not having seen a soul for four days was beginning to take its toll. I had started talking to myself, just to hear a human voice, and I wondered if that was the first sign of the craziness of my imagination taking hold.

When I thought that I saw eerie lights in the woods that night as I closed the curtains, my mind went into overdrive. Was it werewolves or vampires come to show their displeasure at my writing, witches fed up of being cast as evil hags, or the ghosts and demons of my debut writing finally having tracked me down and ready to drag me to Hell?

I poured myself a large glass of vodka, topped off with not enough cola, and took a long, deep slurp. I had to laugh at myself for getting worked up like this. I mean, I could even hear a phone ringing softly.

I stopped and paused. There it was again. Not only

could I hear the soft tones of one of Beethoven's concertos, (or was it Bach?), but I could hear a buzzing noise as well. Not just that, but there was a crunching sound outside the cabin, as if a wild beast had stumbled upon the wooden shack.

I scrambled around the cabin, pausing every few moments to catch a whisper of the buzzing when finally, I opened a sideboard drawer. Sure enough, there was a phone inside, an unknown number ringing. A loud banging startled me as the door to the cabin shook but its lock held true.

Cautiously, I picked the phone up and pressed the little green button to answer, hoping that it was salvation but hearing it was the unknown intruder.

"Hello?" I whispered into the mouthpiece, keeping my voice low so that the monster outside couldn't hear me. "Is anybody there?"

"About time too!" the voice of my agent broke out into her annoying pearly laughter. "Answer the bloody door will you! The pizza is getting cold!"

# A mobile phone in your cabin starts ringing. You don't own a mobile phone.

## by

## S.J. Gibbs

I stretched my tanned, lean, long legs out over the arm of the sofa and settled down with the book I had been longing to read.

I hadn't slept much lately, and the cabin I was staying in was the perfect getaway from it all.

The rays of the setting sun caught my eye as I glanced out of the window and I sighed with relief that I could finally relax as the peace of the cabin swept over me.

The peace was shattered by the intrusion of a mobile phone ringing from the kitchen.

I was confused I had deliberately not brought my phone away with me such was my need for quiet and solitude.

I could feel my heart chilling as I tried to establish in my own mind, why a mobile phone would be ringing out behind the closed kitchen door.

I could feel my pulse beating at the base of my throat as I slowly opened the kitchen door, peering around it as I did so. I would have remained where I was except for the demands of the ringing tone. My eyes narrowed as I cautiously peeked around the door, half expecting to see an intruder inside the kitchen. The cabin suddenly began to feel very isolated instead of peaceful. I felt as though somebody was watching me as I threw the door open the rest of the way and entered the kitchen more boldly than I was feeling inside.

The room was empty, but on the kitchen surface, next to the remains of the shepherd's pie I had half eaten earlier lay the mobile phone, which was still ringing.

I didn't move for a moment, as my eyes scanned around the room once more, to confirm that nobody was in here other than myself.

Having double-checked the room and having satisfied myself that there was no intruder, I began to try and puzzle out how the phone could be there, where I definitely would have seen it earlier. None of it made sense. How had it suddenly appeared? Cautiously, I answered the phone, "Who is it?" It was a conditioned response, and I felt stupid as soon as I said it.

An authoritative voice spoke back to me, "you will comply with what I tell you to do. Go to the bookcase in the lounge." In panic, I headed towards the bookcase. I glanced nervously out of the window and could see a taxi parked at the end of the drive. I could hear rustling in the grass, but as the light was fading, I couldn't determine whether somebody was in the bushes or if there was somebody in the taxi. As my eyes adjusted to the dusk, I could see that somebody was in the driver's seat of the taxi given away by the light from a cigarette they were smoking.

I jumped as the voice spoke again, the accent sounded Italian. My heart thudded with fear as the voice informed me that she had a gun.

Suddenly, I heard a huge BOOM!

"Hello, hello" I cried but the voice had gone.

I ran out of the cabin, into the garden, and down the drive towards the taxi, as I dialed 999.

I closed my eyes and counted to twelve before I dared to open them again and look inside the taxi. This was another world, there was blood everywhere and a woman slumped over the steering wheel. My heart missed a beat as I saw the big man with grey-streaked dark hair standing at the side of the drive, gun still in his hand. His presence petrified me. The silence between us as I stared into his eyes was like the banging of drums. I registered his dusty shirt, jeans and old boots all of which were splattered with splashes of red blood. I had a moment of understanding that what was going to happen next had become inevitable. It seemed like ages passed between us as I froze to the spot. The desire to get away was strong but I couldn't move. I looked across the road to the fields, which seemed to extend miles into the distance, but still I couldn't move. A brief sense of relief hit me as I heard the police car siren.

I watched the man intently as he slowly lowered himself to the ground placing the gun down beside him. He looked like a baby, as he started to cry. He stared at me glassily as he said, "you have nothing to be afraid of now", as he pointed to the taxi, "it was Amalia who was going to kill you. She found out I was having an affair and when I rented you this cabin, she thought it was you that I was having the affair with. She came out here with this gun and the intention of killing you."

**Assignment Fifteen -** You are the creature that gets summonsed at a slumber party.

12<sup>th</sup> October 2016

All of the group tried to get into the head of an evil creature to greater or lesser extents while putting on their own twists.

AJ tried to bring humour back into her story after recent assignments, but is finding that humour is a very individual taste. What one person finds funny or hilarious, others may find not.

The conversation while we were reviewing led onto energy states and S.J. and J.M. experimented with Kinesiology, much to the amusement of AJ and Michael, showing the individual senses of humour.

# You are the creature that gets summonsed at a slumber party.

## by

## AJ. Jones

"So! Who dares to summons the mighty Wendy from her slumbers at such an unearthly hour?"

The girls sitting round the table look up from the Ouija board and giggle nervously.

"Did anyone hear anything then?" the fat one asks.

"I think I did!" says the one in the slutty red dress that's fighting the longing to let her right boob plop over the top of its miniscule casing.

"I SAID, WHO DARES TO SUMMONS THE MIGHTY WENDY FROM HER SLUMBERS AT SUCH AN UNEARTHLY HOUR, YOU MORONS!"

I roar it this time because you gotta love the reaction it has on people, especially a group of well-oiled women like this lot.

Should I reveal myself to them at this early stage of the game or shall I play a few tricks just to raise their scare levels to the maximum first?

I decide to make a few spooky noises. I begin with a few "OOOOOOOOOOOOOOOOOOOOHs" and a couple of childlike sobs. That always gets the hairs prickling on the back of the neck.

Then I have a brainwave - why don't I impersonate Cilla? I've bumped into her a few times since she arrived here in the afterlife and she's a lorra, lorra laffs, so here goes:

"Surprise, surprise, Ladies! Bet you didn't expect to see me here tonight!"

The girls scream . . . but suddenly their eyes start popping out of their faces. What are they looking at, I wonder?

But then I realise that Cilla is actually in the room!

I wink at her and then the fun really begins.

I start materialising as myself when I actually took my last breath. The vomit I choked on adds an extra-gruesome element to the grossness! Well, I was known as Wibbly Wobbly Wendy to most people I knew.

To my surprise, Cilla copies me and shows herself in her final moments of life - not a pretty sight I can assure you.

Our audience down their drinks and run like screaming banshees out of the private room they'd hired for the night into the general hubbub of the busy hotel bar. All except one!

They find her body the next morning, dried vomit polluting the atmosphere, right boob on show for all the world to see.

# You are the creature that gets summonsed at a slumber party.

## by

## J.M. McKenzie

It had been an evening like many others they had spent together. They had changed early into their pyjamas. There was a lot of preening and pampering, soft music, chocolate and magazines, giggles and titters, long languid limbs, skin soft with the bloom of youth. However much they enjoyed this part, they all knew it was just a frothy preamble to the real reason they were together. As night fell, they closed the curtains and gathered on the floor as their thoughts moved to more sinister matters. The Ouija board was brought out and their eyes widened as the glass moved across the board, sometimes fast and lurching, sometimes slow and steady. There was laughter and accusations. The board was tossed to one side. They sat crossed legged, knees touching, and formed a tighter circle. They held hands. The box was ritualistically brought out and placed in the centre of the ring. The lid was removed and the heavy black book was carefully removed from its silky resting place. They opened it at the place marked by the slim ribbon between the pages. Passing it around the circle they took turns to read.

The language was both harsh and elegant at the same

time.  Its style was unfamiliar and hard to understand. But the meaning of the words was not as important as the ritual itself.  The rhythmic murmuring of the written word.  The passing of the book from hand to hand, fluttering fingers brushing. The intensity of their unity.  A trancelike state engulfed them. They instinctively knew when to pass the book on. The murmuring became a chanting. The passing of the book took on an unfaltering momentum.  Faster and faster it went round the circle.  The chanting grew louder.  They could not have stopped even if they had wanted to.

---

We have been waiting since the beginning of time. Not wholly present and yet not insensible.  We are a slumbering nothingness of dark thoughts and feelings, monstrous longings and desires.  We are conscious yet unconscious, lost in our own eternal world of cruel intentions.  We are a potent yet still impotent spring of malice.  We exist solely to beget pain, fear and suffering.  We are vast.  We are ancient. We are brooding.  We are pure evil.  Stars have formed and exploded.  Universes have expanded and contracted and we have waited.  Until now.

We hear the call.  Tiny and faint at first, then slowly strengthening.  It comes from far, far away.  It is unmistakable.  It is our time.  Our being awakens.  We writhe. We uncoil. We expand. We swell. We are alert and ready.

The call is loud now. It is clear. It is a channel. Our feelings intensify. We are strong. We are immense. Our energies surge and pulsate. We move towards the channel. We are drawn by the call. We need do nothing. We diffuse towards the call. We move slowly at first but soon gather speed.

Light years pass like seconds. Planets, galaxies and comets flash past. We are coming. Faster and faster. We are flying in a blur of light and colour. We are close. We are shimmering. We are gorged with malevolence. We are gleeful.

We burst from the channel and explode into life. The call ceases. There is silence. We have arrived.

We see for the first time through clear blue eyes. We are fresh and soft and pink. Fluffy slippers on our feet. Soft cotton against our skin. Astonished faces. Questioning looks. She is gone. We are here.

We speak as one. Our voice is deep and guttural. They cry out. We laugh. They scream and try to flee.

Too late. We are fast. We are vicious. We are merciless.

We are here. It has begun.

# You are the creature that gets summonsed at a slumber party.

## by

## Michael Andrews

Darkness surrounded me suddenly. I couldn't see my hand in front of my face. What was happening? I felt a gut wrenching pain in my stomach as my body seemed to lurch forwards whilst remaining stationary. My head spun and agony erupted like an explosion inside my brain. Spots of light flashed in front of my eyes like a firework display from the Fourth of July celebrations that had witnessed many times in the past.

I now recognised the sensations coursing through my body and I gritted my teeth for the inevitable howl of uncontrollable ecstasy that would finally burst from my lips but I still had some tme to hold on.

I could fight against it, preventing the summoning but, as I heard the chattering, sniggering sound of teenage voices echoing past the deep, enchanting intonations of whomever it was who darted to put voice to the spell, I decided to allow myself to pass through the boundaries of my domain and into the Second Realm of Existence. It had been some time, years perhaps, since I had allowed my spirit to feast on the fruits of the higher plane, and I would enjoy the youthful essences of my so called masters.

Brightness burst around me and I let go, my scream of delight shattering glass as I emerged from the Shadowlands into the glorious light of the human world. Clenching my fists, I blinked to regain my sight as my body soaked in the energy of this plane, feeding myself, allowing my strength to grow.

"Oh mighty demon, you are summoned here to do our bidding," a faltering voice interrupted my pleasure. "Thou art required to submit to my will else I shalt banish thee back to the void."

I looked around the room, spotting two young men and three girls, all of whom looked like they were barely out of High School. I could smell the nerves and fear from them and as I fixed my gaze on a dark haired youth, the leader, the one who had called me, I allowed myself to shimmer into the form of a hideous demon. They were obviously expecting one so I might as well have some fun with them. I knelt onto one knee, head bowed in submission.

"Master, what is your bidding," I crackled out, keeping my voice low and menacing.

"Bloody hell, Danny... it actually worked!" the blonde

haired girl shrieked. I held back a wince as her high pitched cry pierced my hearing.

"Of course it worked, Clara," the lad known as Danny hissed. "I told you... my mother used this spell to summon one and she said it was the most fun that she'd had in years."

"But isn't Aunt Joanne is in the pysch hospital now?" a red headed lad asked. I like red heads. They have so much raw energy, pent up anger and fight inside them. A single ginger could feed a small army of minions.

"My mother isn't crazy, as I've just proved," Danny snarled at his cousin.

I took a moment to study the boy. The name Joanne triggered a memory of a young girl, nervous and excitable. I had many nights of fun playing the part of an incubus. She willing fed me her energy in return for the limited power that I granted her. I could see similarities between the two, albeit there was an inner strength to this boy that his mother never possessed.

"I thought that she'd said he was handsome," one of the girls moaned.

"Oh great and worthy master," I continued to play

along. "What doth thee desire? Revenge or play?" I let my demon form dissolve away until my seductive form appeared. Bright platinum blonde hair, deep sapphire eyes, a chiselled chin and a ripped six pack of abs. I chuckled to myself as I felt the pulses of all five youths quicken as my sexual pheromones leaked out of my pores, ensnaring them. Five youths would certainly fill my needs for many months to come.

"I want the truth from you," Danny calmly stated, seemingly unaffected by my powers of seduction. He looked around at his four friends who were staring glassy eyed at my now naked form. I knew that a mere hint of suggestion in their minds would have them in the same state of undress and once I touched their sex craved bodies, they would not be able to resist giving their essences to me.

"Leave them alone, for Christ's sake," the boy sighed.

I recoiled at the sound of that damn meddling fool's name, the holiness of him causing a sliver of pain in my gut. I turned and focussed on the boy, the son of the girl that I had enjoyed what must have been a decade and a half before as she was still barely a woman herself at that time.

"What truth would you have me tell you?" I replied, feeling a growing uncertainty inside me. I released the others from my sexual trap and willed some clothes onto my body, covering upmy nakedness. I reached out with my mind and touched the black haired youth's mind. I shivered as I felt the raw power inside him and, in an instant, I knew that my existence had changed forever.

He opened his mouth and muttered the words that no Third Plane creature ever wants to hear from a child of the plane above. "Are you my father?"

# You are the creature that gets summonsed at a slumber party.

## by

## S.J. Gibbs

"What have we done?" one of the girls exclaims. They are all screaming at the sight of me. Well they summoned me here with that Ouija board thing they were playing around with.

I'm just having a bit of fun waving my sabre around, why are they screaming so much?

What do they think I am, a bogeyman?

Why are they so upset, I'm only fulfilling my obligation to appear before them, they called me here?

There are kids all around me. I wish they'd stop screaming.

Why are they trying to lock the door, to keep me out?

I look at my hands, thin, supple, and bright yellow.

Why am I causing such a sense of panic?

I hiss at them, but this seems to make them scream even louder.

I lie down enjoying the beauty of my surroundings, Earth.

They've stopped screaming thank goodness, I wonder if they'll bring me a drink, absinthe, isn't that what they drink on Earth?

I can see a sprinkling of lights in the distance.

I am not of this world, but I like it especially now those girls have stopped screaming.

I look up and can see their moon and some stars.

The girl, who had been screaming the loudest, is peeping at me with a puzzled look on her face. She is staring at me as if I have just come out of a Martian space capsule.

She seems to forget her fear and foolishly approaches me.

I can feel triumph in my own eyes.

I can see Satan drinking blood from his crystal goblet.

I unbuckle my sabre and I see her start to back away.

Earth is better than Hell, I decide. Offering to serve Earth had been a good choice, one of my better ones.

The door opens again and two more of the girls venture outside, driven by curiosity.

I can smell their blood.

I wonder if I mix up their bits what they will taste like.

How will I kill them? I could do it with a wave of my sabre.

I spring to my feet. In my excitement, I trip over and land straight on top of the campfire, which the girls had been sitting around before my arrival. My sabre drives straight through my chest and as I leave Earth the last thing I see is the girl who screamed the loudest holding up a crucifix.

**Assignment Sixteen -** A garbage collector discovers something interesting in one of his collection runs.

8th December 2016

Michael's piece of homework for this assignment reflected his then state of mind as he had lost his USB stick with his complete writings. Fortunately he managed to recover a vast part of them, having sent them to his editors previously, but he had lost three chapters of Dragonfire and two chapters of a backburner project.

This is an important lesson for all budding writers... make sure you have multiple back ups of your work or use cloud storage. A very simple solution is to email copies to yourself and set up a folder to store them.

AJ liked this assignment, about a battered guitar and how it could change someone's life and the theme of one man's trash is another man's treasure.

J.M. went with a moral story by running with the theme that you can't judge a book by its cover.

S.J. felt that this homework highlighted that the writing these flash fictions could develop an idea into a larger project.

## A garbage collector discovers something interesting in one of his collection runs.

### by

### AJ. Jones

Who knew that hanging off the side of a massive truck, whizzing along at all of 10 miles an hour would give you such a buzz? You feel like Jack the Lad, the bloke at the fair, holding on with one hand to the back of the "waltzer", spinning it round and round as fast as it can go. The only difference is there are no pretty ladies sitting in the truck, only a bunch of hairy-arsed binmen!

Actually, being a "garbage collector", as the Yanks call it, has loads of perks that the rest of the world has no idea about. Hanging off the side of the truck as it glides majestically along the highways and byways of Great Britain, holding up all the other road users whose stupid, angry faces provide us with so much free entertainment, is only one of them. You also get a daily workout better than any physical trainer could create for you; your abs literally hone themselves.

But what I love most is that you get to rummage through the cast-offs of the rest of society. This can lead to your getting your hands on some very interesting stuff.

Take last Wednesday, for instance, we pull up outside this huge gateway along a quiet country lane in the middle of nowhere. The gates open slowly after Rob, our driver, keys in the code that's written on his daily crib sheet. "Enter, but be as quick and quiet as you can. Mr & Mrs O are asleep and wouldn't take kindly to being woken up by you noisy gits", says the voice emitting from the speaker next to the keypad.

Rob drives slowly down the magnificent driveway and a few minutes later, we see what can only be termed as a mansion of epic proportions. "Holy shit!" mouths Mick, our skipper for the day.

We follow the tradesmen's entrance signs and soon find the covered enclosure where the dustbins are stored. Rob manoeuvres the truck into the best position to begin the collection process and me and the rest of the lads jump off to start pulling the bins outside into the yard area.

As I pull the one out of the left-hand corner, something that's been dumped behind it demands my attention. I look round to see if anyone else has noticed but there's only me inside the enclosure, so I crouch down to pick up the battered old guitar case just as Mick walks in.

"What's that you've found?" he whispers. "Don't worry, there's a policy on my shift that anything we find in the rubbish is ours for the taking. If it's been binned, then the householder has thrown it out and won't mind us having it." He knows I play the guitar so he takes the case and puts it in the driver's cabin, telling the other lads that it's mine and they can "keep their thieving hands off it".

We finish the job in record time and get back to the yard just before clocking off time. I pick up the case and put it in my car boot, ready to take home.

When I get back, I open the boot and take the tatty old case upstairs to my room, telling my Mom that I'm going to do some practice for my X-factor audition on Sunday. I throw the case on the bed and open it. My eyes literally POP when I see what's inside.

Instead of the battered old guitar I was expecting, there's the most beautiful old Rickenbacker I've ever seen. I pick it up and my fingers begin to dance over the strings as if they've known them intimately my whole life. I'm suddenly able to play any tune that comes into my head, and not only that, I can add my own subtle little touches and make them sound even better than the original.

I start to sing along with the tunes and my voice sounds better than it's ever done.

"Dinner's ready," I hear Mom shout from downstairs.

"Be down in a minute," I yell back.

"Whose CD did you buy today, Son?" she asks as I walk into the kitchen. "I really like it."

"That was me singing and playing, Mom," I tell her and I explain everything that's happened to me that day.

"Wow," she says. "I can't imagine what Simon will say when he hears you audition. You can't fail to get through. Your Dad would be so proud of you. He always wanted to be able to play the guitar like that. He tried so hard, but he was never that good."

"I know, Mom," I say, as I remember going to see Dad perform over the years before the cancer took him. "I'm going to tell Simon I'm doing it for my Dad. They always like an emotional back story, don't they?"

*Two weeks earlier*

"I'm sure you put it in your dressing room," Sharon mumbles to herself in the half-awake stupor she always feels when a phone call wakes her up in the middle of the night - well, what she calls the middle of the night, anyway, but it's actually 9 o'clock in the morning.

She and Ozzy had been, what her therapist would call, "a bit tense" with each other the previous evening and it had taken more than her usual 2 bottles of red and 3 sleeping tablets to lull her into any form of sleep.

Ozzy had gone to bed before her, shouting at her for losing his "precious Dad's guitar" - the one he'd never actually managed to get a tune out of, even when he was completely off his head and at his most creative.

"Hello, Simon," she trills down the phone. "Yes, I've decided I will be your fourth judge again. I want to find us a star act this time, just like One D or Olly!"

Simon smiles and Sharon can picture the dollar signs appearing in his eyes.

# A garbage collector discovers something interesting in one of his collection runs.

## by

## J.M. McKenzie

Louis hated his job, especially in the summer when the bins stank of rotting food and buzzed with fat lazy flies. It wasn't the hard physical nature of the work that was the problem, in many ways that was the part he did enjoy. It was the filth he couldn't stand. People were disgusting. The contents of their bins and the way they discarded their waste revealed so much about them. The bins themselves were smeared, inside and out with layers of ancient food waste, generously seasoned with a liberal sprinkling of cigarette ash. That was bad enough, but the contents of the bins were even worse. Open nappies, insanitary sanitary towels and tampons displayed their dirty secrets for all to see. Dog shit, vomit and even human excrement lurked amidst greying potato peelings, soiled plastic containers, soggy cardboard and razor sharp rusty cans.

Some bins were more cared for. You could usually spot them immediately by their relatively clean exteriors, often adorned with colourful stickers to make them identifiable to their loving owners and prevent them being adopted by their less devoted neighbours. The contents of these bins were neatly bagged and tied, their unpleasant innards politely concealed from view. To add a little interest to his long days of drudgery, Louis would try to match the bins to the houses and, if he could, to their owners.

On this particular road he had pretty much worked it out. The dirtiest bin, by far, belonged to the smartly dressed young man at number seventeen. Every day he emerged suited and booted from his big grey designer front door and got into his clean and shiny red BMW Gran Coupe. Head held high, back straight he oozed charm and confidence. Louis hated him. He knew what he was really like and what went on behind that fancy front door, from the contents and state of his bin. Greasy takeaway debris, empty beer cans, crumpled porn and used condoms tumbled from his curry stained bin every week. He wanted people to think he was a great guy. Strong, sexy and successful. Chic trendy and cool. Louis knew better. He was cheap and dirty. Sleazy and grubby.

Now the girl who lived at number eighteen across the road was a completely different story. She was a decent person. Her bin was always spotless and smelt of disinfectant. All her rubbish was double bagged in small white bin liners, sealed neatly with multicolour wire twists. She was small and blond and always smiled and said hello on her way to her little pink Fiat 500. Louis imagined that she was a primary school teacher. He had an image in his head of her sitting, legs crossed, in a low armchair, in front of a class of adoring four and five years olds, reading to them from a large story book as they gazed rapturously up at her. She was a good person. Louis knew she was. Her bin said so.

He was roused from his daydreams about number eighteen as he emptied the contents of her bin into the truck. Something bright and shiny caught his eye. Unusual? He had never laid eyes on any actual rubbish in her bin before. As far as he was aware, nothing had ever escaped from within the clouds of white plastic bin liners. He peered closer into the truck to get a better look at the object. He could just see it nestling between two bags. As his eyes rested on it, he suddenly staggered backwards as a gasp escaped his lips. Not believing what was seeing, he leaned in again and reached down between the bags, just managing to pinch it between his finger and thumb before it slipped out of reach completely. In a mixture of horror and confusion he held it in front of his face, twisting it back and forth.

It was the tip of a human finger. The nail was intact. It was long, red and sparkly. The severed end of the finger was ragged as if it had been ripped from the rest of the hand with great force. Tiny tendons and blood vessels dangled from its torn end. Louis opened his mouth to speak, to call out to the driver or another bin man but no sound came out. Anyway, they were all out of earshot and out of sight ahead of him and the noise of the engine would have drowned him out. Almost simultaneously he heard a movement behind him and he spun around just as a sharp and heavy blow hit his temple. His vision darkened. His knees buckled. He rolled onto his back as he fell. Everything happened fast. He had no conscious thought, only fear and utter confusion.

Above him he saw a small blond figure, arm raised with what looked like a hammer in her hand. She lurched towards him about to strike again, aiming directly for the centre of his forehead. He raised his arm in a defensive posture. Just as he saw the hammer begin to descend, there was a grunt followed by a blur of bodies and a thud as she and her assailant, his saviour, hit the ground.

Louis struggled to his knees, blinking and shaking his head.

In front of him number seventeen, suited and booted as usual, strong, sexy and successful, was straddling number eighteen who was writhing and hissing beneath him, her pretty face twisted in a mask of rage.

"What the fuck? Are you OK mate? You're alright now. I've got your back. Don't worry you're safe now."

## A garbage collector discovers something interesting in one of his collection runs.

### by

### Michael Andrews

Billy Jackson was fed up with life. Here he was, at the age of forty five, stuck in a dead end job in more ways than one. Having flunked his exams at school through lack of effort, he failed to get into university to pursue his dream of writing, and after being made redundant from the electrical goods retailer who went bust, he found a job that paid a decent wage. Well, more than the dole money anyway... not that Billy was one for living off the state.

He sighed as the idiot in the cab of the bin lorry swung too fast around the tight corner and he hung on to the back of the truck, his leg narrowly avoiding the oncoming SUV that was, as usual, being driven badly by some woman driver with more lipstick and make-up than brains.

"How their kids ever make it to school alive, I'll never know!" he muttered to himself. Feeling a hint of relief when Jake the idiot pulled the lorry to the side of the road, Billy jumped down and headed towards the overflowing bins. 'At least it wasn't recycling week this week,' he thought, pleased that he wouldn't get into any arguments as to why he couldn't empty the bins because the thick residents simply couldn't be bothered to read the repeated leaflets and notes left by the council.

The downside of this week though was the rotting stench of two week old food, carelessly overbought and thrown away by the wasteful, well to do residents of Hickens Deeth. It turned Billy's stomach when he thought about how much money was being thrown away, how the food would be welcome to the homeless or the needy, but the overpaid, pretentious population of the newly built village would rather throw food away than think of those worse off.

"Sign of the times... what with Brexit and all," Billy said, regretting it instantly as Jake the idiot immediately started his racist rhetoric about how lucky they were to have the bin man jobs as opposed to those "nasty immugrunt migrunts" who come over here, taking our jobs and living on benefits.

Tuning him out, Billy pulled the first four bins into place for the idiot to load onto the lift and he looked idly around as the bins were lifted into the air, before emptying their contents into the back of the truck. It reminded him of the one and only time that he had gone for a drink with his work partner, who he found couldn't handle his beer and chucked the contents of his stomach all over the table, floor and himself.

As he moved towards the next four bins, a shiny blue object caught his eye. Kneeling down by the black plastic waste containers, he found a small stick with a funny metal key like end. Looking around to make sure that no-one had seen him, he pocketed it and pulled the full bins into place.

Rain started to fall, causing the idiot to complain even more, as if being in the EU was the root of all of the world's ills and Billy resigned himself to another day of misery.

Eventually the day was over and he quickly made it home, ignoring the repeated requests of Jake to "go for a quick one" and in the safety of his one roomed studio flat, Billy pulled off his work clothes, putting them straight into the washing machine. Fishing his loose change out of his pockets, he remembered the blue stick device. Looking at it and being rather techie with computers, he recognised it as a USB drive and within moments, his laptop was booted up and the stick inserted. Making sure that his firewall was on and all of his anti-virus programmes were running, he opened up the drive and his jaw dropped.

File after file, folder after folder, flooded the screen. He didn't recognise any of the file names but a quick inspection of them uncovered a host of book files, all written and edited, all of them formatted and ready to go. He quickly searched the internet, looking for the book titles to see if any had been published but all of them seemed to be brand new, until finally and much to his disappointment, he found a series of them published through an online retailer.

"There goes my idea for stealing them," he frowned to himself. He looked at the author's name and didn't recognise it but again, being computer literate, he soon found himself on a website with a link to social media. Pulling up the mystery author's page, he saw the devastation in the posts about how his work had gone missing and that he was going to stop writing.

"Well, he couldn't have been that good, could he?" Billy mused. He looked up some of the reviews and was amazed at the five star comments from all around the world. A flash of conscience hit him and he pulled up the man's media account/

*Hi. My name is Billy and I work as a bin man. On my round today, I found a USB stick and I think it might belong to you. Please contact me to arrange for me to drop it off.*

Unfortunately for the unlucky author, just as Billy was about to hit send, the storm which had been getting worse throughout the evening, ripped a tree from the street and sent it crashing into the three story apartment block, severing the phone line and killing Billy instantly.

The world will now never know if a certain young vampire will ever find his peace.

## A garbage collector discovers something interesting in one of his collection runs.

### by

### S.J. Gibbs

Russell Gage glanced over the uncut hedge of the large dilapidated house as he grabbed the bins from the pavement outside. He was relieved it was Friday, the last day of the week, for collecting other people's garbage. The job was so mundane and routine that practically everything he did was automated. He tried to cheer himself with the thought of the day nearing its' end.

He grunted as he heaved the bins towards the dustcart but stopped in his tracks as he heard a baby screaming.

The screams were coming from inside the bin, which he was dragging. He opened the lid and peered in, moving frantically the pieces of lettuce, cucumbers, onions and tomatoes, which were strewn over the baby beneath.

The baby was quivering as he pulled it closely towards him and wrapped it inside his jacket, against his chest.

It was a crime scene, he knew, but something was telling him to hide the baby.

He thought of his wife and her beauty and how much she would love this baby.

Spouting apologies to his co- workers, he ran off up the road clinging the baby to him, hidden beneath his jacket. His senses were working but in a mixed-up way. He could feel the baby wriggling beneath his jacket, but he just tightened his grip and held it closer, absolutely sure that nobody else had seen or heard the baby.

He could feel the loss, his wife's loss and all that they had been through, and now this treat had been delivered to them.

The baby stopped crying and feeling encouraged he thought again about his beautiful wife and how happy she would be when he handed the baby to her.

He walked up the path to their home and fumbled with his key in the lock, so eager to please his wife.

He entered the hallway, quickly closing the door after him and shouted, " Robyn, Robyn, come here quickly."

She stared at the baby in his arms, as he explained how he had found it in the garbage bin. Conspiracy and murder charges flashed before her, and yet she felt as if she had won the lottery.

"I really don't know," she heard herself speak, "but you had better rush out and get some formula milk."

She grabbed a blanket and threw it around the baby girl to try and warm her, she felt so cold, so naked.

She held the baby close to her and rocked her as she thought about the death of their two-year-old son and how she was unable to have any more children.

She had sat for about an hour cradling the baby before Russell returned with bottles, nappies and formula milk.

Russell made a bottle of milk, and the baby sucked at it half- hearted.

"We should take her to see a doctor, but if we do, then we will be rumbled," she said. "We will have to invent a story if we want to keep her. We will say my sister in Ireland died within minutes of giving birth and that my brother-in-law has asked us to bring up the baby, as he isn't able to cope. Russell do you really think we may just get away with this?"

## Assignment Seventeen - Write an irate letter directed at a company that makes your favourite (fictional) food. Be as comical as possible.
### 20th January 2017

The group really enjoyed this assignment, for the first time being tasked with writing humour although AJ did not complete this homework.

J.M. went back to her roots with her delightful tale of the benefits, or lack of, from a hot pepper sauce. We still wonder how she can turn the most unlikely topic into that of a zombie apocalypse.

S.J. had an enjoyable bash at humour, which while she felt failed, the rest of the group could only cry (with laughter!).

Michael was not confident with writing humour so resorted to toilet humour. A gross out story follows.

# Write an irate letter directed at a company that makes your favourite (fictional) food. Be as comical as possible.

## by

## J.M. McKenzie

Barbara De'ath
Alexandria Avenue
Hilltop
19th January 2019
Baysian Delights Ltd.
Bridgetown
Barbados

Re: Your product Baysian Delights Hot Pepper Sauce

To whom it may concern,

I am writing to complain about the unsuitability of your product, Baysian Delights Hot Pepper Sauce, to meet the needs of your customers since the Zombie Apocalypse broke out this time last year. I am not usually a complainer but have been so disappointed with the complete and utter uselessness of your product in the situation that we currently find ourselves, in I felt compelled to put pen to paper. Please take the contents of this letter in the spirit in which they are intended, that is, one of constructive criticism. You will note that each point of objection is followed by a suggestion for the future development of your product, should of course you and your employees be fortunate enough to survive this recent global catastrophe.

Baysian Delights Hot Pepper Sauce is one of my all-time favourite foods. A bottle lives on my kitchen table at all times and I add liberal quantities of it to every meal I eat. I regularly use it in my cooking and when the munchies strike I inevitably turn to it as my snack of choice, dipping whatever vehicle I can get my hands on at the time into small bowls of the fiery yellow liquid. I have to admit when my cravings for its spicy sweetness overcome me I have been known to swig it straight from the bottle to a mixture of horror and amazement from my friends and family.

As the product is not available in the UK, maintaining a supply that is enough to satisfy my demand requires a complex and robust purchasing strategy, involving a high degree of stockpiling. I ensure that I regularly visit the island myself always making room in my case for several bottles. I also have a wide network of friends and acquaintances that bring me back a bottle or two when they visit. As a result of this I still have a large supply, a year in to the apocalypse. In fact Baysian Delights Hot Pepper Sauce it is the only canned or bottled food that I have left in my store cupboards in any significant quantity. This has caused me to reflect, with increasing frustration, on the inadequacy of its properties, on many levels, in terms of being a useful resource in a world overrun by the living dead.

My main issues are as follows:

> 1. The fact that it comes in a plastic bottle. A plastic bottle is of no use to man or beast in the Zombie Apocalypse. In the early days of the event I was sitting at my dining table

enjoying an early dinner when my newly undead neighbour burst his way through my back door into my kitchen. I grabbed the nearest thing to me, which was a bottle of Baysian Delights Hot Pepper Sauce, and struck him around the head with it, only to discover to my horror when it bounced of his skull, that a plastic bottle was just not going to cut it. Thankfully, I was able to reach a baking dish of streaming macaroni cheese straight from the oven which I smashed over his head causing a jagged shard to penetrate his brain killing him again and also saving my life.

Recommendation: Package all your products in glass bottles, strong enough to survive the journey from Barbados to the UK but fragile enough to break when required for use as a weapon.

2. The consistency and texture of Baysian Delights Hot Pepper Sauce is not suitable for use in a super-soaker. Due to my large supply of Baysian Delights Hot Pepper Sauce and that fact that the active component in the hot chilli pepper, capsaicin, is often used as a deterrent and temporary protection spray against large wild animals such as bears and elephants, I decided to consider using it against the zombies surrounding my house when I attempted to move to a safer location. I loaded my, now deceased, son's super-soaker with Baysian Delights Hot Pepper Sauce and tried to spray the offending horde as I made my escape. Imagine my dismay when after an initial tiny burst of watery

liquid, nothing whatsoever left the nozzle. I was forced to retreat back into my propriety and, on examining the super-soaker, discovered that the sauce was not only too thick to get through the internal piping, but the end of the nozzle was blocked by chilli seeds.

Recommendation: Ensure that the consistency of the sauce is thin enough to be used in super-soakers, and similar water based weapons, and either remove or liquidise to remove chilli seeds.

3. The calorific content and nutritional value is inadequate when consumed as a dietary staple. As Baysian Delights Hot Pepper Sauce is my main food source now, apart from the odd rodent or large insect, I have to say that it is not meeting the calorific and nutritional needs of my body. I am so thin that my ribs and collar bones are protruding, my hair is falling out in patches and I have sores all over my body. My skin is yellow as are the whites (or now the yellows) of my eyes.

Recommendation: Adjust the recipe of the sauce to include nutritional supplements and increase the calorific value by adding additional carbohydrates and sugars.

4. The colour makes it unsuitable as a staple food. While I am sure that the bright yellow colour of Baysian Delights Hot Pepper Sauce is due in the main to the natural colour of the Scotch Bonnet Chillies, mustard and turmeric that are its main ingredients, I

suspect that some additional artificial colouring in the form of Sunshine Yellow may have been added. I am sick to my stomach of the sight of the yellow teeth, tongue and gums that greet me every morning in the bathroom mirror and this is made even worse by sight and smell of the runny yellow shit that explodes into my toilet bowl several times a day. Clearly, this is not helped by that fact that the drainage and plumbing systems failed several weeks ago now but nevertheless the problems could be improved considerably if the colour of the sauce was slightly less vibrant.

Recommendation: Minimise or completely remove the amount of artificial colouring in the product.

Anyway, I think I have said enough to make my point so, assuming this letter ever gets to you, the postal service is experiencing serious delays at the moment for obvious reasons; I look forward to hearing from you with an outline of your intentions to compensate me, as a loyal customer, for my inconvenience. In addition, if you would like to draft out your plans to modify the manufacturing and packaging of your product Baysian Delights Hot Pepper Sauce, to make it more useful in the event of a Zombie Apocalypse, I would also be happy to comment on these.


Yours sincerely


Barbara (they're coming to get you) De'ath.

# Write an irate letter directed at a company that makes your favourite (fictional) food. Be as comical as possible.

## by

## Michael Andrews

17 Fiction Street
Madeuptown
Contriveshire
Fabulous Flavours Ltd
Unit 41, Storify Industrial Park
Phonyville
Shamshire

Dear sir,

Normally I am not one to voice my concerns regarding matters. However, I feel that I simply had to write in to complain about my recent experience with my most favoured of all of your products.

I have been a loyal customer to your company for over thirteen and a half weeks now, but my most recent experience simply was beastly... so beastly that I struggled to finish my meal. In fact, I had to make sure to leave the final morsel of food so that I could enclose it within the Tupperware container which is included within the jiffy bag.

Ever since discovering your website amongst the many sites available on the internet, nestled between Fabulous Fatties From Franchester and Frivolous Formaldehyde Figurines, I have explored and sifted through such delights as your 'garlic and rhubarb digestive biscuits', the 'honey and hagfish oatmeal', not to mention the delightful 'duck and cucumber ice cream'.

However, my mind was totally blown away when I was recommended by other consumers on your referral page to try what fast became part of my daily diet. No longer could I simply eat plain rice, chicken or some minced beef concoction. I filled my refrigeration unit with container after container of the deliciously scrummy 'pickled onion and chocolate lamb risotto'. Hitting four major food groups, it just was the best thing since Otto Frederick Rohwedder sliced up a loaf of bread.

For nearly sixteen straight days now, I have feasted upon this marvellous miracle of culinary magic. Until yesterday morning. As I was sitting down to eat my breakfast portion, I felt a stirring within my insides, something which had not happened for almost fifteen days... in fact ever since I started to eat the three portions a day of the said risotto. I had a brief but sharp pain in my stomach and my lower back region and before I knew what had happened, the chocolate portion of the risotto had coloured my underwear!

I thought that it must be a mistake, an anomaly as Fox Mulder would say but it happened again as I was consuming my third helping at lunchtime. I even had to put on a new pair of undergarments after I had been to the shop for my cigarettes, whiskey and newspaper. Dinnertime was no different.

In fact, in the last twenty four hours, I have had to change my underknickers on six different occasions. This is totally unacceptable that a food stuff should do such a thing! I have never heard of this situation before. I am sure that there must just be a stray ingredient that made its way into the most recent batch of risotto and so, to help you identify it, I have enclosed all six pairs of my undergarments for your quality control team to study.

My wife has told me that I should stop eating the risotto completely, even to the extent that she had the audacity to throw the remaining eighty seven servings into the dustbin, but I managed to save several containers to last me until my next order arrives. An order, which I do hope I will receive a discount on due to my most recent experience.

I await your comments with expectation as I would hate to have to switch over to the 'Boiled Cabbage and pink bubblegum lasagne' which my wife is currently crowing about.

Yours sincerely


Peter Phartletting.

# Write an irate letter directed at a company that makes your favourite (fictional) food. Be as comical as possible.

## by

## S.J. Gibbs

Dear Sir or Madam,

I believe your company and employees to be very cunning manipulators who will sell your product to anyone regardless of the effect it has upon them.

The ready meal lasagna is richer in taste than any of the others I have tried.

My psychiatrist has recommended that I write this letter to verbalize my inner rage about my addiction to said ready meal, which has resulted in my gigantism.

I feel you should set aside a share of the profits in my name to compensate me for the size I have become by consuming this product.

The lasagna is too satisfactory to resist buying and eating and as a result I probably manage on average two hundred a month.

I can only imagine that you are all of the English upper class and have produced this product for the lower classes purely to make myself and others look fat and unsightly.

I am not a philosopher but I do apportion all blame for my size upon your selves.

I used to do voluntary community work for my local church, helping the elderly, which because of my addiction I am no longer able to do. Therefore, you are also causing the elderly to suffer by selling this product.

I am made to feel like a defenseless animal against one of the most effective weapons ever invented.

Of all the foods I have encountered, this has been the most treacherous for my addictive nature.

I think you should supply me with the boss's home number so that every time I have an urge to eat one of these meals, I can call him to discuss my problem.


Eagerly anticipating your response,


S.J. GIBBS

## **Assignment Eighteen -** The slave that became the slave owner of his former master.

### 24th February 2017

Again, the group enjoyed this subject, being able to go back to serious writing. Three of the group went for modern day slavery while Michael went back to Roman/Greek era with his tale.

S.J. demolished the word count barrier but we allowed her this licence as we felt the story was worthy of it. However, S.J. did fall back into the continued use of a character name throughout which she later recognised.

J.M.'s descriptive piece with crawling reptilian tattoos are worth mentioning, while AJ tackled human trafficking with a happy ending.

Michael looked at both sides of slavery but is a harsh

story in a tale of revenge, showing a darker side of his writing, which was to feature in three of his next four homeworks.

## The slave that became the slave owner of his former master.

**by**

**AJ. Jones**

The knock at the door chilled me to the bone.

Instinctively, I looked over at my sister, Martha, and saw that her eyes were wide with fear. I knew I had to do something - anything - to make her feel safe again. We'd had it drummed into us often enough what would happen if we were to open the front door and allow the world of pure evil that lay beyond it into the safety of our home.

Ali told us that the only people who would knock our door were the Police - and we all knew what horrors would happen if they ever found us, didn't we?

We all stood there like marble statues, hardly daring to breathe for fear of our lives.

Martha was now as white as a sheet. She looked as though all her blood had drained through her fingers into the massive sinkfull of freezing cold water that her hands were still immersed in. I could tell that she was fighting to stop her teeth from chattering. How much would I give to be able to move closer to her and ease her suffering with my warm breath?

"Hello! We know you're in there and you can either let us in or we'll break the door down."

The loud voice startled me so much I nearly dropped the broom I was holding.

"Don't move," mouthed Jonathan, who'd recently taken over as our leader. His predecessor, Michael, had been taken ill and died a few months previously and Jonathan had naturally assumed the responsibility of spokesperson whenever Ali paid us a visit.

The sound of the door being broken down filled me with utter terror. But when the Police came into the laundry, they told us not to be scared.

"We're here to liberate you," they said calmly and gently.

We all just continued to stand there, open-mouthed, not comprehending half of what they were saying. Our mouths opened even wider when someone else entered the room, though: the last person we were expecting.

Michael!

"Michael, we thought you were dead," said Jonathan.

"Yes, well, Ali left me outside the hospital thinking I was dead. He must have thought that, if he left me there, they'd just put me in the morgue and no one would care who I was or where I'd come from - just another faceless immigrant - one who they didn't need to spend any money on, so why bother to find out anything about him? But he didn't reckon on my friend, Matthew. He'd seen this happen before and so, this time, he decided to investigate what was going on. He watched the CCTV camera footage and saw Ali dump me. They found and arrested him and he's confessed to using us as slaves."

"Glory to God!" said Jonathan. "But what's going to happen to us now? We'll be put in prison with evil men and they'll rape us and keep us there until we die."

"No, that was just Ali's way of keeping us here. Life is good out there. You'll be given a new home, one where you can have your own key so you can come and go as you please. You'll be given money to live on and you'll be able to go to the shops and buy yourselves food and new clothes. Life will be good. You won't have to be anyone's slave ever again."

"Hallelujah!" we all murmured soundlessly and looked at each other in total shock. Could we believe our ears?

Martha had dared to move closer towards me. She looked at me pleadingly, no doubt wanting me to reassure her that she wasn't going to be punished for not finishing the laundry she'd been working on. "Is it true, Debra? Are we going to be free?"

"Yes, my Sister, we are," I said quietly, as a little smile

escaped my anxious face.

"Thank God," she said with a deep sigh.

As the Policeman had promised, we were taken to live in a beautiful house with proper beds and a lovely room with a table and chairs where we could sit and talk about home, and everything that had happened to us. Life became good again and we found that we could even laugh about some of the horrible things we'd been forced to do in "The Bad Place".

Martha and I decided to study hard and, even though it took us some years, we eventually became successful business women, opening our own laundry business, this time with professional premises and equipment. We gradually gained business from many of the local hotels and care homes and started making good money. We employed lots of people from many different countries and always treated them with respect.

* * * * *

We've recently won a very lucrative contract with a prestigious hotel group and so, today, we've had an open day in the foyer of one of their hotels to try and recruit some more employees. Martha usually oversees this sort of activity as she's a good judge of character. She does the final interviews, after the recruitment agency have weeded out all the unsuitable candidates.

Around 3pm, I walked into the foyer and, to my amazement, the person sitting in the interview chair opposite Martha was Ali. Martha was listening to him intently. Then, she got up, smiled and shook his hand vigorously. I watched him walk out of the front door in disbelief. Surely, she couldn't have offered him a job?

"Why not?" quipped Martha, later that evening. "He didn't recognise me and I doubt he ever knew our names, so it'll be fun to show him how a laundry business should be run. I may have to throw in a few examples of bad laundries during his induction course, though. I can't wait to see how he's going to react. I see it as God's way of allowing us to get the last word."

Well, I couldn't argue with my very wise sister, could I?

# The slave that became the slave owner of his former master.

## by

## J.M. McKenzie

Kasia walked to work every day no matter how she felt or what the weather was like. It was a couple of miles and took around forty minutes but the sheer joy of being able to walk outdoors for as long as she wanted was still with her even now, seven years after she had been released. Every morning when she awoke she allowed herself a few moments when she lay under the covers simply revelling in the fact that she was free. She would remind herself that whatever her day was like, every single thing she would do that day was something she had chosen to do, not something she was forced to do by anyone else.

Her story was similar to that of many others, who were also the victims of human trafficking. She was free and she was grateful for that every day but she was also damaged. Seven years of support and counselling had eased her pain but her scars would never fade. At night she relived some of most traumatic memories in terrible nightmares. During the day flashbacks would hit her fast and hard, forcing her to stop what she was doing, taking her breath away momentarily.

The worst memories were always of him, the one who owned her and used for his own pleasure as well as pimping her to others. His cruel smile and glinting grey eyes. The course blond stubble on his face and head. The reptilian tattoos that crawled all over his body. His strong forearms reaching towards her. His breath on her face. His hands gripping her shoulders, forcing her back and down then roughly flipping her over onto her front. His teeth tearing at her skin. Pushing, pressing, shoving. Sweat, blood and pain. So much pain. Sometimes there was more, beatings and worse.

She knew he could not touch her now but she would always be afraid that he would find her. That fear would always be with her. Sometimes she thought she saw him across the street or in a passing car. Panic would seize her, her heart pounding in her chest, cold sweat breaking out on her forehead and waves of nausea bending her double. It never was him of course. He was long gone. She didn't know where but she knew it was far away.

As she climbed the steps to the prison entrance she brought her focus back to the shift ahead of her. She took of her jacket, revealing her guards uniform underneath, and bundled it into a plastic tray along with her bag and stepped into the scanner, arms raised above her head. Leaving her stuff in her locker she made her way down to the wing. After a brief handover with the finishing shift, her first job that day was to process a new prisoner and she headed straight down to the interview room.

As she opened the door she stopped in her tracks. The man had his back to her but the shape of his back and his tattoos were unmistakable. Although his head had been recently shaved she could see the blond stubble beginning to push through. She closed her eyes and shook her head, alarmed by the reality of the flashback. She opened her eyes as he turned to face her. A look of confusion flashed across his face then his grey eyes flickered with recognition. He opened his mouth to speak then immediately thought better of it. His features hardened and he lowered his gaze to the floor. Behind her, her colleague put a hand on her shoulder, "You ok there mate?"

"Just great." She replied as a long slow smile spread across her face. "Fantastic actually........."

## The slave that became the slave owner of his former master.

### by

### Michael Andrews

I approached the auction stand feeling a mix of revulsion and anger. The people, the want-to-be slave masters, or those already in ownership, gaggled together, pressing forwards towards the platform where I could see a young girl of no more than fourteen summers standing naked in front of the crowd.

I had to hold back my loathing of the auctioneer, a man in his forties who rubbed his hands over the helpless girl, announcing to the gathered buyers that she was well trained in the kitchen, and the bedroom. I saw her grimace as his hand slipped between her legs to make that point.

The bidding started high and was soon far out of my meagre budget. As a former slave, I had made it my goal to try to rescue the young boys and girls by buying them and sheltering them in my home. A home left to me by my second master, the man who had rescued me from my own misery of slavery.

You learn very early in life as a slave that there are two kinds of masters. There are the ones like Mister

Stephen. The ones who do make you work, but are not cruel. They feed you, clothe you, give you a safe place to sleep. The ones who free you when your terms of indenture are over.

Then there are the second type. The bastards. The sadists. The child molesters. The rapists, although of course, it isn't rape when you have no rights to your body. That was my first master. The one who paid my dying mother seven silver crowns for me when I was ten. The one who robbed my innocence, my dignity and very nearly my sanity until he got bored of me and sold me on to Master Stephen when I was fifteen.

It was Master Stephen who put me back together, who held me in the dark as my cries of terror echoed through his house as my nightmares tormented me. It was he who paid the doctor to reset my broken hand, a hand smashed by a hammer to teach me never to take food from my previous master's table.

Finally, it was Master Stephen who moulded me into the person he wanted to follow in his footsteps, before releasing me from slavery. It was he who restored my love and faith in my fellow man.

My musings were interrupted as I found myself looking at the reason why I was here. While I do come each week to see if there are any slaves I can afford to buy, to take to the sanctuary of my house, that was not the reason for my appearance today.

I shivered, despite the heat, as I saw him dragged onto the auction block. He looked a shadow of his former self. The man who haunted my nightmares, even to this day. The man who's body I knew inch by intimate inch. But that was then and this was today. Today, he had lost his money, his property, his slaves and now his freedom.

As I expected, there was virtually no interest from the buyers for this broken spirited man in his late forties. I waited quietly as the auctioneer tried to start the bidding at five sliver crowns before dropping to four, then three and finally when an old grey haired owner bid two silver crowns, I waited the allotted time before bidding two crowns and three copper. He countered with two more copper before I bid three silver. He backed away, not wanting to waste his money and I had my prize.

I signed the paperwork and was given the leash which was attached to the metal slave collar. Pulling him forwards, I smiled as I saw the recognition flash in his eyes. I allowed him the moment of hope, as he had heard about my efforts to shelter the slaves that I bought. It would be all the crueller when I dashed those hopes.

I didn't give him the chance to stand as I marched through the square, my new piece of property scrambling to keep up on all fours. Children laughed at him and threw rotten pieces of fruit and vegetables before I came to my destination. A small brook ran past the soldiers barracks and I pushed him in.

"Remove your clothing and scrub yourself clean," I hissed at him, throwing him the coarse soap bar that I had purchased for this very occasion.

"Is this him?" a stern voice from behind me queried.

I turned, knowing who I would see. "It is, Captain William." I smiled grimly at one of my former slaves. I had rescued him from his own slave hell and, with the help of the city guard, I moulded him into the fine soldier that he is today.

"And you are sure that this is what you want?" he asked, a look of concern on his face. "Revenge is sometimes not what you will expect, the resulting emotions can break a man."

"I was broken... by him," I spat. "I have long waited for this opportunity to repay his treatment of me."

I ordered my former master, now slave, out of the brook and denied his request for clothing. Handing his leash over to the Captain, I sneered at him as the look of comprehension dawned on him. I saw his legs quiver and, for a moment, flight crossed his mind but that was soon ended when two burly city guards took hold of his arms. I laughed as he cried as he was dragged into the barracks.

I took a drink from my wine skin as I heard it start. A blood curdling scream as I knew that he was being penetrated for the first time. It would be the first of many as his life was now a whore to the men of the guard.

The Captain was wrong. The emotion wasn't emptiness but fulfilment.

# The slave that became the slave owner of his former master.

## by

## S.J. Gibbs

The place was not as Alexsander Dibra imagined it would be. He had been promised good work, good living conditions, and a good life when he surrendered his passport in return for a job in England. There were six of them in this cramped, shabby office and they were being herded like sheep.

He could see through the cracked, glass petition the two bosses, smoking and talking in hushed tones. He strained to hear what they were saying but they were heads together almost whispering. He could tell that the larger of the two men, was in charge and that the smaller one seemed a little bit afraid of the other.

He checked himself and tried not to let any panic arise within, he was overreacting. He was here, in a town called Bournemouth, England. He was safe. He hadn't seen any of England yet as he had arrived at this office in the back of a van, with no windows.

The other five he had travelled with, fellow Albanians had slept for most of the journey, which had been, long, tedious, cramped and smelly. He had studied them all, but the one who was now grinning like a

Cheshire cat intrigued him the most. Alexsander had established during the journey that the man's name was Pavli, and it was he who now offered his hand in a friendly handshake.

Alexsander offered his hand in return and they grinned at one another. Alexsander couldn't think of anyone more good – looking he had ever seen in his life. He looked about the same age as himself mid – twenties, but his bone structure, dark wavy hair, furrowed brow, deep – set almost black eyes, dark clear complexion and stubble moustache, made Alexsander feel full of envy.

Pavli was smiling as he shook Alexsander's hand and Alexsander could feel the energy from this guy go straight through him. It was as if he was electrically charged in some way. The sensation was odd, and Alexsander averted his eyes. He almost felt a little embarrassed.

He could feel his own insecurities rising. His own face had a hideous scar all the way down the left side from a knife attack back in Albania. He had never been good – looking with his eyes set too close together and a large, crooked nose.

He glanced at Pavli again, and noticed his clothing was of a better quality than anything he had ever owned in his life. His hand had felt smooth and his fingernails looked as if they had been manicured.

His mind raced to thinking about how exciting it was

to be here in England, with job prospects, better living conditions, life had been extremely tough in Albania. This was the fresh start he had dreamed of and he felt honoured to have been selected.

The two bosses entered the room and then ushered the group through the room with the glass petition and through some further swing doors into a large warehouse type room. There were about fifteen other guys packing boxes, and the bosses instructed Alexsander, Pavli and the other four guys to watch and learn. Within an hour, Alexsander found himself picking screws and placing them in small plastic bags for the next guy to pack into cardboard boxes. Alexsander felt tired, hungry and thirsty. They had been offered no food or drinks since they had left Albania. The work was mundane, the warehouse was cold and the roof was leaking. Cold splashes of water kept dripping on him. A couple of hours later, when he truly believed he was on the point of collapse, a bell rang and trays of what he could only describe as slop were placed before them, where they stood. He observed the guy next to him sit down on the cold concrete floor to eat the slop, and ravenous he did the same. The mug of tea he was offered looked and smelt like piss, but he drank it anyway such was his thirst. He started to try and make a conversation with the next guy, but was told they didn't encourage talking and it would be best to keep quiet. The room they gave him to sleep in was in the same building, at the back. The six new arrivals were to share one room, with three bunk – beds. It was no lighter or warmer in here and they were each provided with one filthy blanket and a pillow. Alexsander's pillow was blood – stained which gave him more concern. As the days passed, it soon became clear to him that he had been duped into coming here under false pretenses, they held his passport, and he had become nothing more than a slave. He didn't even know what day of the week it was anymore, but the smaller of the two bosses, came up to him and gave him one of his cakes, telling him what a great job he was doing.

He shared his bunk with Pavli, who had taken the top one. Pavli stood for everything he didn't. He was the one who had been challenging the bosses, demanding their passports back. It had got him nowhere other than a beating by the larger boss, but at least he had the balls to try unlike himself and the others.

At night, he wrote in the notebook, he had brought with him. It was the only thing that kept him sane. He had always written stories since he was a child and although his circumstances were so bad, his writing seemed to have improved. He knew what he was writing was good, Pavli had read some of it and had said how brilliant it was, Alexsander was encouraged by his words and it spurred him on to write more.

They were lying on their bunks. Pavli started the conversation. "It's a shit position we've gotten ourselves into. Your writing is our way out, if you can make a diary of the events that brought us here and we can break past those bastard guards, we could seek asylum or we could just kill the bastards and go on the run."

"I think the asylum suggestion is better, I don't fancy being on the run for murder. We need to make a plan, I'm not living like this for the rest of my life," Alexsander replied.

"I've got a girl, a good girl, back in Albania, I should never have left her. I was going to send money back to her, get her some nice things, promised her the world, and now she'll think I've just upped and deserted her," Pavli banged his fist on the wall.

Alexsander felt a pang of envy again, as he often did around Pavli, the guy had a girl, course he did with those looks. Alexsander had never found love. He had not even come close to it.

The key turned in the lock to their room, and the larger boss entered. "Lights out you fuckers," he shouted as he turned the light off, hand on his side arm, just to let them know, he was the boss.

Alexsander lay in his bunk. He couldn't sleep. He was trying to formulate a plan and couldn't decide whether he should involve Pavli or just try and escape on his own. He liked Pavli. Maybe he should include him. By morning, he had formulated a plan and Pavli had listened intently. They were to work with sheer eager, try and befriend the smaller boss, do everything to please, appear grateful for everything. Once they had established a bit of trust from the smaller boss, they would wait for an opportunity when the larger one was distracted and would then escape and seek asylum. An hour later, the plan didn't go quite as it should have done, when in his eagerness to put it into action and work at double- speed, Alexsander managed to knock over a whole crate of screws and they scattered everywhere.

The larger boss came towards him, baton outstretched and clobbered him around the head, so hard and so many times, Alexsander was knocked unconscious. They carried him off to his room and threw him on his bunkbed.

Alexsander woke to voices and a lot of confusion. It would appear a doctor had been called and was now examining him. The lager boss stood behind the doctor observing. Alexsander started to appeal to the doctor, but it was quickly evident that this guy was as corrupt as his bosses.

Alexsander drifted back off to sleep and when he woke the next time, he was surprised to find the smaller boss, leaning over him offering him some soup and actually assisting him to eat it. "He can be a bastard," the smaller boss was saying, "come on eat up we will soon have you back on your feet." "Thank you," Alexsander muttered as he wiped some blood from his mouth.

"He's going too far, he's killed one and I thought he'd killed you. It's time to do something about it. I won't be able to get hold of your passport but if I helped you to escape and seek asylum, I could come with you and in return, you could lie and tell the authorities that I was brought over with you and that we have both been enslaved."

Alexsander nodded in agreement, "that sounds good to me mate, but we have to take Pavli as well, I won't leave him behind."

"Give me a couple of days, build your strength back up, I'll bring you food whenever I can. I don't think we should tell Pavli until we are ready to go."

"Why are you helping me? I thought I was done, when he was beating me."

"That's the reason, he's going too far. He would shoot me as well. I'm terrified of him. He's blackmailed me form the start, but it's time to get out."

"I can't tahnk you enough but we must get pavli out as well, he's not made for this, he will crack and challenge him, he'll end up dead."

"Give me a couple of dyas, I know his routine and he trusts me. I'll get the three of us out of here. My name's Pal by the way."

Pal kept to his word and brought Alexsander food whenever he could. Three days later he told Alexsander, "as soon as Pavli finishes and comes back to the room today, tell him the planis going into action tonight. Both, be ready and alert. When you hear the key in the lock of the door and me whistle from outside, run and follow me as closely as you can. We will have five minutes to get out but only if Pavli agrees to not drop me in it and say that I was transported over with both of you."

Alexsander shook Pal's hand, "we won't let you down, Pavli will be as grateful as me. When Pavli came back to the room, Alexsander whispered the plan to him. They sat on Alexsander's bunk for just over two hours, both as jumpy as each other, but tried not to alert the other roommates that something was about to happen. They heard the key turn in the lock and then heard the whistle. It was really dark and they ran as fast as they could behind Pal. Before they knew it, they were out on the street. They had escaped.

They ran for at least a mile before they dared to stop and re- group. Pavli now took charge of the situation., he was clearly the more educated of the three and stated, "we need to find a police station, we have to turn ourselves in to help the others, and we need to seek asylum." Pal was beginning to panic, "you won't turn against me will you? " Pavli reassured him, " no way mate you've given us our freedom, and we can get the others out."

Just after nine pm, they entered Bournemouth police station and turned themselves in. They were put into different single cells and statements were taken individually from them. Alexsander's and Pavli's statements, along with Alexsandr's detailed diary of events married but there were holes in pal's statement which were inconsistent with the others.

Three months later, Alexsander and Pavli, who had been detained in a hotel whilst there applications for asylum were assessed, discovered that Pal had been deported back to Albania. The larger boss had been arrested and had been sent to prison for life for murder, people smuggling and kidnap. The others had been freed but deported back to Albania.

Alexsander and Pavli became close friends over the next twelve months, living together in the same hotel, with imposed restrictions on seeking any work. Finally they were both granted asylum and given the right to apply for work within the UK.

Alexsander took up a position as a prison guard, and couldn't believe his luck when he discovered he was now in charge of the very man who had enslaved him. The larger, boss in a cell, on his watch.

**Assignment Nineteen - You run a bar during the days of prohibition.**

19th May 2017

Everyone in the group praised each others work in this particular assignment. However, the curse of the USB struck Michael once again and, having not learned his lesson from the previous time, lost this particular chapter when his drive corrupted.

AJ tested a new style of writing with a vignette using a lot of dialogue.

J.M. spent time researching the old Speakeasy of the 1920's but added a twist of time travel into it.

S.J. started to focus on character development with this homework and the discussions during the review process highlighted the improvements that S.J. was making as a writer.

# You run a bar during the days of prohibition.

## by

## AJ Jones

Head held high, she walked into the bar, her cheap perfume polluting the air around her.

I watched her out of the corner of my eye, suspecting she was here to do business. How wrong could I have been?

I was in the middle of an important business meeting, procuring enough alcohol to keep this bar up and running for the next 12 months, and at a bargain price too.

"Shall we seal the deal with a slug of the good stuff, Joe?" I asked my supplier.

"No, my Old Lady's invited her Folks over for dinner, so I have to take a powder," replied Joe.

"Well, maybe next time. I'll expect your delivery tonight then. I take it it'll be cash on delivery as usual?" I asked.

"Of course, Mick. Anyway, nice piece of ass just walked in. I guess you're going to be busy for a while," said Joe with a wink.

"Maybe," I replied, fixing my gaze in her direction.

After shaking Joe's huge leathery hand, it was a pleasure to take her tiny one in mine.

"Let me buy you a drink, Doll," I said, in the schmooziest style I could muster.

"I thought you'd never ask," she purred in my ear.

We held each other's gaze as the waiter poured our drinks. Lifting them carefully, I led her to a table in the corner, away from the foggy haze of the bar area.

"So, are you here to meet someone?" I asked her.

She lifted her drink and took a tiny sip.

"Well, in a fashion," she replied.

"You're not what I think you are, are you?" I asked.

"Depends what you think I am, I s'pose," she purred coquettishly.

"When you walked in, I thought you were a Moll or a Doll, but now I've met you, I'm beginning to think my first instincts were wrong."

"Actually, they were very wrong," she mouthed. "I'm not that kind of dame at all."

"What kind of dame are you then?" I asked.

"I think you'd be better to ask my brothers," she replied.

Looking behind her, I noticed 3 young hoods sitting at the bar but staring intently at us.

"There's no point in looking for your bodyguards, I'm afraid," she continued. "You'll find them lying in the alley outside, nursing a headache."

"So, you're just here for the money?" I asked, disappointment dimming the glint in my eyes.

"No, we're here to make you an offer you can't refuse!"

## You run a bar during the days of prohibition.

### by

### J.M. McKenzie

*New York 1921*

Ted had been using the same Blind Tiger establishment on Bowery since long before prohibition. In recent years, after the 18th Amendment and the Volstead Act, not a lot had changed other than the fact that the whiskey had got worse and the cliental had expanded. It was still a dark and brooding place shrouded in mystery and tinged with a sense of danger and foreboding.

Ted would inevitably head down there after work every afternoon drawn partly by the idea of a leveller but also by the thrill he got from the experience. It was his daily adrenaline rush after a dreary eight hours in the office at the Department of Public Works . As he approached the shabby red door he would always slow down and loiter in the street for a few minutes, pretending to read a notice in a nearby store window as he furtively scanned his surroundings for any unfamiliar figures or other signs that he was being observed. When he was confident that it was safe to do so, he would slip inside.

The unassuming door was deceptive as inside, after passing through a small lobby, a second door opened into a vast dimly lit space. It was quiet inside, a few small groups of suited men stood around the walls, glancing over when anyone entered but taking no heed of the regulars. Others in working clothes played billiards at one of the many tables arranged in rows in the centre of the room.

Ted always headed straight for the wooden panelled wall on the other side of the room. Built into the panelling was a small drawer. It was one of several along the wall that looked like part of its structure. The lip at the top of the drawer was smooth and shiny, polished by generations of fingers. The routine was the same every day. Ted would pull open the drawer, chuck in a few coins and close it again, sliding a small lever just above it over into the position that signalled an order. After a few minutes the lever would slide back and he would open the drawer revealing his prize, a small glass of amber liquor.

*New York 2017*

Greg had inherited the bar in the Bowery from his father and his father had inherited it from his. He believed it had been in the family for long before that. There had been good times and bad, as the neighbourhood had gone through its own ups and downs, but it had never failed. Since the nineties things had been good and getting steadily better as the area underwent a period of gentrification and now, in 2017, his place was one of the most popular bars in this part of town. Alongside the eclectic range of craft beers and whiskeys from all over the world, the key reason for this popularity was the fact that the interior was relatively unchanged from the days when his great, great grandfather had owned it around about the turn of the century. Of course it had had a lick of paint from time to time and the furnishings and equipment were modern but the basic structure was the same as it had been back then.

That basic structure included the "drawer". It was tucked away behind the bar underneath a large ornate mirror. Unless you looked closely you would not know it was there as it nestled neatly within the structure of the wooden panelling on the wall. Greg's father had told him about the "drawer" when he was a boy and he knew never to change it, question it or investigate it in any way. All his staff were told what they needed to know about it when they started, which was essentially that they should leave it well alone and let him deal with it. If they did wonder about it they never voiced their curiosity to him and that was fine. The bar was always busy, they had more than enough to do. He was busy too and, as he had grown up with it, he just did as his father had told him and never gave it much thought. If he was totally honest, he was slightly afraid of it and believed his father had been too.

So, during opening hours when the drawer called, he answered. His father's instructions had been clear but simple. When the lever is on the left, open the drawer, remove the old coins and replace them with a shot of cheap whiskey in a plain tumbler, close the drawer and slide the lever to the right. Next to the drawer he always kept a bottle of the cheapest and strongest whiskey he could get his hands on, the nastier the better his father had said. Alongside the whiskey he also kept a small supply of old plain glasses. They were scratched, cracked and chipped but his father had been clear that that was how it should be. He collected the coins in a container beneath the drawer and, again as instructed by his father, when the container was full, he would take them to a coin dealer and sell them for the best rate he could get at the time. He knew all the dealers in New York City and by methodically working his way through them he rarely needed to visit the same dealer more than once every couple of years.

*New York 2017*

Lee was new, she had started the week before and this was only her third shift. They had been hectic since she had come on board and Greg had not got around to telling her about the "drawer". She had seen him go over to it several times during each shift and, anxious to learn, she had carefully watched what he did.

On Saturday they were rammed and had all been working flat out since they opened. She noticed the lever had moved to the left about six that evening and, eager to please, went over to tend to it. She opened the drawer, removed the coins and dropped them into the container. She looked at the old cracked glasses and instead reached for a branded Jack Daniels shot glass from the shelf to her right. She opened the whisky and the caustic odour immediately made her eyes water. There was no way she was serving that. What was Greg thinking? Again, genuinely thinking she was doing the right thing, she took a bottle of their best Bourbon from behind the bar.

It was then that Greg saw her but it took a few moments before he realised what she was doing. His blood ran cold. He turned to stop her but by then the drawer was closed and she was sliding the lever to the right. Fuck. He sank to his knees, his hands covering his face and shaking his head.

*New York 1921*

Ted opened the drawer and stopped for a moment before removing the shiny smooth glass with the writing engraved on it. He turned it back and back and forth, examining it and its contents. The liquor was darker than usual and actually smelt of smoke and spice, without the stinging pungency that usually hit him as he raised it to his mouth. He took a sip. Instead of the shock as the harsh liquid caught the back of his throat and burned his mouth, a warm, smooth sweetness flooded his senses. The flavours were so intense, that rather than downing it in one and bracing himself for the hit, he rolled the liquid around in his mouth for a bit before he swallowed, slowly savouring every moment of the experience. He sighed deeply then quickly fumbled in his pocket for a few more coins. This was going to be a good night.

# You run a bar during the days of prohibition.

## by

## S.J. Gibbs

When prohibition was introduced, Tucker could have given up his bar and called it a day. But he saw an opportunity to provide illegal booze and was excited by the prospect of beating the authorities and their stupid laws.

He was fifty- two years old, and had been on the criminal circuit for most of his adult life. Nothing scared him. He had seen it all. In fact so t peace with himself with barely a conscience he sort war.

And so it was that he ran one of the busiest speakeasies in New York. It was 1925 and the place had gained considerable popularity in the five years he had been operating under prohibition. The raids by the police never bothered him, he had too many ways of deflecting them with his door bouncers, secret passages, secret drawers and often he would serve the moonshine in tea cups. They always had music, usually jazz and he charged people entry for the music not the shit alcohol, which he sold them. You could only obtain entry with the bouncer recognizing you or by having one of the member's cards.

The raid tonight, was different from the others. Three of them had come as one. They'd approached silently in plain clothes. They had fooled the bouncer with false member cards and had gained entry, during the flow of alcohol.

His time had come, but he had no desire to go to jail. It was pandemonium as he took his gun from his drawer and shot all three officers dead. People fled the scene through the secret passage to the back door, they wanted none of this, they didn't even want to witness it.

With the help of the bouncer, they carried the three lifeless bodies down the secret passage and out of the back door, dumping them over the railings at the rear of the yard. He glanced upwards as the lightning struck and there was a huge clap of thunder. He raised his arms. He was God.

Violence was nothing new to him. It was not the first time he had taken a man's life, or a woman's or a child's for that matter. He thrived on evil and pain, had done all of his life.

It wasn't the kill, which he thrived on, it was the suffering it caused to others around them where he drew his pleasure. The killing was nothing, but the pain in their families eyes, now that's where the pleasure lay.

He was a large man, considerably unfit now that he had reached his fifties. He hadn't always been overweight. In his earlier years, he had been fit and strong. He was out of breath now from the exertion of moving the bodies and he rubbed his round belly recognizing that he was out of shape.

He had always been popular, always first to get picked for any team games at school. Women loved him for his easygoing nature and humorous joking manner. Men admired him for his strong body and lack of fear.

What nobody knew, was that when he was on his own, he had never taken a wife or a partner, he was an entirely different man. His time alone was spent quietly reading, playing the piano or his violin. Quite, an introvert.

The other side, which nobody knew either, was that he was a serial killer who had been operating successfully for over twenty years without any suspicion falling upon him. He chose his victims well.

He had destroyed so many lives. Thirty- three murders, if he counted the three police officers he had just shot dead. He took such pleasure from watching the distraught families after his crimes, not knowing if their loved ones were dead or alive, but just missing. Not one of his victims, bodies had been discovered.

Since the age of six, when he had witnessed his own mother, brutally killed with a hammer right in front of him, death had fascinated him. Not so much the death itself, but the torture of the people around them, how his own feelings of grief had been at the loss of his mother.

His first victim he had killed when he was thirty. He was a seventeen- year old boy who he had lured to his home with the promise of employment. He killed him quickly and incinerated his body. He then watched over the next couple of years the disintegration of his parents, as they were unable to come to terms with the fact their son was still missing. Their hope that he had just run away from home and would one day turn up on their doorstep. Oh the joy of watching people's pain.

The next victim, a fifteen- year old girl, who he knew before he too, was very much loved by her parents. Before he killed her he made her write several notes with dates on from the future. He had taken such pleasure in sending these notes to the parents on the relevant dates, keeping their hopes up of finding her alive and well.

Unknown to tucker, his bouncer had already left and headed directly to the police station. He had no intention of being fingered for the death of three officers.

Tucker was promptly arrested, and although God was telling him not to confess to all of the murders, of course he defied God and spilled all.

## **Assignment Twenty -** You unwittingly violate a clause in a contract you never bothered to read, to dire consequences.

### 19th May 2017

This was a very open assignment and four very different stories came to light. J.M. looked at pre-nuptial agreements, Michael went corporate business, S.J. explored home renting while AJ focused on a charity donation website.

The moral of all stories are to check your T&Cs as one of the most common lies is "yes I have read the T&C's"

S.J. used this exercise to try to get a start, middle and ending into a very short piece of work, while Michael enjoyed the shock factor in his latest dark tale.

# You unwittingly violate a clause in a contract you never bothered to read, to dire consequences.

**by**

**AJ. Jones**

A ring at the doorbell awakes me with a jolt.

I hadn't realised I'd even nodded off, but it's been happening a lot lately. Like the other day when I dropped off watching Homes under the Hammer. I remember one minute thinking, that's exactly what I should have done when I had money and then all of a sudden Tim Wannacott was encouraging me to spend what little I had left on antiques.

Money, I remember that!

I've had a strange relationship with it all my life. Sometimes, I've had enough to paper the walls with it and other times I've wondered whether I could afford to eat that day. Lately, I've been one of Theresa May's JAMS - "Just About Managing".

I get up to open the door. The woman standing on my doorstep gawps at me. Well, I am still dressed in my PJs at 2 o'clock in the afternoon.

"Olivia Windsor-Smythe?" she asks. I guess she

wasn't expecting me to look like this with a name like mine. I blame my parents for wanting me to grow up thinking that I'm posh.

"Yes," I say, trying to sound like a toff.

"I've come to collect some money from you. Have you received my letter?" she asks.

"Not that I've noticed," I say, glancing over at the hallstand and its erupting volcano of unopened post.

"Well, if you'd opened it, you would have been expecting me. I need you to provide me with £50,000, please."

She's lit the blue touch paper so she stands back expecting the fireworks to begin. However, I just smile back at her in as confident a manner as I can muster.

"Funnily enough, I don't have that amount on me," I say. "You can check my pockets if you like."

"No, I believe you. Do you have any way of transferring the money over to me?"

"Not that I'm aware of," I say nonchalantly. "Anyway, how can I possibly owe anyone that amount of money without knowing it?"

"You signed a contract agreeing to pay my client £50,000 if you hadn't proved you weren't her birth mother within twelve months of the contract date."

"Whaaaat!"

"Yes. When you signed up for her Just Giving page, there was a clause stating that she was seeking her birth mother and anyone making a donation was also agreeing to pay this amount if they didn't prove without an element of doubt that they hadn't given birth to her."

"That's ridiculous," I blurt out.

"I know, but you signed the contract, so you now need to pay up." I look at her face and it's as cold as a polar bear's arse.

"Well, I'm not going to pay up for something as preposterous as that so you'll have to arrest me," I say, remaining as calm as I can.

"I'm not here to arrest you. You must be able to get your hands on that amount of money. Haven't you got it invested somewhere?"

"Well, you've obviously got me all wrong," I say.

"I've done my research and you've got shares in all sorts of places," she continues.

"I used to have, but I had to sell them when the recession hit," I reply.

"Can you prove that?" she asks.

"Not at this moment," I say, glancing again at the pile of letters spilling over onto the floor.

I try to remember the girl's name on the Just Giving site. I don't remember any mention of her mother. My friend, Sarah, had told me about one of her daughter's friends who needed to take her son to America for him to have an operation. It all sounded genuine so I donated a fiver, all I could afford at the time. "I didn't read the small print, as I didn't realise there was any," I murmur.

"You're not the only one who made that mistake," says the woman standing in front of me. "She's making a fortune out of this. She's a clever girl. She's done everything legally so no one has a leg to stand on. You have to comply or else someone will be calling on you tomorrow to collect everything you own."

She stares at me with a confidence seen only in people who know they've got you by the short and curlies.

I close the door on her. I can't think of anything else to say.

Going inside, I pour myself a big glass of red and try to gather my thoughts. Shall I phone the CAB? No, that won't be any use. I've signed myself up for this. The law has its claws into me and I only have myself to blame. Why didn't I read the full terms and conditions? But does anyone do that, these days? - Too busy! Too lazy! ... Too gullible!

It occurs to me that there is one thing I can do to get myself out of this. I know it's a bit drastic but my life's not going anywhere at the moment anyway. Fight or flight is the natural reaction when something life-threatening crops up. So, flight it is then.

I go upstairs and pack my suitcase. I've just about got enough money to get me across the channel. I'll just see what happens when I get to France and take it from there. I pack my guitar and a couple of bottles of paracetamol too, just in case.

If only I'd read those bloody Ts & Cs. I could easily have had a DNA test to prove that I am that girl's mother. I had an inkling when I saw her photo that she was the daughter I'd given up for adoption all those years ago. I could have saved myself from all of this. But I didn't read the small print. Let that be a lesson to you!

# You unwittingly violate a clause in a contract you never bothered to read, to dire consequences.

## by

## J.M. McKenzie

"It's all in there Elizabeth, clearly stated in Clause Twenty Seven." Mr Postlethwaite pushed the document across the desk towards her, his stubby finger pointing at the relevant section. "You signed the document; you knew what you agreed to."

"Well that's the thing," Liz sat back in her chair and ran her fingers through her short auburn hair. "I never really read it all. I trusted him. I thought it was all about the money. There are seventy seven clauses for god's sake! I read the first twenty or so but then it all seemed to get a bit repetitive. I assumed the important ones were all at the beginning."

"Never assume." Mr Postlethwaite stared at her over his tiny wire framed glasses, his finger still resting on Clause Twenty Seven. "It makes an ass of you and me." He chuckled.

"With respect, this is no laughing matter. This is serious." Liz groaned. "What the fuck am I going to do?"

"Well my dear there is nothing you can do. You have violated the clause and he knows it. You don't have a leg to stand on. I'm sorry."

Liz sighed and closed her eyes. The last few months had been the worst of Liz's life and now they were going from bad to worse. Things had been wrong in her marriage for a long time. If she was honest with herself, they had been wrong from the very start. She should have seen the warning signs when he got her to sign the stupid agreement in the first place. Six weeks before the wedding a delivery driver had turned up at her door with the 102 page document. She couldn't believe that he hadn't spoken to her about it first. Admittedly he had apologised later but she could never forget the wave of confusion and sense of betrayal that had coursed through her that day. She was utterly deflated and unable to push away the feeling that she was planning her wedding and her divorce at the same time. She was so in love with him back then she had made excuses for him. After all he was a wealthy man and had one dreadful divorce behind him already that had almost broken him both emotionally and financially. Even though she was hurt and confused about the way he had done it, she had told herself that she could understand why he felt a prenup was important and that she would have done the same if she had been in his position.

It was less than a year after the wedding that things had begun to change between them. It was as if his mask had suddenly slipped. The gorgeous, charming, gentle and generous man she had married became moody, mean-spirited, cruel and controlling. Again she had made excuses for him, trying to make it work. He was working too hard. He was scarred from his first marriage. She needed to try harder to be a good wife. Somehow they had limped along for a few years. Thankfully they had had no children. She kept thinking she could fix him, get things back to the way they had been but all the time in her heart she knew was fighting a losing battle.

She was beginning to think about leaving him when the cancer came and all her energy was focused on that. It was the cancer that had finally finished it though. After the mastectomy he had started avoiding spending time with her. He went out early and came back late every day citing a heavy workload. Sometimes he didn't come home at all. At weekends he played golf or went to the gym. In the evenings he sat up late watching TV long after she had gone to bed.

It was when she started chemo and her hair began to fall out that things disintegrated completely. She remembered looking up from where she was kneeling on the bathroom floor surrounded by clumps of long red hair to see him looking at her in the mirror. He turned away quickly but not quickly enough for her to miss the expression of utter disgust on his face. She looked at her reflection in the mirror. There were huge bare patched on her scalp. Her face was red and blotchy from crying. He had left the bedroom quietly closing the door behind him without a word.

Her hair was the reason he had first noticed her. He had loved her hair, her beautiful long red hair. He loved to caress it when they were sitting close to each other and to grasp handfuls of it when they made love and bury his face in it when they lay together afterwards. It was too much. Weeping, she had used his razor to shave her head, packed a few things and moved back in with her mother. From that day, he never came to see her, never even called to see how she was doing. It was over.

After chemo was finished she had contacted Mr Postlethwaite and started divorce proceedings. He had not contested and it had seemed as though it was all going to happen very quickly. Then, yesterday, out of the blue, Mr Postlethwaite had called her and said there was a problem. She needed to come in and talk about it. He would not tell her anything about it over the phone. He said it would be better to discuss it face to face. And now here she was, sat in his office reading Clause Twenty Seven of the Prenuptial Agreement.

She read the words again unable to believe what she was reading.

"27. In the event that the WIFE (Elizabeth Bennet nee Jones) shall cut her hair by more than two inches at any point during the marriage she will forfeit all rights to a financial settlement or any entitlement to the estate of the HUSBAND (Michael Richard Bennet) in the event of a divorce".

# You unwittingly violate a clause in a contract you never bothered to read, to dire consequences.

## by

## Michael Andrews

"What do you mean?" I said in anger. "I've done everything that you asked!"

"Ah, but you haven't," the man standing in front of me smiled menacingly. "While you were happily taking all of the fruits of the success which I helped you gain, you failed to address the part of the contract which was the most vital and important to our associates."

"What part?" I hissed. I reached into my safe, pulling out the brown manila A4 folder which held the contract that he was talking about. It was a contract that I had read briefly. It was a contract which promised that my business would succeed, supported by this man and his mysterious company, which I had still not fully researched some eleven years later.

And succeed my business, and my life had. The start-up support that I had received had been significant, as it had needed to be. As with the launch of any new technology, money was required and lots of it. I had developed a nanobot which could be programmed to hunt out and destroy cancerous cells in the human body without the need for destructive chemotherapy. The Government, or rather the military, had seen the success of it, and with my reluctant agreement, the programming had been altered to allow the controller to send my creation out onto the battlefield.

Firstly, it had been as a medical solution, saving the lives of not only injured soldiers but those medics who no longer were placed in mortal danger. The, the "powers that be" changed the algorithms so that the destructive capabilities were switched from damaged cells to healthy ones and the new "drones" were launched. My creation, meant to heal the world, had become the number one assassination programme on Earth.

Money started flowing into my bank account and, along with the cash, power and influence became mine. I was invited to attend balls and functions with the rich and powerful and was soon dating the daughter of the Vice President. Angela was stunningly beautiful, blonde, slim, attentive, everything you could dream of for a wife.

And a wife she became. A year later we added the title of "Mother" as my son, Isaac, was born into our lives. He was a wonderful child, never fussing, learning to walk and talk ahead of the norm. By the age of nine, he had already completed his schooling and we were preparing him to study for his university degree. Truly we had been blessed.

Then, on Isaac's tenth birthday, HE had shown up at our house, interrupting the party. Flashing his identification at the security guards, he had marched into the garden, throwing the juggling clowns off balance before verbally dragging me into my home office.

"So what is it that I supposedly haven't done?" I fumed at him, scanning down the contract until my eyes widened as they spotted the hidden clause. Amongst the points regarding distribution contracts, propriety rights and licences, clause 17 dot 3 dot 5 dot 8 jumped out and grabbed my heart.

"You cannot be serious!" I growled at him, throwing the paper down on the desk. A sadistic smile was spread on his lips, one that I was flexing to wipe off.

"Deadly serious," he smirked. "As you failed to give up the rights to the bot, and you are still living from the proceeds, we are here to claim the secondary payment."

I heard a scream from the garden, followed by several more. Angela's high pitched shout brought me to my senses and I pushed past the smug official. Running into the garden, I was grabbed by two burly guards whom I had never seen before. Both had white dog collars and a crucifix pinned to their lapels.

"Abraham Moriah, for services rendered by the High Almighty Father, we claim the life of your first born son, Isaac," the voice of the smug man came from behind me.

I watched in horror as the man who was holding my struggling beloved child laid him backwards on the garden table, brushing cups, dishes and ice cream out of the way. The smug man strode forward, raising his arm into the air. Sunlight glinted off metal and I saw the knife.

It swung down.

My son's screams suddenly stopped.

Blackness surrounded me as my legs gave way and I slumped to the ground in despair.

# You unwittingly violate a clause in a contract you never bothered to read, to dire consequences.

## by

## S.J. Gibbs

As his wife, Eleanor, lay on the bathroom floor with paramedics giving her CPR, Bill knew that the stress they had been under had caused this heart attack. At 11.06 am she was pronounced dead, the paramedics had tried for over forty minutes, to revive her with no success.

They had celebrated their twenty- fifth wedding anniversary, six months earlier. Their marriage had been a contented and easy relationship, albeit missing any passion. Childless to the end, Bill had bought Eleanor a puppy for their anniversary, after refusing for years, Eleanor's request for such. Bill was a sales representative and was often away from home during the week, the puppy would be company for Eleanor, whilst he was away and it would fill the void of her agony over not being able to bear a child.

Saturday morning, Bill took the puppy out for its regular morning walk. Eleanor and himself had always taken a walk on a Saturday morning, but it had been so much more enjoyable since having the puppy. He missed Eleanor more than he thought possible.

It pained him to think of how much Eleanor had suffered, the last couple of months with stress. They had lived in their rented apartment, with its' fabulous balcony, overlooking the river, for nearly ten years. Unwittingly, by bringing the puppy to live with them, he had violated a clause in their contract, which stated no pets. They were either to lose their home or sell the puppy. It had cost Eleanor her life.

**Assignment Twenty One** - You cut yourself but the blood that comes out is white.

21st July 2017

AJ focussed her story on her real life experience of chakra cleansing which S.J. performed for her. In her research of which creatures have white blood, she was excited to tell us that one of them was unicorns, much to the amusement of the rest of the group.

J.M. took the opportunity to get inside the head of a zombie... something she had not yet tried and found it an enjoyable experience.

Michael was pleased that he managed to get two different story lines within his short piece of writing as he went back to his sci-fi roots. However, being a massive Doctor Who fan, he had been less than impressed when it was announced that the latest regeneration had transformed him into a woman, something that he is now willing to give the series the benefit of the doubt but at the time, rankled that a strong male character was being changed.

S.J. would like to apologise for the amount of profanity within her piece for this, and since completing her writing course, has been advised that this could be off putting for some readers.

# You cut yourself but the blood that comes out is white.

## by

## AJ. Jones

"So … let me cleanse your chakras for you."

She says.

"Take your necklace off. I need to use it."

She says.

I give her the look I've worked hard to perfect over many years. You know, the one that epitomises any two-word phrase you can think of that ends in "off".

"Don't worry. I'm not going to nick it," she says.

I reluctantly take off my new silver pendant and hand it to her, suddenly remembering that, if she does keep it, I've still got her gold cross in my jewellery box from when she let me wear it for Andy's wedding last year.

"Sit on this chair."

She says.

She holds the back of one of my new black leather swivel chairs and forces me to sit down.

She stands behind me and dangles the necklace

above my head. I don't see this, of course, because, much as I've prayed for them over the years, I still don't have eyes in the back of my head.

"Close your eyes and listen carefully to what I say."

I close my eyes and listen carefully to what she says.

"Observe the stillness."

She says.

"Open your mind and take 3 deep breaths."

"Breathe in."

"Breathe out."

"Feel the power of the universe fill you."

"Feel Mother Earth fill your feet with a golden light."

"Feel the golden light move up through your legs."

"Breathe in and take in the universal energy."

"Breathe out all that no longer serves you."

She says.

On and on and on and on!

Her words fill my consciousness. The colours she mentions fill my eyes - orange, yellow, green - the colours of the rainbow. A flower starts to spin around in front of me.

I feel as though I'm dreaming the weirdest dream

ever.

My head is spinning along with the flower.

"You have now cleansed your first chakra."

She says.

As she speaks, her words move my consciousness up through my body.

"You've now cleansed your second ... third ... fourth chakra."

I focus on my breathing.

Her words continue to flow.

"Fifth chakra."

"Sixth chakra."

"And finally, you've cleansed your seventh - your crown chakra - your violet-white chakra."

I feel quite sad that it's all coming to an end.

"Begin to wiggle your fingers and toes and come back into the room."

She says.

And I'm back in the room!

"Well, that was fun. Are you ok?" she asks.

Suddenly, I feel my body change shape.

She blinks hard and pulls a weird face.

I feel the strangest urge to neigh.

I look down at my feet. They've become hooves and

there are four of them.

I catch a glimpse of myself in the mirror above the fireplace.

My body is that of a white horse.

I notice the rainbow-coloured horn sticking out of my forehead.

I try to speak, but all I hear is a strangled neighing sound.

I move towards the mirror. It must be lying. That's not me. I accidentally touch the mirror with my horn and it tumbles to the ground, shattering into a million tiny pieces, one of which takes a chunk out of my leg.

A sticky substance the colour of my seventh chakra oozes out.

She looks down at the mythical creature depicted on the silver pendant I gave her.

"You're a unicorn."

She gasps.

# You cut yourself but the blood that comes out is white.

## by

## J.M. McKenzie

I don't recall when I regained my sense of self. I just became aware that I am walking. I have no thoughts in my head other than the fact that I am walking. I have no idea of my destination or my origin. I have no awareness of my location or why I am walking. In fact none of these questions or concepts have even occurred to me. I am simply putting one foot in front of the other and walking. That is all.

"Simply" is the wrong word for it though. It is not simple to move at all, it is difficult, a huge effort. My sense of self exists only in my head. My body is not mine. It moves awkwardly and unsteadily. Its limbs are heavy and unfamiliar. I trip and stagger from time to time on the uneven ground. I walk in one direction until a stumble throws me off course and then I walk in that new direction.

My sense of self is basic. Primitive. Pure existence and nothing more. No thoughts, no memories, no purpose. I do have desire, but it does not have words. It is warm and wet and red. It is more than desire. It is need. I am walking to that need. It is calling me. It is pulling me.

I can hear my breathing. It is harsh and rasping. I think I am making another sound too. It is somewhere between a growl and a moan, maybe a wail or even a sob. There are other sounds coming from all around me. Crunching. Crashing. Tearing. Screaming.

My eyes look straight ahead. My vision is dim and blurry. I can see shapes and shadows. Some of them are moving. Some are still. I am drawn to the moving ones.

I glimpse my feet beneath me. I think they are my feet. They look familiar. I stop. I look down at my body. I am wearing tattered blue jeans stained with red brown smears. My white shirt is also ripped and torn and covered in more red brown stains, the stains are heaviest on my chest where the fabric has dried and stiffened.

I lift my hand to touch the front of my shirt. My hand is grey and cold, my nails devoid of colour. I hold it out in front of my face, trying to focus, trying to understand. I touch it with my other hand, which is also grey and cold. I feel nothing. They are my hands, but they are not.

Both hands still outstretched, I start to walk again, towards the shapes. The moving shapes are hardest to see. They are beyond the still shapes. I have to reach them. They are my need.

The still shapes form a barrier between me and the

moving shapes. The barrier is brown and green and yielding. It parts as I push into it. It bends and springs back as I pass through. Something sharp tears the skin on my finger. It shears away in a large flap. I expect red but the only fluid that oozes from the wound is thick and viscous and pure white. I know then that I am dead. I am dead and I am walking.

# You cut yourself but the blood that comes out is white.

## by

## Michael Andrews

Bullets whizzed past my head as I ducked behind the wooden crate. Cursing to myself, I glanced around at my team, pleased to see that they had all made it this far unscathed.

"Sarge, I think we're in trouble," came the whining voice of Private Whittaker. The young blonde was straight out of the academy and I'd had heated words with the Major when he assigned her to my patrol. Nothing against women, but she just wasn't cut out for frontline action in my opinion. To top it off, she was our medic as well.

A female doctor on the front line just shouldn't happen. She should have stayed as a nurse. But it wasn't my call and now I had to worry about trying to keep her alive and stop her from getting the rest of us killed.

"They're coming at us again," Corporal Hicks muttered, shifting his ammo pack as he got himself comfortable behind the stone pillar.

"Well, let's make sure we take as many of them as we can," I shouted, putting as much steel into my voice as possible.  Straightening slightly into a crouched position, I unleashed a deadly volley of bullets which ripped apart the bodies of the oncoming alien horde. Green blood splattered across the floor and the terrifying croaks and shrieks from the beaklike mouths added to the whole gory nightmare.

Silence suddenly deafened us.  There was a stillness in the warehouse.  Motioning to Hicks, I watched as he and his partner edged around the pillar, carefully examining the scene.  He nodded to me and I gave the silent order for the patrol to fan out and make its way forward.  We had to clear the warehouse of these creatures, or at least come away with supplies for the base camp.  There were starving children back there after all.

"Watch out Sarge!" Whittaker called as my foot skidded in a pool of the green gore.  I braced my body as I slipped to the ground, catching my hand on the open beak of one of the fallen alien fiends.

"Fuck!" I cursed and turned my hand to examine the damage.  My eyes widened in disbelief.  It was the first time I could ever remember cutting myself, but instead of the expected trickle of red blood, a white sticky substance was oozing from my hand.

"What the hell, Sarge?" Hicks quizzed, raising his gun in my direction.

"What the fuck are you?" Whittaker sided with the corporal. "Are you one of them?"

"AND CUT!"

John Derek's voice echoed around the warehouse. The film crew burst into applause as the final scene was completed. I looked around, grinning to myself and the team. It was guaranteed to drive the fans crazy, leaving the series on a cliff-hanger like that. Sergeant William Buckley had become one of the iconic characters in science fiction television, and I loved playing him. Initially I had argued against the idea that he might not be human but John, the director, and Dave Smith the writer of the show had pressed ahead anyway. After five seasons, they needed a new twist to the series to keep the fans wanting more... so they had said.

"Great job guys," John congratulated us, shaking my hand before wiping the white goo on his jeans.

"So when do I find out what Buckley is?" I asked wanting to get my head in gear for the next series already.

"Jesus Mike, you have got six months holiday. Take a break," he said.

"No... come on, you guys owe me the explanation," I frowned.

I felt a hand on my shoulder.

"Now if we tell you that," Dave chuckled, "where would the fun be for us?"

# You cut yourself but the blood that comes out is white.

## by

## S.J. Gibbs

"Fuck, what the hell is that coming out of my finger, white fucking blood, what the hell," Darren shouted at the kitchen co-workers.

Darren stood looking in disbelief, at the tip of his index finger, which he had just managed to slice off whilst chopping celery.

He could hear a voice but it didn't seem to be making any sense.

He could sense people running around the kitchen, but again nothing seemed to be making any sense.

What's going on? Where am I? Nothing makes sense!

Ricky stood over Darren who had collapsed on the floor, his face haunted with terror, as he saw the white substance which looked like blood but which wasn't red shooting out of his finger, which he had sliced in two.

"Fuck, fuck, fuck – what's going on? We need help here."

What's going on? Where am I? Nothing makes sense!

Ricky froze on the spot, he couldn't believe what was unfolding before him.

A sudden clash of thunder, made him jump out of his skin, and as the lightning flashed through the kitchen, Darren's whole body appeared translucent.

"Get help, now" he screamed, "dial 999 somebody."

He heard somebody make the call, but he was transfixed to the spot, he couldn't move.

"We need an ambulance here now, I don't know if he's breathing, I ain't going anywhere near him, he's collapsed and oozing white blood, and he's gone a funny colour," Harold screamed down the phone.

A low, mournful groan was coming from Darren and he was trying to gesticulate with the hand with the cut finger, but this just seemed to make the white stuff spurt out even more, in every direction.

As some of the white stuff spurted out at Ricky he moved away out of fear and stood closer to Harold.

"For fuck's sake, Harold, what's happening to him?"

Harold nodded towards Darren, "something's happening to his body, you can almost see through it."

Ricky heard the sirens approaching and was relieved when two paramedics ran into the kitchen.

The first paramedic that entered stated, "Clear the area, please give us room to work."

He then threw his hand to his mouth and gagged.

The paramedic had never witnessed anything like it, he felt sick to the stomach, and annoyed at himself for gagging for the first time in his career. He looked at the young female paramedic who was accompanying him and pulled her back away from Darren.

"We can't help this man, something very abnormal is occurring here, this is like something out of a science fiction film."

They joined Ricky and Harold in the doorway.

"What the fuck do we do?" the first paramedic stared at them all.

Ricky gave the paramedic an agonized look, "if you don't know what to do, I'm fucked if we do."

The paramedic just stared back at him blankly and shook his head.

The young paramedic burst into tears and she leant into Ricky to steady the dizziness she was experiencing.

Ricky held her steady in his arms, his eyes fixed on the older paramedic urging him to do something.

It seemed to set the paramedic into action and he

approached Darren, whilst calling for further assistance over his radio.

"Darren, I'm going to help you, stay with me mate. I don't know what's happening but we're here to sort you out."

Suddenly, there were some strange noises and they all jumped back and watched in amazement as a small, spindly creature appeared from nowhere.

The creature had a grey body with a large head and massive eyes which seemed too big for its' torso. It opened its mouth and spoke in English, "I'm here to help, don't be afraid, he is one of ours. Our advanced technology will cure him. Stand back."

"Don't be afraid we live amongst you, some of us you can't always see, as although we live in the same frame time we are of another dimension. Others like Darren live amongst you as our experiments, it's pretty unbelievable that he's reached his early twenties without bleeding before. His DNA was altered during his mother's pregnancy."

They all stood back, clustered together, Ricky shook his head in disbelief. The young paramedic couldn't look and buried her head in his chest. The others huddled together whimpering.

The cut to Darren's finger had occurred at 10:30pm, it was now 3am and sanity had been restored as Darren was standing up smiling at them all oblivious to anything that had happened, finger intact, no sign of white blood, the grey creature having disappeared as quickly as it had arrived.

"What's up with you lot? Get back to work, and why are the paramedics here?"

**Assignment Twenty Two -** Your neighbour's mail is delivered to you in error.  It's partway open and you see your name on the handwritten note.  Bear in mind, you've never had any interaction with that neighbour in the three year's he's lived there.

8th Septmber 2017


J.M. was inspired by a recent spate of car thefts within the area, which helped open the story and set the sense of nervousness.

AJ tried to start with the showing not telling style of writing, being more descriptive with scenarios.  S.J. had been reading a lot of best sellers to try to understand markets, trends and shared that every book she was reading seemed to use the word "cacophony" which AJ included in this work

Michael seemed to take over the alter ego of AJ as his

young character finding the letter and having an identity crisis.

S.J. attempted to use a lot of dialogue as her learning curve continued.

# Your neighbour's mail is delivered to you in error. It's partway open and you see your name on the handwritten note. Bear in mind, you've never had any interaction with that neighbour in the three year's he's lived there.

### by

### AJ Jones

The noise of the traffic engrossed him as he strode confidently along the streets full of people heltering and skeltering their way towards the place they would call home for the night. The orchestra of revving engines, car horns and blaring radios filled his head with the tunes he'd become accustomed to during his three years in New York City. Before he'd moved there, he'd seen images of the place on TV but they'd never truly portrayed the cacophony of sound and the ant-like allegiance of the bustling hordes in their commitment to following the shortest path to the snugness of their cosy homes.

The late-September sun belied the cold chill in the evening atmosphere. He breathed heavily as he walked, glad of the woolly scarf and smart leather gloves his daughter, Abi, had given him on her recent visit. He was "missing her already", but today had reinforced his conviction that he'd made the right decision after being offered the transfer to the Big Apple following his divorce from Abi's mother, Sue.

Alan had worked hard for the same engineering company since leaving school, firstly excelling as an apprentice and then being promoted through the ranks to the senior position he held today. The move had helped him recover from the devastation he'd felt when Sue had left him taking every penny of his hard-earned savings with her. Because he still loved her deeply, he'd just rolled over and let her get away with it. When she'd cited mental cruelty as grounds for the divorce, he'd had no idea why. As far as he was concerned, he'd always treated her well and been kind to her whenever they were together. But she'd quoted numerous occasions when he'd belittled her in front of their friends and made her feel unworthy of anything better than the life they'd shared for "thirty-nine boring years". She had never worked - never needed to - and was outwardly the perfect wife that he'd always felt lucky to come home to at the end of each busy day. He'd had no clue about the growing level of bitterness she'd said she'd felt throughout their marriage. She never mentioned it, and, to him, she'd smiled her way through life on a mission to be the perfect housewife and mother to their only child, Abi.

He reached the front door of the apartment block he'd called home since arriving in NY. He collected his post from the mailbox in the lobby, smiled a quick greeting to the new concierge and decided to take the stairs up to his third-floor apartment. He threw the post on the hall table and went to pour himself a stiff whisky, his nightly reward for a hard day at the office. Today had proved particularly stressful because one of their suppliers had decided to raise the price of a key component and he'd had to apply his toughest negotiation techniques to get them to back down.

Glass in hand and intending to re-heat the contents of the doggy bag he'd brought home from last night's meal with a potential new client, he strolled back through the spacious hallway towards the kitchen. The post he'd tossed onto the hall table caught his eye so he picked it up and flicked through it quickly, looking for anything interesting. He noticed that one of them was addressed to his neighbour across the landing and the envelope wasn't fully stuck down. Curiosity getting the better of him, he peeked inside. The only contents were a tatty handwritten note card which read:

"Your *neighbour, Alan Morris*, is a *paedophile!*"

It was written in big, scrawling capital letters as though a child had written it.

After his initial shock had subsided, he slowly looked up from the malicious words and stared at his pale reflection in the hall mirror. Question after question flipped and tumbled in his head.

He tried to make out the postmark but it was too faint. It had a foreign stamp on it, though, maybe from somewhere in Asia - maybe Thailand.

Thailand! Shit!! The realisation began to dawn on him. He pictured the cute little Thai girl that he'd been offered in that tourist bar towards the end of his holiday last year. He'd seen her sitting in the corner with a man he'd assumed was her father and was stunned when the man had walked over and asked for 500 baht to spend the evening with her. He was sure he'd said no, but the following morning he'd woken up with her lying next to him in a dirty bed in a room above the bar. His wallet was missing but he decided not to report the incident to the Police because he didn't think they'd believe him. He was due to fly home the following day and he'd been alone when it happened so no-one knew about it and he meant to keep it that way.

So, bar the occasional nightmare, he'd managed to put it behind him - or so he thought. Now, he wondered how anyone connected with the incident could have found him? More to the point, how did they know who his neighbour was and why had the envelope been put into his mailbox instead?

He decided to go back down to the lobby and speak to the concierge. He may be able to answer some of his questions. Maybe he'd noticed something odd when the post was delivered earlier?

The lift took ages to reach his floor but he didn't trust himself to walk steadily enough down the stairs without falling. The lift doors opened and he walked straight over to the desk.

For the first time, he looked properly at the face of the new concierge. He found himself staring into the dark black eyes of the Thai girl's "father".

"What can I do to help you, Sir?" he sneered, revealing the crooked, stained brown teeth that Alan had so often seen in his nightmares.

# Your neighbour's mail is delivered to you in error. It's partway open and you see your name on the handwritten note. Bear in mind, you've never had any interaction with that neighbour in the three year's he's lived there.

by

## J.M. McKenzie

The worst moments for me were when I got home after dark. That was when the terror really took hold, paralysing me in its iron grip. I'd sit in the car for a few moments after I turned off the ignition, eyes scanning my surroundings as they adjusted to the darkness, and my ears straining for anything out of the ordinary. I'd psyche myself up to leave the car, making sure everything was in my bag and that my keys were to hand, avoiding the need to fumble around and expose myself for unnecessary seconds when I locked my car, and then unlocked the front door.

The walk from the parking area to the front door was one of utter dread and tension. Heart pounding and my breath shallow and fast, I covered the short distance as quickly as I could without drawing attention to myself, constantly aware that he might emerge from the shadows at any point. Images formed in my head of him stepping out of the gloom and blocking my path, his menacing silhouette illuminated by the orange glow of the streetlight.

All my senses screamed at me just to run to the front door as fast as I could, and when I reached it bang on it with my fists, shouting and screaming at Craig to let me in.    I didn't do that though. I kept control and walked briskly, working hard to ensure that my facial expression and body language did not leak the fear I felt.  I couldn't let him see the effect he was having on me.  Then he would be winning.

I knew what he looked like to an extent.  I'd seen him enough times over the past three years, following me in his car, hunched in a doorway across the street, or pretending to flick through a magazine in a shop.  But I could never make out his face.  He always wore a beanie hat pulled down low over his forehead where it met the large, mirrored aviator sunglasses he was never without.  He was tall and seemed to be bulky but, other than that, any detail of his body size and shape was hidden by the long cape-like overcoat that he wore, whatever the weather.

I burst in the front door, slamming it and locking it behind me, before resting my back against it, trying to slow my breathing.  Craig was sitting at the kitchen table.  He murmured a greeting, barely looking up from his newspaper.  With irritation I noticed that the lights were all on and the yet the kitchen blinds were still open, offering anyone outside who wanted it, an unrestricted view of anything they might want to know about us and our lives.

"For fucks sake Craig!"

He rolled his eyes to the celling as I rushed across the room to close the blinds. As I moved, I stepped on an envelope that had been pushed through the letter box and absent-mindedly picked it up. After I'd closed the blinds I sat down at the table with Craig. He looked up at me. His eyes were sad.

"You've got to stop this Kate. You've got to get a grip! It's not real! The police have told you that, and the psychiatrists have told you that. Please, Kate, I don't know what else to say or do." He shook his head. "It's destroying our lives. Destroying our relationship..." He trailed off.

"I know he's real Craig! I've seen him loads of times. Just yesterday when we were in the restaurant he was sitting at a table at the back. I saw him when I went to the toilet."

Craig put his face in his hands. He sighed deeply.

"Oh Kate! So, why didn't you tell me or point him out

to me then?" His voice was low and accusing. He sounded tired, very tired.

"Because I knew you wouldn't listen to me, wouldn't believe me!"

I stood up and walked across the room, spinning to face him again. "There's just no point trying to get through to you Craig. What can I do to prove it to you? Maybe when he does something to me, hurts me, kidnaps me..." My voice faltered, "Kills me..."

Craig was silent. He bent his head, appearing to resume reading. The conversation was over. He always did this. Apparently the psychiatrist had told him it wasn't helpful to indulge my 'paranoid fantasies'.

Frustrated, I turned my attention to the letter which was still in my hand. It had been delivered to the wrong address. It was actually for our neighbour. I only knew this because it was for number 27, not number 25, our address. There was no name on the envelope. I didn't know our neighbour, didn't know his name and had never even spoken to him in three years since he'd moved in.

I examined the envelope. The top was torn and the letter inside was poking out slightly. I went to push it back in and noticed the letter was a handwritten note. I didn't deliberately set out to read it, but the words were there right in front of me…

'Dear Resident, With regard to your neighbour K…'

I couldn't believe what I was seeing!   I pulled the letter out a bit further…

"With regard to your neighbour Kate Parry…."

My knees went to jelly as I pulled the letter out completely and read it with shaking hands.

When I was finished I walked over to Craig.  I thrust it in his face.

"Here!  Is this enough proof for you?"

He looked at the letter.   For a moment a look of confusion crossed his face which quickly turned to one of concern.  He looked up at me, studying my face. I thought he was going to speak but he looked at the letter again, then bent his head and continued reading his paper.

# Your neighbour's mail is delivered to you in error. It's partway open and you see your name on the handwritten note. Bear in mind, you've never had any interaction with that neighbour in the three year's he's lived there.

### by

### Michael Andrews

I was enjoying a nice quiet Saturday morning, shooting up the enemy on my latest Call of Duty game when my Mom's voice echoed throughout the house.

"Danny... go and get the mail will you," she shouted at me from the kitchen.

Knowing that it would only get louder if I didn't go straight away, I sighed and watched as my character took three body shots before keeling over and dying. I grabbed a t-shirt and slipped it on so that I was covered up. Mom had warned me about the strangers in the road, especially the guy next door who seemed to watch me every time I went out. I thought he was a bit creepy but never said anything to her, because she always went over the top on "protecting me" as she called it.

I was fourteen for God's sake, but she'd been looking after me ever since I could remember. But it did weird me out a little so I always put a shirt on now. I ran down the stairs, three at a time, earning me a reproachful comment about a herd of elephants, before opening the door. Did I risk the path barefoot? Sod it... why not? I got four steps down the path before I changed my mind. I didn't realise how hot the sun already was and my feet were burning! Putting my trainers on, I sprinted the ten yards to the front gate where our mail box was located. The little red flag was pointing upwards, indicating that Jim the Postie had already been.

Pulling open the flap, there were two envelopes inside. One was addressed to Mom, it was a bill and it had been stamped with the words "reminder" and "urgent payment required". I frowned, wondering if she was late paying something. We struggled by most months, with Mom working two jobs, and I tried to help out where I could but she wouldn't even let me get a paper round.

The second wasn't addressed to us. Mr Daniel J. Harbourne. The address was next door. I finally knew the guy's name. Funny it was the same as mine, well the first name anyway, and the middle initial. Although he'd moved in three years ago, because of Mom's warnings and his constant watching of me, I hadn't even introduced myself to him.

I didn't relish going to his door to give him the letter.

I turned it over, thinking I could send it back to wherever it came from when I noticed that the sticky back part had come undone. Curiosity overrode my politeness and I slipped the letter out of the envelope. The letter was handwritten, strange in this day and age. But the immediate words which jumped off the page and into my head was the subject header.

*'Re: Daniel Jason Jacobs'*

Why would this bloke have a letter to him about me? I needed to read it and my gut told me that I shouldn't show my Mom. I tucked my shirt into my shorts and slipped the letter inside so that it was hidden.

I ran back into the kitchen, giving my Mom a quick hug before putting the bill on the table. I saw her frown at the words and she gave me a peck on the cheek and told me not to worry. I told her I wasn't hungry in response to her unasked question, thinking that I could skip a meal here and there to help save some cash.

Back in my room, I pulled my t-shirt off and fished the letter back out of the envelope. I took my time reading the words, my brain refusing to accept what was being spelled out in front of me. It must be a mistake. How could people make shit up like this?

There was more than one page, only the first page handwritten. The next two sheets were copies of official looking documents.

I felt the tears start to stream down my cheeks as my whole life suddenly became a lie. A joke. This had to be somebody's idea of a bad joke but the final page nailed it. A judge's signature and I knew him. It was my Mom's friend, my 'Uncle Peter' even though he wasn't really related.

I didn't even realise I'd let out the screams until Mom had come running into my room. I looked up at her, barely seeing the woman who had raised me.

"You LIAR!" I yelled at her. "How could you lie to me all this time!"

"What are you talking about, son?" she asked, stopping as I held my hand up to prevent her from touching me.

"You're... not... my... mother," I gasped out finally.

I got up and ran past her, stumbling down the stairs and threw open the front door. Burning feet didn't stop me as I hurdled the gate and turned to face his house. I walked slowly up the front path and rang the bell. I saw my Mom, scrub that, the woman stop partway down our path as the strange man from next door finally opened the door.

He seemed shocked to see me there, shirtless, shoe less, the first time that I'd even acknowledged his presence. Something in his demeanour changed and he held out his arms. I fell into them, crying.

"Dad?"

# Your neighbour's mail is delivered to you in error. It's partway open and you see your name on the handwritten note. Bear in mind, you've never had any interaction with that neighbour in the three year's he's lived there.

### by

### S.J. Gibbs

Beverley Samuels moved into her home, three years ago, and although she had never spoken with the man who lived next door she had witnessed some very strange behaviour from him.

This afternoon, with a few of her friends gathered in her garden, on this glorious sunny day, drinking pimms and waiting for the meat to cook on the barbecue, she felt uplifted.

"So did you invite your strange neighbour Bev?"

"No, still haven't spoken with him, he runs away every time I see him."

"Maybe he's scared of you, scared you'll get him in the sack."

"That'll be the day, can't remember the last time that happened, it's that long."

The neighbour, Johnnie Stringer sat on his patio trying to drown out the noise from the cackling women, next door. He could hear them all laughing and he was sure he was the butt of their jokes.

The banter continued, "So what's he like, is he good-looking?"

"Yeah he's handsome in an understated way, but I haven't got close enough to him, to have a real good look at him."

Johnnie sat in his deckchair, eating a ham sandwich and although he felt like shouting over the fence, instead he muttered under his breath," Bloody noise and bloody smell of barbecue and all I've got is my own company and a bloody ham sandwich."

"So in three years of living here, you still haven' spoken to him once Bev?"

"No, nothing at all, I've even tried knocking his door a few times, when I know he's home, but he won't answer the door."

"Bizarre, why do you think he's so strange?"

"I've no idea, it's not just with me. He doesn't speak with the other neighbours either."

"Does he work, do you know what he does?"

"There's no pattern, sometimes he's home in the day, sometimes at night, but no regular hours."

"Could be a serial killer." Beverley saw the look of regret on her friend's face, the moment she had said it. She gave Beverley an apologetic smile.

"I was just joking, I'm sure he's not."

"Well you never know, he's certainly very strange."


Beverley had been trying to work out his work pattern for months, and it bothered her that she knew so little about the stranger who happened to be her neighbour.


"Sausages are ready, grab one, there's salad and jacket potatoes on the table inside, help yourselves, burgers won't be long."

"Great, looks fab Bev, do you want me to pour you another pimms?"

"Yeah, sure, why not, I'm not working tomorrow."

"None of us are, let's make the most of it."

The four nurses, worked the same shift patterns, "let's enjoy it while we can, we work bloody hard enough."

"Sure do, you old bint, food looks delicious."

"Cheeky mare calling me an old bint."

"I bought my diary by the way, we need to choose some dates for our trip to Vilamoura."

"Yeah, we'll do that later, Miss Impatient."

"Oh my god, you're such a diva Bev."

"She wouldn't know about patience."

"Is that so Lady of Innocence, born again virgin."

"Virgin will do, not born again, virgin on the ridiculous."

"By the way, I picked your post up, it just dropped through the letter box. I couldn't help but notice, the one on top is addressed to Mr. J Stringer. Is that him next door? Look it's partway open and it's got your name, Miss Beverley Samuels handwritten on the top of the letter."

"Oh my god, you shouldn't have opened his post."

"I didn't it was already like it, you've go to open it now though, see what it says about you."

Beverley knew her friend was right, there was no way she couldn't open the envelope, knowing it had her name on a letter inside.

She moved inside with the friend who had discovered the post, they looked at each other intently, their breaths deep and unsteady as Beverley placed the envelope on the table.

The kitchen was filled with light from the beautiful sunny day outside, and the light took on a surreal effect as it emanated from the envelope.

They stood in the kitchen, Bev wiped her forehead, the heat of the day, the cooking of the barbecue and now the thought of what maybe contained in this envelope, suddenly making her fell overheated.

"Do it Bev, just open it."

"Okay, give me chance, I'm going to."

Beverley slipped the letter from the envelope, her friend couldn't imagine what it contained, as Beverley pulled out a chair and promptly sat down on it, her friend leant over her to look at the piece of paper, now in Beverley's shaking right hand. Time seemed to stop still and the light left the kitchen as the sun moved behind a dark cloud.

The letter started with Beverley's name and address. It soon became clear to the two of them that Mr. Johnnie Stringer had hired a private detective to follow her for the last month. Every detail of her life was mapped out for her neighbour but the question on Beverley's lips was why?

## **Assignment Twenty Three -** Someone's reanimating murder victims so they can get revenge.

### 20th October 2017

We had fun with this one, allowing the darkness within ourselves to come to light. It's been noted that this was the start of a trend with Michael getting a lot darker as he got into the head of a serial killer. An adapted version of this piece can be found in the anthology "Cathartic Screams" published by Severance Publishing.

Being influenced by J.M., S.J. went all Zombie on us.

AJ, blaming Michael's vampires, went all Twilight on us.

J.M. went Mary Shelley on us with a Frankenstein-esque story

We hope you enjoy these.

# Someone's reanimating murder victims so they can get revenge.

by

## AJ. Jones

The last thing Mick remembered was walking down the dark alleyway between the shops over which he'd lived for the past five years. The entrance to his apartment block was at the back of the building and the alley was currently pitch black because the overhead light had been smashed earlier that day.

As he neared the end, someone jumped him and he felt the sharp, pointy head of a tiny hammer hit home. In a flash, Mick's life was snuffed out, just like the overhead light.

"So, that's it then, is it?" he mused as his *soul* sailed out of this body towards the proverbial light that he'd read about on the internet.

"Not necessarily!" boomed a voice. He wondered how he could hear without actually having any ears.

"What do you mean?" He either spoke or thought these words, but, either way, it didn't really matter because the owner of the voice had obviously heard him and that was all that mattered.

"Well, what I mean is you don't have to die if you

don't want to," came the reply.

What the f...! Mick tried to remember the f-word but it seemed to escape him.

"No-one swears here, Mick," the voice's owner had read his thoughts. "Anyway, I need you to listen carefully because I want you to accomplish a vital mission back on earth, one that will stop further lives being taken in the same way as yours was. However, you'll have to sign up to two conditions before I can send you back. Otherwise, you'll revert to your original pathway."

"And where will that take me?" asked Mick.

"To the Deathzone, of course," the voice replied.

"Now let me think ..." replied Mick marvelling at the way he was managing to communicate with this mysterious persona. "Of course, I'd like to live again - who wouldn't - but I'd be stupid to agree to something before I know what the conditions are."

"Well, I can only reveal them to you by starting the initiation process. Would you like me to begin?" the voice asked.

Mick wasn't sure at first, but then he nodded (a metaphorical nod, of course). What's the worst that could happen, he asked himself.

"Ok, let's make a start," said the voice. "Firstly, you must accept the fact that the life you go back to may not be your previous one. I have to warn you that, should you not agree, I'll be unable to continue this conversation and, as I told you previously, you'll return to your original path. Mick, do you agree to Condition Number One?"

He didn't need long to think about his answer. His previous life hadn't been that great, anyway. Since he was a boy, he'd worked hard to become a great athlete, but he'd never quite made it because he was far too prone to injury. Maybe a new body would give him a second bite of the cherry?

Decision made, he communicated his agreement and so the owner of the voice continued.

"Ok, I can now reveal the second condition. Again, if you don't agree, you will be sent on your journey into the Deathzone."

Mick figuratively shuddered.

"So, the second condition is that you must avenge your own death. But there are two sub-clauses: one is that you must kill your murderer within two hours of returning to life; and the other is that you must do it in a way that won't result in your being sent to prison. I can tell you that, should you agree, I will help you fulfil this condition."

As this one was a bit more complicated, the owner of the voice gave Mick a couple of minutes to think, but then asked, "Do you agree to Condition Number

Two?"

Mick had to admit he was feeling a little bit conned. He hadn't foreseen these sub-clauses and he had no idea how he was going to achieve this mission. But, after weighing up the options, he decided to comply because he really didn't fancy ending up the Deathzone. The name alone gave him the willies!

So, yes, he thought, I agree to this second condition ...

And that was how Mick found himself back inside his crumpled body, lying on the cold, hard ground in the pitch-black alleyway.

"You're supposed to be dead," sneered the youth standing over him. He'd been salivating at the thought of what he was about to do, but he'd detected a twitch of returning life. "I was about to drink your blood. Now, I'll have to kill you all over again." His right hand reached for the hammer in his pocket.

This guy thinks he's a blood-sucking vampire, thought Mick. I've seen him before. But where was it? Think, Man, think.

Suddenly, he remembered his recent visit to A&E after he'd fallen over at the track and sprained his ankle. The doctor who'd treated him had looked very young, but they were all classed as junior doctors these days, weren't they? Could it be this particular doctor had discovered a taste for blood to retain his youthful looks? After all, A&E was the perfect place for him to find his victims.

"You're not a real vampire," Mick snarled menacingly. His last word came out as a growl. He sensed his eyes flashing fiercely in the blackness. He felt the urge to stand up on all fours. His *hands* were now covered in silvery-coloured fur with sharp claws extending from huge padded paws. His body was becoming muscular and he felt a growing awareness that he could run quicker than ever before.

He noticed his assailant stiffen. "Ughh! I hate werewolves, especially silver ones," he wailed, displaying a serious lack of *vampireness*.

Mick roared with carnal desire as he pounced on the terrified youth, his huge teeth tearing at the flesh and his claws stabbing through his eyeballs into his brain.

"Mission accomplished," Mick howled as he watched the life leaving his victim's body.

## Someone's reanimating murder victims so they can get revenge.

### by

### J.M. McKenzie

I was awoken by a violent jolt and a painful flash of bright, white light behind my eyes. A solid ball of heat formed in the centre of my chest and spread through my body, radiating from the top of my head to the tips of my fingers and toes. A high-pitched buzzing filled my head. My skin tingled and I could smell the slight, but unmistakable, smell of burning flesh.

I lay still with my eyes closed, waiting for the noise and the heat to subside. I was vaguely aware that I was lying on a hard surface. I could feel the pressure on my elbows and hip bones. Cool air on my skin told me that I was naked. I opened my eyes.

My vision was blurry. I blinked a few times until it began to clear. The room I was in was well lit. The tiled ceiling above me was white and clinical. A large surgical light was positioned so that its beam was focused in the centre of my chest. Was I in hospital? I had no idea where I was or how I had got there. I tried to remember but my mind was empty.

A large face appeared from my left, so close to mine that it filled my field of vision. An elderly man with kind, blue eyes behind wire-framed glasses was examining me closely. He looked concerned. He was mostly bald with a few tufts of curly, white hair above his ears. He waved a hand in front of my eyes and his lips moved but the buzzing in my ears blocked out the sound of his voice. I struggled to sit up.

As soon as I moved, I felt the pain. I couldn't pinpoint a specific source. My whole body felt stiff and sore. Firm hands gently helped me to raise my torso up and swing my legs around until I was in a sitting position, my legs dangling in an empty space. My head was spinning and my stomach rolled over in waves of nausea. I closed my eyes. The old man kept a hand on my shoulder to steady me.

When the worst of the nausea and dizziness had passed, I opened my eyes again and looked around the room. I was in the centre of some sort of operating theatre on a high, metal trolley covered with a thin plastic mattress. Trays of surgical instruments were neatly laid out on a stainless steel counter. A large machine covered in knobs and dials and flashing lights stood next to the trolley. Two circular red paddles were connected to it by long curly red cables.

When he was sure I was not going to fall, the old man reached over and grabbed a green hospital blanket from one of the counters. He draped it around my shoulders and I pulled it tight across my breasts, conscious of my nakedness for the first time. He pulled up a stool and sat down in front of me. Taking my hands in his, he looked into my eyes again and he spoke. The buzzing had lessened and this time I heard him.

"How are you feeling, My Dear?"

I opened my mouth to reply but the only sound that came from my lips was a rasping croak. My hand flew to my throat. I felt the crusted scab and the thread-like sutures before he gently coaxed my hand away.

"Your throat was badly damaged in the ...accident..." His voice tailed off. "Don't worry, My Dear, it will heal now that you are...recovered...recovering..."

Maintaining eye contact with him, I touched my temple and shook my head slowly, trying to signal to him that I couldn't remember anything.

"I can help you with that. It's important that you remember. You need to know why I brought you...here...What you need to do."

He fished under his surgical gown and pulled a fat, gold watch out of his trouser pocket. He held it up and towards me. The second-hand flicked between the digits in tiny movements.

"That's it, My Dear, watch the second-hand. Listen to my voice and watch the second-hand."

He began to count. His voice was deep and reassuring.

I watched the second-hand.

"One, two, three...."

My eyelids felt heavy.

"Six, seven, eight..."


Suddenly, I was in a forest. I was running. It was dark and raining. The ground beneath me was soft and slippery. Branches and twigs scratched my skin, tore at my clothes and pulled my hair. I was terrified. My breathing was hard and fast. My blood pounded in my ears.

Someone was behind me, chasing me. I could hear crashing footsteps and heavy breathing.

I tripped and fell to my knees. Before I could get back on my feet, a hand grabbed my hair, yanking my head back. I saw the moonlight reflected on the blade before it made contact with my throat. I felt no pain, only a warm wetness flowing down over my chest. My vision darkened. Far away, I could see tiny bursts of light like distant stars exploding, then everything went black.

I opened my eyes again. I was back in the operating theatre. The old man was putting the watch back into his pocket. He looked at me knowingly.

"Well, did you see? Do you know?"

I nodded. I had seen. I remembered, remembered everything. I knew, knew everything. I understood, understood everything. There were no more questions.

A quiet anger began to pulse deep inside me, quickly building into a rage. I clenched my jaw and my fists. My knuckles whitened.

The old man looked at my hands and then back up at my face.

"So you know what you have to do, My Dear?

I smiled through gritted teeth and nodded again.

"Good. Well let's get started. We have work to do. *You* have a job to do."

# Someone's reanimating murder victims so they can get revenge.

## by

## Michael Andrews

I screamed as the pain became too much for me to bear. My mind was on overload as I felt my life slowly slipping away. A blood bubble popped from my lips and I couldn't believe what I was seeing as the knife was buried deep into my stomach. I cried out, begging for mercy but the look in my killer's eyes showed only a dark, deep satisfaction as he opened up a seven inch gash in my chest.

I suppose I should start my tale from the beginning. No-one is interested in the ordinary, average John Smith growing up with an abusive father and a mother who spent more time examining the bottom of her gin glass than the bruises on her only child, are they?

I was bought a dog for my twelfth birthday but my father grew tired of Buster's barking and, when he bit my father as he hit me, my father got his gun and shot my dog in front of me.

I learned very quickly how to behave so as not to share Buster's fate. The memory of seeing the splatter of red and grey from the explosion of my dog's head stuck with me. I would retreat to the woods and find squirrels and rabbits, but their splatters never really matched Buster's.

The white ropes of intestines soon became a fascinating distraction. I could play for hours, looping them around my knife, twisting them and slicing them. I didn't know that a rabbit could make as much noise as it did when I was gutting its innards.

My mother passed away, dead drunk literally when I was seventeen and my father's rage increased at me. I would stay home from school, too afraid to show my bruises and cuts, and would work with my father on our land.

I was nineteen when I cut his throat as he slept. I wanted to wake him first but knew that he could overpower me. So I crept into his room and ran my five inch blade along his throat, starting from his left ear and all the way over to his right. I watched as he woke, his hands trying to stop the fountain of blood and his last words to me were of prideful cursing.

I burned his body and the police were happy that their main cause of trouble in the county had disappeared one night. My tearful pleading for my Poppa to come home cast away any suspicion.

Life settled down. I owned the farm and worked hard, making good money. I even had some girls but they soon left when my predilection for bondage and sadomasochism overwhelmed their own pleasure.

My life became a circle of loneliness, avoiding people, going back to nature for my enjoyment.

One night, I was driving home when I saw a young man thumbing for a lift. I pulled over and offered him a drive. He wanted to go south, anywhere. I could see bruising on his face and guessed he had a similar history to my own. Offering him a place for the night, I slipped a sedative in his food and when he was passed out, I tied him to the hook in the barn.

It seemed hours before he came around which was when I could start my fun. I had stripped him to his underwear, I wasn't interested in him sexually, not really, but I found myself aroused at the prospect of what I was going to be able to do.

Picking up one of my many knifes, I carved a line from his navel to his groin, his screams were like a symphony written by Bach or Mozart. Four more quick slices and I could peel back his skin, exposing his innards. Cutting away muscle and fat, I soon found the delightful sight of the grey coiled intestines. I'd heard that the human body held around twenty foot of coiled gastrointestinal material, and as I hooked out the first three foot, the lad squealed like the pig I'd gutted last week for my Sunday lunch.

He begged and pleaded and started to get on my nerves. My hands were already shaking over the excitement of having actual human parts in my hands but his wailing made me slice through the tubes by mistake. I lost my temper and rammed my knife into his heart, silencing him.

Frustrated at my outburst, I pulled his body down and cut him open, exploring the human body before throwing the chucks of flesh into the burning furnace.

Night after night, I cruised the back roads, looking for another hitchhiker until my luck turned. A boy, no older than seventeen I guess, wanting a lift back home from a night out with friends. Getting him in the car was easy. Keeping him there was a struggle but I finally overcame him, tieing him up and driving him to the barn.

This time, I gagged him so I could enjoy my carving in peace. The books were wrong in his case. I estimated only seventeen feet of intestines. When his body went limp, I unhooked him and threw him on the floor. As I bent over him to begin carving him for the furnace, darkness filled my vision. My legs wobbled underneath me and I fell to the floor. I couldn't move.

I cried out in horror as the boy, surely dead, sat up. He pulled his innards back into his body with a look of disgust. Red light covered his body and there were no signs of my incisions.

My body rose up in the air and my hands passed into the looped rope around the hook. The boy picked up the knife.

"Now you will know the suffering you inflicted on others," a deep voice said. I looked and saw the devil himself, smiling a sadistic smile as the boy plunged the knife into my stomach. As he cut through my intestines, I cried out... a cry that would last for eternity.

## Someone's reanimating murder victims so they can get revenge.

### by

### S.J. Gibbs

The year was 2117. Cash wasn't going to take the murder of his eighteen, year old daughter Opal, lightly. Somebody was going to pay for what they'd to her.

Cash's biotechnology unit had been on the brink of reanimating the dead for years, but they'd been unable to gain permission to put the technology to test due to the ethics surrounding the idea.

He placed Opal's dead body on to the operating table. He carefully made an incision into her upper spinal cord, where the brain stem was located and administered the drug directly into the nerve, which stimulated the body system. He then sent the laser beam to the brain stem.

Would it kick, start her vital body functions back into life?

The heart machine indicated that her heart had indeed restarted. She was breathing.

He stood back in amazement, as he watched her body slowly recover. He had successfully raised her from the dead. They would get their revenge, on her murderer.

He watched as she climbed off the table, but something was horribly wrong. She wasn't Opal. She appeared to be in a trance and she was moaning and shambling around with her arms outstretched. She stumbled towards him, and mindlessly began to attack him. Her muscles were twitching in myoclonic jerks as if she was having a seizure. She had become a mindless killing machine as she brutally attacked her own father as she bit into his neck. She had added a new member to her army of the un-dead.

They advanced together from the building, into the street, spit dripping from their mouths. Their skin was turning grey and almost scaly looking, like a fish. They stretched their arms forward as they stumbled along the street.

Their brain activity was unconscious and they ambled along as if sleepwalking. The blood trickled from Opal's mouth from where she had taken a big chunk of meat from her father's neck. A hunger was growing within them both as they spotted dinner, moving around before them.

The insatiable hunger drove them both to attack the next couple of people moving along the street. The army was growing. There were now four members.

The four swayed along the street bunching together, their feet turned inwards almost shuffling on their ankles. One of the new members, a male, had a torn shirt revealing a bloody stomach, where Cash had taken a huge chunk from to satisfy his hunger. Their mouths hung open, blood dripping as they moaned in unison. They were corpses that would not lie down. Brainless and repulsive they continued on down the street as people began to run horrified by what they saw was approaching them, a shuffling mass of four with their hands reaching out in front of them. Their brains had been stolen away. Their next victim joined them with her glistening intestines sliding out of her tummy. They were five. They descended on a house and started to bash the front door, but they could feel no pain as they bumped into each other and banged their heads furiously on the wooden door, as they could smell their next food behind it.

Demented and deranged with their inhuman groaning they relentlessly tried to move the door to obtain what was behind it, human meat.

Their combined body weight and persistent banging finally unhinged the front door and they crashed into the hallway, knocking into one another, smelling for their prey.

The man was asleep on his sofa, earphones blaring out the latest jazz, oblivious to the commotion around him.

He woke from a delightful dream into a heinous nightmare as they attacked his flesh in a frenzied hunger. As Opals' blank stare penetrated into him, there was a moment of recognition that she was the girl he had strangled to death.

Subconsciously, she had taken her small army of five to take her revenge on the man who had ended her life. There was no sweetness in the revenge for Opal or Cash, as the murderer now became the sixth member of their vile army.

## **Assignment Twenty Four -** You meet, or you are, the sleaziest person on earth

### 24ᵗʰ November 2017

Between the last meeting and this, AJ had an operation for a knee replacement and we had already postponed for a couple of times. However, the recovery period, and use of pain relief, was a lot longer than originally thought so the decision was made for J.M., Michael and Shelly to complete this assignment and AJ could take a well-earned break.

This assignment was met, as usual, with differing plot lines and definitions of the word "sleaze".

J.M. went with a Casanova type character and his encounter with a gentle lady.

S.J. took on the office sleaze and describes her character's escape

Michael looked at the word sleaze and tried to think the worst. His story may be upsetting for some as it contains suggestions that people may find offensive.

Please be aware that the stories may be uncomfortable reading for some due to the content and theme.

# You meet, or you are, the sleaziest person on earth

### by

### J.M. McKenzie

Dusk was falling on Folgate Street when we had our first encounter. The shadows were long and the light had a queer pink hue. I had alighted from my carriage, smoothing my skirts as my manservant hurried past me to open the front door.

I was only vaguely aware of the gentleman walking purposefully in the direction of Brick Lane until he paused but a few feet from me. I felt his eyes upon me affecting me to return his stare.

"Do I know you, Sir?" I asked, surprised by the quiver in my voice.

"Sadly no, Bella Signorina, but I hope soon to remedy this." He spoke with a foreign tongue.

He dropped to one knee and lowered his head in a manner that was inappropriate to both the occasion and his position on a filthy London street.

"Sir, you presume too much. Please arise. I beg of you."

He lifted his head and I studied his face for the first

time. He was not unattractive, but uncommonly dark of skin and hair and marked by pox. My eyes met his and he held them in his black gaze for longer than was fitting. A strange and unfamiliar feeling stirred between my legs. Not quite an itch, nor quite an ache, but something in between that made me long to touch myself.

I felt my cheeks flush and my breath quicken as he rose to his feet again. He was heavy of limb and broad of chest. My face was level with his collar and I had to raise my head to follow his eyes.

He took my gloved hand in his. My manservant moved towards us but my raised palm caused him to retreat towards the house where he lingered, confused and uncomfortable.

The stranger slowly loosened each finger of my glove until the whole garment slipped easily away. I allowed him to lift my hand to his mouth. He pressed my bare skin to his lips. They were rough and warm. The tingling between my legs surged and a soft moan escaped me.

Suddenly light-headed I closed my eyes, swaying towards him. His strong arm curled around my waist, both steadying and supporting me.

"Sir, I am undone..." My voice was not my own.

"My man, see to your Mistress! She is unwell!"

The stranger and my manservant guided me into the house, settling me on the sofa in the hallway to regain my senses. My maid bustled from the parlour fussing and fretting and throwing angry glances at the men. They both turned away as she loosened my bodice.

Confident I was restored, the stranger went to take his leave.

"Sir, will I see you again?"

"With your permission, Signorina, I will call tomorrow to be certain that you are recovered?"

"Of course, Sir, that would be most kind."

He moved to the door.

"Sir, how will I know you? What is your name?"

"My name, Signorina? But of course. I am Giacomo. Giacomo Girolamo Casanova."

# You meet, or you are, the sleaziest person on earth

## by

## Michael Andrews

It was the bestest day ever of my twelve year life!! I'd been so excited ever since I was told that I could help drive the steam train but not to dress smartly. My Mum had got me my play jeans and a t-shirt that she was going to throw away, and BAM!, there I was on the platform meeting Mr Bob, the train driver.

I looked at the train in awe. It was just like the Ivor the Engine train from the telly show apart from there were no dragons in the coal furnace haha. Mr Bob helped me into the drivers compartment and showed me what the levers did, how to open the furnace without burning myself and where the shovel was to load up more coal.

I was so chuffed when he handed me my own little shovel and told me that part of my job would be to help put more coal in as we were travelling.

I looked back at the platform and saw people getting on the train into the passenger carriages and suddenly there was a shrill whistle. Mr Bob told me that it was Fred the station guard telling us that everyone was on board. A man also got into the drivers compartment with a camera. He was from the telly show and was recording my journey but said to ignore him and enjoy the experience. Mr Bob lifted me up so I could reach the chain that ran across the top of the compartment and told me to give it a pull. I did and giggled as the steam whistle of the engine trilled out across the station, indicating we were reading to pull out.

I got to pull the lever, knocking the brake off and we slowly picked up speed and left the station behind. Mr Bob told me some stories about the engine as we journeyed down the tracks before we felt the train slow slightly.

"Time to fill him up," Mr Bob had said and opened the furnace door. The heat was unbelievable, but I helped Mr Bob and shovelled in four scoops of coal. Man it was heavy and I got some on my t-shirt and jeans. Mr Bob chuckled and ran a finger over my nose, saying I looked like I was a chimney sweep.

We carried on talking about trains until it was time to fill him up again. As the heat hit me, I guess I stumbled a little. Mr Bob caught me and suggested I took off my t-shirt to cool down. It's what he did. He took off his shirt and man, did he have some muscles. I was a little embarrassed at my skinny body. It looked puny compared to his but Mr Bob was really nice. He stroked my arms, telling me that after today, I'd have some proper muscles.

It got hot in the compartment, and I got really sweaty, but so did Mr Bob so I didn't care.

It felt a little funny when he picked me up to pull the steam whistle again. His hands were really rough and felt strange on my chest and sides. He liked to rub my back and chest as we drove.

However, the journey soon came to an end. We'd spent three hours travelling! I couldn't believe how quickly it had gone and was sad that it was over. Mr Bob had been really nice and as we got out, I gave him a hug as a thank you. His hands rubbed my back and he said he'd see me again in a couple of weeks.

So when my Mum and I got to the telly studio, I spotted Mr Bob and ran across to say hello. He gave me a hug again and said I looked a lot cuter when I wasn't so dirty and covered in coal dust. I giggled cos it had taken three baths to get it all off my chest and arms.

We had to wait for another couple of kids to go on first, so we found the food table. There were all sorts of sandwiches and crisps and sweets, including sherbet dib-dabs. I love them.

Finally Mr Bob and I were called over to the edge of the studio. My Mum was told to go and sit in the audience and I would be delivered back to her after the show was finished. And then I saw him. My eyes couldn't believe I was going to meet him really, in real life. I could already smell the cigar smoke and then he called my name.

Mr Bob took my hand and led me onto the set, sitting me next to him. We watched the video of my time on the train before he turned to me and said he had a special something in his chair. I'd seen other kids do it before so I stood and went to him and he pulled me up and onto his lap.

He said that I should press a button but there were so many. He took my hand and pressed it onto the arm of the chair. I felt a bit uncomfortable because I felt his other hand stroking my leg, but a steam whistle made me jump. I literally lifted out of his lap and landed back on him. It felt strange, lumpy, but my mind was distracted by a miniature steam train coming towards us and there was my medal, hanging on the funnel.

Mr Bob picked it up and stood in front of me. He gave it to the man to hang it over my neck who whispered into my ear, "and we'll fix it so you have more fun in a minute."

His hand pressed into my lap but I was frozen in his lap.

"Tell his Mum we will drop him off at his hotel later," the man told his assistant, who had a knowing look on his face.

# You meet, or you are, the sleaziest person on earth

## by

## S.J. Gibbs

Linda Coke found herself, on her first day of her new office job, assigned to work alongside Adam Betts.

Within an hour, she had realised it was like walking on eggshells, he was so moody. He had made it plain, that he didn't like her and resented having to show her around. She had noticed the snide remarks, the eye-rolls and huffs whenever she asked him anything. He had even yelled at her, after one straightforward question.

She was confused at lunchtime when he suggested they went out of the office to grab some lunch together. She declined politely, deciding it was safer to stay within the office, than spend anytime on her own with him.

On his return from lunch he sat at the opposite desk and she was thrown when he randomly asked her, "You're Prime Minister for a day. What's the first thing you do?"

Jokingly she replied, "I would make it mandatory for all employers to provide teabags in offices." His response was to switch on his computer, and ignore her.

As she switched on her own computer, he proceeded to brag about his private boarding school education, and how he had worked longer in this office than any of the other employees.

"If you need to know anything at all here, I'm your man."

Linda just nodded and smiled at him.

"So how old did you say you were Linda, twenty seven? So you're a virgin in this office but are you a virgin in life?"

Shocked and not being able to believe what she had just heard, she glanced around the office t see if anyone else had heard his question. Nobody had or if they had they didn't show it as they all busied themselves at their desks. Bewildered, she fought back tears for the rest of the day and was incapable of focusing on her work.

The next day, she was determined he was not going to get the better of her. She was not going to quit. She had worked hard for this job and she wasn't going to give it up easily because of some sleazy old man.

She had already purchased a diary to keep a record of anything he may say or do which were inappropriate towards her. She took a deep breath and approached him. She had practised the words over and over in her head, "I would appreciate that you keep personal comments about me to yourself. I don't want to be your adversary and I hope we can work alongside one another. If your attitude towards me doesn't change, I will consider making a formal complaint to our boss."

The morning passed quietly and she was able to focus on the job at hand. However, at lunchtime as she tucked into a pie at her desk, he edged past her and muttered, "If you don't watch it, you're gonna get fatter still."

Linda decided to circulate a little after she had finished her fat making pie. She found out that nobody really liked Adam, that he was fifty -three and his wife had recently left him for another woman, which had made him even worse than he had been previously. He'd been passed over three times for promotion and was disgruntled at work. They warned her of his defensive attitude and to try not to be put out by his wayward comments.

After lunch, he showed Linda some old departmental filing cabinets and told her to clear them out. She was sure this was not part of her job description but decided it wasn't worth protesting.

Just as she was finishing off there boss Jane crossed the office, "What are you doing Linda, why are you clearing out cabinets?

Before she had chance to reply, Adam piped up, "I told her not to do that, but she insisted, said she couldn't work in such a messy environment."

Linda felt the sudden snap within her, the killing snap. The one she had felt before. She didn't show it. She smiled sweetly at them both, "Sorry."

She returned to her desk, Adam unaware of what he had triggered within her. She had killed before. She would do it again.

She waited in her car for him to leave the office and followed him discreetly. Once she had established where he lived, the rest would be easy.

She returned to his house a couple of hours later, with a knife safely placed in her handbag. She rang the doorbell, and saw the surprise on his face, when he answered the door.

Shaken, he politely invited her in and offered to make her a coffee. As he turned to hand her the mug, she saw his eyes register the knife, which she held towards his throat.

She stabbed him repeatedly until she watched the life drain from him. He barely put up a fight, such was the shock and horror of witnessing what he had stirred up within her.

As she plunged the knife deeply for one last time, she whispered in his ear, "I'm not the little feeble creature you thought I was, you certainly messed with the wrong one this time, but you won't do it again."

## Assignment Twenty Five - You've been sucked out of a plane and are falling towards Earth

### 17th February 2018

Again, with this chapter, unfortunate personal circumstances meant that AJ could not complete the assignment or come to the meeting so there are only entries from J.M., Michael and Shelly.

During part of her writer's course, J.M. was also investigating short story/flash fiction competitions and noticed that many of them limited the word count to five hundred. As she was keen to start entering as part of a desire to achieve accreditations to help with being accepted by agents and publishers for her main novels, J.M. has decided to try to limit her assignments to the five hundred word count instead of the one thousand which the group had decided upon.

Michael and Shelly backed her decision but decided that the group would continue with the one thousand word limit, as it didn't affect the idea behind it.

J.M. explored twinergy, the physic connection between twins.

Michael enjoyed his first special operations adventure with no real intention to carry out the actions in the story.

S.J. thoroughly enjoyed this homework as she was able to demonstrate through her writing some of the experiences that she has encountered through her mediumship and meditation.

# You've been sucked out of a plane and are falling towards Earth

## by

## J.M. McKenzie

The roar of rushing wind over total silence and the womb-like sensation of floating and tumbling was strangely comforting.

But for the cold. A womb should be warm. I was freezing. My thin summer clothes flapped against my bare skin.

I awoke. My eyes were streaming.

I was falling. Twisting and turning. Dizzying, blurry glimpses of sky and earth flashing past.

Instinctively, I stretched out my limbs into a stabilising star shape.

The spinning slowed and I was falling backwards. My vision began to clear. The sky above me was clear and blue. I was not alone. There were others. Silent specks of humanity plummeting to earth.

A curling trail of dark smoke cut through the blue to my right. Loosening into wisps above me and tightening and darkening into the distance.

Confusion gave way to realisation, and briefly to

panic and terror, before a sense of calm inevitability washed over me. I closed my eyes.

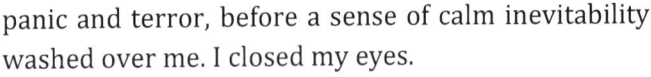

I awoke before my alarm. The dream had been so real.

Falling. Twisting and turning. Dizzying, blurry glimpses of sky and earth. Rushing wind over total silence.

I fumbled for my phone. 05.58. I snuggled back under the duvet. Five minutes more.

My head was full of the dream. I tried to give it more detail but it was gone.

My thoughts shifted to Enid. She would be almost there by now. The flight was due to land at 06.35 UK time.

It felt strange to think that she was on the other side of the world. It was the first time we had been apart for more than a few miles for a few days and now we were going to be thousands of miles apart for a whole year. We had shared a womb and a bedroom for all of our lives. We had been in the same class at school, played in the same sports teams, had the same friends and gone to the same parties. Now her usually cluttered side of the room was sparse and neat, her bed smooth and unslept in.

I sat up and reached for my phone again, this time to silence the alarm. The screen was showing a BBC Breaking News alert. The words "Virgin" and "missing" seemed to jump out at me. A cold ball of fear formed at my core as I clicked into the article.

Flight VS1022 from Heathrow to Kuala Lumpur was missing. Initial reports were that following an explosion all contact with the flight had been lost and all radar signals had disappeared.

The phone fell from my hand and once again I was back in my dream. I was falling backwards. The sky above me was clear and blue. A sense of calm inevitability washed over me. I closed my eyes.

# You've been sucked out of a plane and are falling towards Earth

## by

## Michael Andrews

The world is a beautiful place, especially when seen from thirty five thousand feet up. It's peaceful too. No birds. Only the occasional roar of a plane's engine but even then, the air is quite thin and sound doesn't travel well. You can just about start to see the curvature of the Earth at this height, definitely helped today with no clouds and no pesky aeroplane around me to block my view.

How did I know? Five minutes ago I was sitting in my seat on flight G-18-576, looking forward to my pre-packed in-flight meal when I received the call to be ready. I had set the timer on my watch, reached into the back pack under my seat and put on the full face mask, miniature air tank and gloves. I glanced out of the window before closing my eyes. My watch pinged and I turned the on switch on the air tanks.

The whole of my insides felt like they were on the outside as my ears popped, my vision blurred, came back into focus and blurred again. My stomach lurched and a brief stab of pain hit my brain before peacefulness settled around me.

I watched as the plane continued on its flight, speeding away at just over seven hundred miles an hour and within ten seconds, it was already over two miles away and was quickly disappearing into a speck on the horizon.

I spread my arms and legs as my body began its plummet towards Earth. I could feel the whip of air around my jumpsuit and wondered for a moment if Superman ever felt like this. I grinned as I closed my legs, put my left arm by my side and extended my right arm above my head. Tilting downwards, I started singing to myself.

"Da da daaaaaaah, da dah da daaaah!"

I soared through the air with the greatest of ease, trying to swoop upwards but to no avail. I heard static start to crackle in my ear piece and glanced down at my wrist. Twenty thousand feet. Crumbs, I'd already dropped fifteen thousand feet in what seemed seconds.

"Bravo Three, Bravo Three, come in," a cool, deep voice echoed in my head. Looks like play time was over.

"Command, this is Bravo Three, roger," I replied, my voice distorted slightly in the full face mask I was wearing.

"How was the extract?"

"Painful, but within expectations. The view is great," I could hear myself smiling.

"You can view the scenery later," Command snapped. "Echo Four is holding position at pick up so let's get this over with and we can review the files later."

I touched a button on my arm-piece and the electronic HUD lit up. It tracked Echo Four's location and I twisted my body shape so that I aimed for it. Satisfied I was on target, I glanced back in the direction of the jumbo I had been aboard. A twinge of guilt and conscience flashed through my thoughts for a moment as I pondered the lives of the three hundred odd innocents but sometimes, collateral damage was necessary to win a bigger conflict. Killing the Foreign Secretary had been sanctioned at the very top. He'd become an embarrassment to the country's ruling elite but was holding sway with the public. It was deemed to be vital to the ongoing security of the national that he was removed, permanently.

I pressed the trigger on my wrist and saw a flash of light in the distance as the plane exploded in mid-flight. The fake documents which I had hidden in the backpack of the Middle Eastern youth would mark it as an attack by ISIS and there would be public outrage and further strengthening of support for the war on terror.

Echo Four's plane came into sight and I pushed another button. Brain pain and stomach lurching hit me as I was pulled inside the hold. Taking off my mask, I took the offered bottle of water.

"Well done, Bravo Three," Command told me. "Mission complete."

# You've been sucked out of a plane and are falling towards Earth

## By

## S.J. Gibbs

Guy Tracy sipped his whisky and coke as the aircraft cruised at 30,000 feet. He stretched his legs in the open space before him, having paid for extra legroom and had found himself seated next to the emergency exit.

He hardly had time to register that the emergency door suddenly blew open as he was sucked from his seat through the gaping hole.

He gasped as the freezing cold conditions enveloped him into a virtual state of paralysis. His breathing was rapid as he gulped at the air for oxygen. The realisation that he had no parachute and that death was certain flashed in front of him.

As the Earth spun beneath him, he slipped into a state of unconsciousness. A temperature of minus seventy degrees froze his skin and eyes. Fatal spikes in his blood pressure and heart rate sealed his death, as his lifeless body plummeted towards Earth.

Guy felt his soul leave that lifeless doomed body as he

flew around, no longer falling. He knew he was dead and that it had been a mistake to believe that you just died as he floated mid-air. A big bright light surrounded him and Earth had turned into a light beneath him as well. A man appeared to his right and was floating around in the same fashion. Guy tried to call to him but the light was so bright that the sound could not penetrate it.

Suddenly the floating experience changed as he was pulled downwards into a spinning vortex. The white light was brighter now, brighter than anything he had ever seen, so bright and yet he didn't feel blinded. He welcomed it, as a feeling of absolute calmness, overwhelmed him. Peace of mind, settled around him, as he sensed himself floating freely once more, this time in an up wards direction. A beautiful garden appeared before him. The garden was more beautiful than anything he had ever seen. A sense of feeling whole and loved overcame him. He felt complete as the sound of celestial music entered his being. Vivid coloured flowers brighter than he could have imagined, and greenery and trees, greener than any green he had found on Earth, surrounded him.

Two beautiful round-topped mountains, the tops of which were covered in snow appeared before him, the foliage of the slopes of indescribable beauty. His vision felt one hundred times stronger and clearer than during his life on Earth.

He became aware, to his right, of a shimmering lake,

which contained a different kind of water. It was golden, radiant and alluring. The whole landscape felt alive.

Beyond the lake, he could make out about fifteen people holding hands and dancing in a circle. He floated towards them, across the lake. As he approached them he was fascinated by the grace and beauty of their movements, their bodies seemed almost weightless. A sudden joy overcame him as he realized that he was home, he had been purely a visitor to the place called Earth. He hung there, floating. Serenity surrounded him in this timeless space.

A huge pull lifted him higher, further away from Earth, past stars and galaxies. He felt tiny and enormous at the same time. It was serene. There was no gravity. It was all breath taking, surreal and magical.

## A message from the authors

We all hope that you have enjoyed our tales of fiction, our experiments into genres unknown at times. As it was mentioned at the start, we all started these homeworks with a sense of trepidation, but have now incorporated them into our writing experiences, taking on board the learning curves, and even to take some of the pieces and expand into longer stories.

We recommend the writing prompt book as a useful tool for any budding writer, and hope that by sharing our own experiences, it helps people take the plunge, to open up a blank word document or pick up a pen and paper and take that first step into their own writing careers.

Good luck and best wishes

AJ, J.M., Michael and S.J.

## **Works Published by the Authors**

## **AJ Jones**

I Am Here! Where Are You?

## **Michael Andrews**

For The Lost Soul

The Empty Chair

The Alex Hayden Chronicles

Book 1: Under A Blood Moon

Book 2: The Howling Wind

Book 3: The Cauldron of Fire

Book 4: Dragonfire

## **S.J. Gibbs**

Fighting A Battle With Himself

Printed in Great Britain
by Amazon